HORSE SENSE

HORSE SENSE

What's in it for Billy Brent?

GODFRAY AMY

The Book Guild Ltd

First published in Great Britain in 2022 by
The Book Guild Ltd
Unit E2 Airfield Business Park,
Harrison Road, Market Harborough,
Leicestershire. LE16 7WB
Tel: 0116 2792299
www.bookguild.co.uk
Email: info@bookguild.co.uk
Twitter: @bookguild

Typeset in 11pt Adobe Jenson Pro

Printed on FSC accredited paper
Printed and bound in Great Britain by 4edge Limited

ISBN 978 1914471 001

British Library Cataloguing in Publication Data.
A catalogue record for this book is available from the British Library.

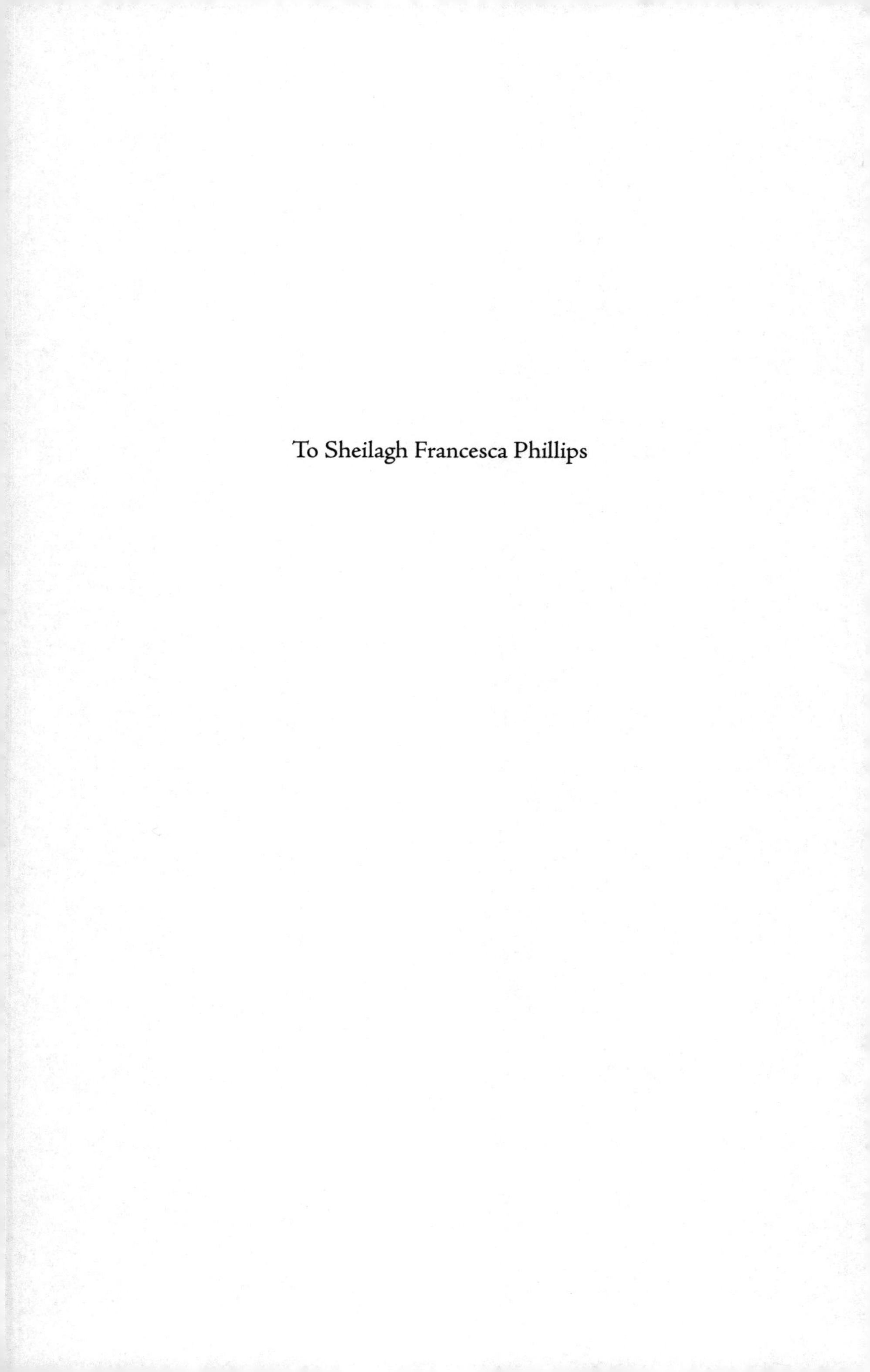

To Sheilagh Francesca Phillips

ONE

Walking across the playground, the boy tried to distance himself from the other children. It was raining, chilly and grey. He had no coat, just a tatty short-sleeved jumper with holes in the elbows to protect him from the cold and wet.

As he passed through the school gates to make his way home, two older boys pushed him off the pavement. Thinking it funny, they laughed and shouted abuse, calling out at him, "Filthy, smelly rat face." The boy pretended to take no notice; he'd come to accept it. Head down, he increased his pace as the traffic roared past, drowning out the catcalls behind him.

Billy Brent was thirteen years old, small for his age and stick-thin. School was something new to him as he'd never been to primary school. Well, only the once when he was sent home for not having the required uniform, never to return. Starting secondary school was a frightening experience for him. Life was bad enough before this, and now he was on the verge of deep depression, but, not knowing what this was, he just tried to cope.

Turning off the main road and passing by the multistorey council flats, he turned into his street and entered the side door of the old second-hand furniture shop. He ran up the stairs to their one-bedroom flat above and tried the door; he knocked and waited. No, nothing. A minute later he tried again, to no effect. Sighing, his legs aching, and out of breath, he realised the door was locked – well, nothing unusual in that. Knowing that the doorbell had long been broken, he knocked more loudly this time; still no answer. No one came; no sign or sound from inside. With a silent groan, Billy slid down and sat on the cold stone floor, wrapped his arms around his chest to find some warmth, and wondered whether he'd get anything to eat today; this was not an unusual situation to him.

Billy woke up with a start. The door opened, and a man he'd not seen before stepped over him. "Sorry, lad." The man smiled and disappeared down the creaky stars. Billy scrambled up and went inside. His mother, Lucy, was stretched out on her chair, seemingly in a daze. A half bottle of whisky with an empty glass sat on a small table next to her. Her bottle of prescription drugs had fallen onto the floor, with several pills having spilt out. Billy bent down and picked them up, slipped them back into the bottle and tightened the cap. Gently shaking his mother, she focussed from her dazed state.

"How was school?" she drawled.

Billy didn't answer and went and opened the fridge. A half bottle of yesterday's milk and two remaining fish fingers left over from the night before. Taking them out, he put them in the microwave. Two minutes later, he took them out and scoffed them down. There was nothing else. Zilch, zero. He went back into the front room.

"Mum, can't I go get something for us to eat? There's nothing left, Mum, I'm starving."

"Sorry, love, I must have forgot." She fumbled about in a plastic bag she'd been leaning against and gave him a crumpled fiver and a handful of change. "See what you can get with this. It should see us out through the weekend."

Turning away from him she reached for the zapper and settled back to watch whatever was on TV.

—

Next morning, no breakfast, no clean clothes, Billy walked to school, just ten minutes away, and after the class had settled down his form teacher asked Billy to follow him; he was taken to the headmaster's office.

"This is the boy, sir, I'll leave him with you." The headmaster nodded and gestured for Billy to sit down in front of him. He seemed kindly.

"Now, Billy, I think we have a problem, don't we? Did you have any breakfast this morning?"

Billy averted his gaze, feeling ashamed. "No."

"Did you have a proper meal when you got home yesterday?"

"Not really."

"Are you happy at home?"

"No, my mum's not well. She can't look after us proper."

"Well, Billy, we must do something about this, mustn't we? I shall contact social services and perhaps they can help us, eh?"

"Don't know. They did come to see us months ago but never came again."

"Look here, Billy, you will have a proper meal at dinner break, and if you go along to the canteen now I'll call Mrs Williams to rustle up a hot breakfast for you. Off you go, now, and I'll try to get things moving to straighten things out for you both."

Billy nodded, still making no eye contact, not fully understanding what might happen, but the thought of a hot breakfast brightened him up just a little.

TWO

It must have been just after two o'clock. Students were starting to file back to their classrooms when the two women arrived and were taken to the head's office. He explained his concerns. They admitted that the department had been aware of the family's problems some time ago, but couldn't explain how they had somehow dropped out of their system. They asked if they could see the boy now. Billy was fetched. It was immediately obvious to the two ladies from social services that something was seriously wrong. The boy was malnourished, not properly clothed, and none too clean. They spoke kindly to him, and asked if he would accompany them to see his mother.

Billy became nervous, not wanting them to see his mother in the state she'd become, but he knew deep down she needed help.

The headmaster agreed he could leave school early, and suggested that Billy needed to change to a school that had facilities for children with learning difficulties, adding that Billy seemed a bright child who wanted to learn but had little to no schooling, and needed to be brought up to the standard of his classmates.

–

Having appraised the flat, its contents and the condition of Lucy, the ladies made contact with their superior and it was decided to take immediate action. They sat Billy down and helped Lucy to sit up from her slouch.

"Lucy, if we may call you that... Lucy, you need help to get nourished, fit and together again. We need to get you into hospital where you can be assessed, and with treatment, returned to good health, and strong enough to live a normal life... and, Billy... you can't be left on your own so you'll come with us and be taken into care until we can find you a nice foster home. We will also find you a more suitable school that specialises in one-to-one teaching that will give you the grounding of a future education you deserve."

Billy sat sullen and silent, trying to take in what all this would mean. He moved up closely to his mother.

"I love you, Mum. I know you need to get better, but I don't want to lose you."

"Sorry, love, I'm no good to you like this. Be a good boy and go with the nice ladies, and when I'm better we can get somewhere nice to live and be together again."

Billy put his arms around her and kissed her cheek. "Someday," he said with the seriousness of a grown-up. "Someday I will make enough money to buy us a house and buy you lovely dresses."

"That will be nice," she said, and, before Billy knew it, they were in the car speeding off to God knows where.

Leaving the junior carer with Lucy to wait for the ambulance, the senior of the two women drove on erratically; a nervous Billy clung on in the back. Not a word was spoken.

—

It was a surgery for privately insured patients and provided dedicated services to "The Indigo Boys Home" in Finsbury Park. Billy was given a thorough medical examination by a doctor who showed little empathy to what stood before him.

Told to remove his clothes, ashamed and embarrassed at the state of them, and of himself, he stood there, in front of Marjorie and the doctor. Billy was near to tears; he let out a sob.

"Open your mouth, boy. Stick out your tongue." Cold metal pushed down on it so hard it hurt and a light was shone down his throat. And so it carried on. It seemed to take ages, but Billy had taught himself long ago to cope in the knowledge that nothing lasts forever, and this didn't.

Putting his clothes back on, he was told to wait outside and that the receptionist might give him a cup of tea.

"The boy is underweight for his age and seems to be short of breath, but at this point all he needs is feeding up. Three hot meals a day, I'd say. Bring him in again in six weeks' time and we might take an X-ray of his lungs."

–

Six weeks had passed, no mention of returning to the doctor; that at least was something, he supposed. Billy was homesick. He didn't know what homesickness was, but he had it. It was missing his mother, the only person that had ever loved or really cared about him. He had asked them where she was. Was she better? No one had spoken to him about her; no one seemed to have the time to bother. He hated it here. Yes, he was clean, had new fresh clothes. Three meals a day but little else.

Attending classes four days a week, he and a twelve-year-old boy were taught by a kindly middle-aged lady. They had made some progress with their reading, he was keen to learn, but, then, the weekends seemed to last forever. No TV, no phones allowed; not that he had one, of course.

The other boys in the home, fifteen of them, were all older. He was the outsider – well, nothing new there – and was left out of anything that might have provided some much-needed fun.

Billy made up his mind. Yes, he'd do it. He would slip out when the chance came and go find his mum.

THREE

He thought things through. First he decided to make his move after lights out, after everyone was asleep, but then he would have to get up and dress in the dark and surely one of the boys in his dormitory would spot him. No, Sunday. On Sundays the staff were replaced by part-time relief carers who were easier on discipline and allowed the boys out to play and wander through the grounds of this old abbey, long ago abandoned by its nuns, or monks, or whatever.

But Sunday came, and being the beginning of March it was cold windy and wet. No one would want to go outside on a day like this. Then perhaps it might be to his advantage. Perhaps the staff might be less concerned as to where everyone was. No... Decision made: he would go today. When the bell was rung for lunch, there was always a stampede to get to the canteen first.

The carers ate in a separate room. No one in reception.

Billy took his chance and slipped through the front door, down the steps and skirted the lawn.

Passing under the impressive stone arch and once into the road, he felt free. Excitement welled up inside him, but then it came to him in a bolt of indecision. Which way should he go, to the left or right? Hardly ever having ventured anywhere other than Finsbury Park, he had no idea of where he was.

Turning left, he ran along the pavement, rain dripping down his hair and face. He stopped to shelter in a shop doorway for a minute to get his breath back. A family came out of the shop, stopping at the sight of him. Billy asked if they knew the way to Finsbury Park. Worrying why a young child should be without a coat in this appalling weather, they asked why he was here and on his own.

"I got on the wrong bus and I'm lost, and I haven't any money to get me home," he said with a pretend half sob.

The couple looked concerned and were sorry for him. "Can we phone your parents to come and get you?"

"We're not on the phone."

"Well, it's a long way from here… Look." The man took out his wallet and handed Billy a five-pound note. "Best grab a taxi; this should cover it… Better still, take the Tube. Kilburn station is just down the road."

Billy marvelled at this generosity and of someone being kind to him. He thanked the couple politely, and they made off in the opposite direction.

—

It was around four o'clock before anyone noticed that Billy was not in the building. Worried for the trouble they would be in rather than for the boy, they rang the police.

"We, I mean… This is the Indigo Boys Home, Willesden Green. One of our boys is missing." After a few minutes' holding on, they were told that someone would be sent over within the hour.

Meanwhile, Billy walked on, and a few minutes later saw the station. The man behind the ticket desk took pity on him and wrote down the changes he would have to make. Change at Baker Street to the Metropolitan Line to King's Cross, then change to the Piccadilly Line and four stops on was Finsbury Park.

Sounded simple but Billy felt very nervous. Somehow he would manage it; he would just ask each time he had to make a change. Actually, he surprised himself as just thirty-three minutes later he exited the Tube station and immediately recognised his surroundings. He walked on.

The second-hand furniture shop was still open even though it was a Sunday. Billy tried the front door to their flat above, but it was locked. He banged on the door, standing despondently on the doorstep for several minutes. No one answered, no movement above. He went into the shop.

Mr Bruce was sitting behind the counter reading his paper. He looked up.

"Hello, Billy. My goodness, you're soaking wet. What you doing back here?"

"I've come to find Mum, but no one's in."

"No, Billy, we haven't seen her since she was taken to hospital and you'd disappeared too. Have heard nothing since. That was over six weeks ago. Just a week ago I rented the flat to someone else. Now, you come in the back and I'll make you a hot drink and we can work out where she might be."

Mr Bruce phoned the nearest hospital and asked whether they had an admission of a Lucy Brent about six weeks ago and, if so, was she still there? After three or four minutes they confirmed she had been there, but was now recuperating in the rest home in Alderman Street just half a mile away.

"Billy, I'm shutting up shop. We'll go right now and find her."

FOUR

The day had gone well for David Clayton. The weather had been kind, and Grace had just got back from collecting their new purchase. A nice-looking seven-year-old gelding* racehorse, now retired. An addition to their eight other horses all acquired to be retrained, calmed down, and then resold on as manageable, quiet and sensible horses, ready for a new career.

They had just turned him out in the schooling paddock, and, with a series of snorts and three huge bucks, he galloped around three or four times before stopping and going up to the rails and touching noses with the two yearling* thoroughbreds in the adjoining paddock, both curious of this new addition. Snowy: that was his stable name but he was registered at racing headquarters as Snow Chief Mystery.

Snorting again, he turned away, put his head down and started to graze. The yearlings stood their ground and watched him. "Just got him from a racing yard for a thousand." David smiled to himself. "A good buy, for sure."

–

David and Grace Clayton had started this business four years ago and were becoming well known amongst the racing industry as the solution of what to do with a racehorse when his racing days were over. Eight years was considered to be old in racing but young in the other world of equestrian pursuits.

David's dad, Hugh, had trained from their farm of fifteen acres with an attached yard of twenty boxes.* David had been his head lad. Hugh and his wife, Jennie, had passed away several years ago and David had taken over, but, as with most small trainers and the poor prize money on offer at the lower end of British racing, they'd found it hard to make ends meet.

They had two children, now grown up and in their twenties. The youngest, Patsy, had not long left home, whilst their boy was in a well-known Australian trainer's racing yard in Melbourne.

Yes, still a busy yard, but the house seemed empty. The young had flown the nest.

The business of retraining these horses was paying dividends and becoming increasingly profitable. In the four years, they had already sold and rehomed forty-two of them, with another nine currently in the yard.

Grace rode out once a day; they had Celine, who worked full time, plus several part timers.

David himself rode as many times as was necessary so that each horse was exercised and schooled each day.

—

Filling the hay nets and making up their feed for the night, the horses and the new one were brought in from grass, brushed over, and checked for any cuts or heat* in their legs. No problems, all OK, fed, and bedded down. David thanked Celine and said that she could get off home. Last job, he carried the two bowls of feed out to the yearlings, who were left out in the paddocks overnight unless the weather turned nasty.

David went back through the back door to the kitchen. It was warm cosy and spacious. Grace stood at the Aga finishing off preparing supper...

"Be another twenty minutes," she said. He sat down at the head of the long oak table, its gnarls and cracks depicting its huge age.

"Has our new boy settled down?" she asked.

"He seems quite laid back; we'll see more of what he's made of tomorrow. A good sort, I think." The house phone rang. David reached over for it. He listened.

"My wife? She's busy at the moment. Who is that? Oh yes, sorry. That's OK. Really... Why, what's happened?" Grace caught his tone and tried to catch what was up. "Well, it's not that easy for us; we're very tied up here. Is everything still on, though? All right then, if we must. We'll just have to wait, but it's very upsetting. We'll wait to hear from you then."

FIVE

Billy felt so relieved. Getting across London had been a testing experience, and now he'd made it. Forgotten were the soaked clothes, but, as he waited for the kind shopkeeper he hardly knew to close up, he started to shiver with the cold.

As the old man pulled the shutters down and locked the shop door, both were startled by the screech of tyres of a police car pulling up not a foot away from them.

A woman officer got out of the passenger door.

"Are you Billy Brent?" she asked. Not unkindly. Billy nodded. She lifted her eyes to Mr Bruce; her attitude seemed to change. The other policeman now got out of the car.

"And what are you doing with this child?" he asked. The old man was shaken.

"We're just off to try and find his mother. She used to live above my shop. I couldn't leave this little chap on his own. Look at the state of him."

The police asked whether they knew where she was, and yes they did: she was in a care home near the hospital in Alderman Street.

"And you've come all the way from Willesden Green on your own, have you, Billy? They were very worried about you at Indigo's." Billy was close to tears. The policeman put his hand on Billy's shoulder; he smiled down at him. "Well," he said. "Let's go find her."

The car drove up to the front entrance. The policewoman got out and Billy followed. The driver stayed put. "I'll wait here for you," he said, "and radio in to say we've found Billy safe, and are taking him to see his mum, who we think is in the nursing home on Alderman Street. We'll drop the boy back to Indigo's later."

The two of them walked into reception. Billy's heart was pounding. The policewoman rang the bell on the desk and they waited.

–

There were perhaps fifteen people sat around the room; some seemed to be asleep.

Billy scanned the room, and there she was. Once he'd spotted her he simply stood and stared, almost too overcome to move. She was talking to someone. Gathering himself and taking a deep breath, he walked over. "Mum?"

She turned, with a look of astonishment and surprise, eyes wide with shock. "Billy," she gasped, reaching for him, both arms stretched out to hold him. "But you're all wet, you poor boy. Oh, Billy, it's so good to see you. Tell me, are they treating you well? They told me where you were. I was going to phone you." She let go of him. She turned back to the old man she'd been talking to. "This is my son, Billy; he took care of me for two years. God knows how I'd have managed without him."

"Mum, they're taking me back to the boy's home. I ran away. Mr Bruce has let our flat to someone else. What's going to happen, Mum?"

She gave his hand a squeeze. "Billy, you have to be brave; they won't let you be with me. You know I can't look after you properly. They're letting me out of here as soon as they find me somewhere nearby where they can monitor me. I still need looking after. I'm not well, love."

Just then he noticed the policewoman standing at the door. "I've got to go now, Mum, they're taking me back."

"Be a good boy, then. I promise I'll keep in touch and let you know where I am."

She kissed him on the cheek. Still looking at her, he stepped away backwards; she was not looking at him but already talking to the man next to her.

Billy wiped the tears from his eyes; the policewoman held out her hand to him. He grabbed hold and they walked out back to the police car.

"Did you find her?" asked the policeman. Billy said nothing.

"Yes, we found her," said the police lady as she helped Billy back into the car. "It's upset the little lad; let's get him back and get them to give him a warm bath and into some dry clothes."

—

Back at the home, getting out of the car, the policewoman took him to Matron's office. Billy looked up to her. "She loves me really," he said. "It's just she's not well."

"I'm sure she does, my love. Now, sit down there and I'll have a chat with Matron to explain what happened." Five minutes later she came back out. "I'll leave you now; it was nice meeting you, Billy. Matron's not cross with you. In you go and be a good boy. We don't want to come looking for you again." She reopened the office door and was gone.

Matron was quietly nice to him. He sat, hardly seeing over the desk to this woman that he'd only seen a few times, yet this was the person whose whims governed their days for weeks and sometimes years. "William, I am not going to make it an issue that you ran away. I know you went to find your mother, and I think you were rather clever to do so. Now." She had a file in front of her and she flipped over several sheets. She continued, "It's a pity you went off like that because we had someone coming to see you tomorrow and we've had to cancel it. Never mind, all is not lost. We're taking you to see another doctor tomorrow instead, and, if he's pleased with how you are, we'll rearrange their visit. If they like the look of you, they may want to give you a lovely home." She picked up the phone. "Muriel, come and take William from me, run him a hot bath and find him a full set a set of new clothes from the store."

Billy had wanted to ask why someone was coming to see him, but was so tired he just couldn't find the words.

SIX

A week had passed since the phone call cancelling their appointment in London. It had upset Grace more than it had her husband. The week had had its compensations, though, as they'd sold one of the horses deemed ready to the parents of a young woman wanting to train on for cross-country eventing. Then today a gentleman, a very competent rider, had come to try out two of the others and he agreed to take them both. So now only six were left in the yard, none of which were yet ready enough to sell on. David would never let a horse of his be sold out of the yard unless he felt the person he was selling to was well able to cope with what they were taking on.

Going into the house for lunch, or rather a bowl of Grace's vegetable soup and a slice of the fresh baguette, he asked Grace to find the list of people waiting to disencumber themselves of the high cost of keeping their horses in training. Yes, of course he trained them too, at his own cost, not to race but to slow down, to be quiet, gentle and safe.

He was about to make the first call and the phone rang. "Hello, who's that… Who, sorry? Oh, yes… fine, thank you. Is it good news? Can you hold on? I need to check with my wife." Grace was looking on nervously. "Can we do next Tuesday? Yes, it's them." Grace hurried across the room to her desk to check their diary. She nodded back to him. "Hello, still there? We can come down then, what time? Yes, we could just manage to get down by 9.30 but could we make it ten to be on the safe side? Yes, that'll be fine, thank you. Ten o'clock, then. Can you tell us what caused the delay? Never mind… we'll see you Tuesday, then… and thank you… Bye."

They were up at 5.45. Celine came in early, and between them they turned the horses out into the field and gave them a feed. After a hurried breakfast, David and Grace tided themselves up, leaving Celine to muck out and return later to bring the horses back later in the afternoon at 4pm. It was now just after seven as they drove out of the yard and into the road.

With a two-hour drive ahead of them plus an allowance for probable traffic delays getting into Finsbury Park and the Town Hall, it was a close call to be there for ten.

For a while there was a silence between them, both deep in thought. Grace was the first to break the ice. "Are you as nervous as I am, love?"

David didn't answer straight away. "I don't really know how I feel. We've been so long with this, not knowing if we've been accepted or not. I just want get it all settled and move on."

Grace leaned over and squeezed his arm. "Today's the day, love. We'll either be driving home alone or we'll have someone with us."

"That's the thing, though, isn't it?" he replied. "We've had to get everything organised and ready, and it all could have been a waste of time and money."

He gave out a deep sigh. Grace shook her head. "I don't think so; I'm pretty sure they want us, surely. Why would they have been so thorough and checked every aspect of who we are and how we live, just to reject us? No, it's going to be OK, and now I'm really excited."

SEVEN

The boys were got up each morning at six and Billy had been separated from the others as they went down for breakfast. He didn't understand why they were checking up on what he was to wear, slicking down his hair, polishing his shoes, checking his fingernails. Was he clean behind his ears? Nothing was said; he was afraid to ask. The female assistant sensed his concern. "You might be leaving us today, Billy. Now." She put her hands on his shoulders, bent down and looked into his face. "You must be on your best behaviour, and for goodness' sake speak up when you're asked a question."

Taken down to the canteen, Billy ate his breakfast, his head spinning. If he might be leaving, what did it mean for him? Why just him? Why none of the others? Why?

Lost in thought, someone tapped his shoulder. It was Wendy, the only member of staff he almost liked. She was carrying a backpack. "Come with me, Billy, and take this: all your own stuff's in here and a change of clean clothes. Should be enough to keep you going for a while."

Finishing off his breakfast, the other lads looked at each other as Wendy came to collect him, and as he got up someone called out, "Good luck, mate." It was one of the older boys at the next table. "And don't worry too much. Anything's gotta be better than this place." The whole room erupted with shouts of approval. Wendy gave him a look, trying not to smile. She pushed Billy in front of her and headed him out of the room, towards the office.

Matron was sitting behind her desk but to Billy's surprise Marjorie from social services was sitting in front of her. Wendy patted him on the shoulder and left him to it.

"Hello again, Billy." Marjorie indicated him to sit in the other chair. "We understand that you've not been too happy here, but we do understand. Life has not been easy for you. It was always our intention to find you a nice family who can give you a better life and a chance to make something of yourself. We have, of course, been in touch with your mother, and she agrees that it is for best. Also, the doctors have advised that you should get out of London to somewhere where you can breathe fresh country air. You have a slight asthmatic condition that London's poor air quality will only make worse. Now, I know this is a lot to take in, but in the next few minutes Mr and Mrs Clayton will be here to meet you and I think you'll find a whole new life and opportunity with them."

Billy looked forlorn. "When will I see my mum again?"

They told him they would keep him in touch with Lucy, and always let him know how she was getting on and where she was. Matron called for Wendy to come back and take Billy into the reading room and to stay with him until called.

With a book in his hand an hour passed; it seemed ages. The school had broken up on Friday for the end of term and Easter holidays, and for a rare treat the boys were to be taken by coach for a camping holiday by the sea. Billy had never seen the sea, let alone gone on holiday, and he'd been really looking forward to it. And now he was going to miss it, and miss it for what?

He couldn't focus on the reading. Wendy was trying to encourage him, but, realising his concerns, shut the book. "Billy, it's not that bad, you know. These people who are going to look after you live in a lovely old farmhouse with lots of animals." Just then the buzzer went, and, as Wendy walked him back to the office, he whispered that he didn't like animals because they ate each other. She laughed, not knowing if he was being serious or had managed a joke.

As he walked into the room he saw a middle-aged couple sat there, both turning to look at him. They smiled; the man stood up, and went to shake Billy's hand, but sat down again when Billy didn't respond. Matron introduced the couple, and said he was to go with them and to try very hard to be a good boy. Marjorie also added that after three weeks she would telephone and, if he was not happy and settled, he could come back.

EIGHT

There were three seats in the front of the pickup truck, Mr Clayton drove out of the Indigo grounds with Billy sat in the middle and Mrs Clayton by the passenger door.

Having to concentrate and not used to the heavy traffic, little or nothing was said, but as soon as they pulled onto the M25 David broke the ice.

"Billy... we're not going to ask you loads of questions just now. I think it best if we tell you about us, where we live, and what we do. Is that OK with you?" Billy looked straight ahead. David continued, "We live in an old farmhouse just outside Fordham, three miles from Newmarket. I buy and sell ex-racehorses; Grace helps me, looks after us, and keeps the accounts. Have you heard of Newmarket? No, well, it's the centre of the British racing industry and has over 3,500 horses being trained there. We have two children, both grown up and both have left home. We have lots of room now and the house feels empty, so, after much thought, we decided to offer a loving home and care to someone who has had a very hard time of it."

Billy took it all in, but still said nothing. He was more interested in marvelling at the sights they were passing by, things he'd never seen before, going through the Dartford Tunnel and seeing the huge suspension bridge opposite.

The journey took three hours and as they pulled up into the yard curiosity lifted his spirits. He could hardly wait to get out of the car quick enough. David reached in the back, picked up Billy's rucksack and walked to the front door and into the house. Grace and Billy followed on. She asked if he was hungry. He nodded. "Well," she said, "David will show you to your room whilst I rustle up something to eat."

Billy followed David and the rucksack up the stairs; they walked to the end of the corridor. A heavy gnarled oak door was open and they walked into the room. Billy stood transfixed. The bed was made up, there was a comfy-looking chair, a desk and its chair, a wardrobe, polished oak flooring, and he could smell the paint of a newly decorated room.

Billy looked up at David. "Will I be sharing this with someone else?"

David laughed as he dropped the rucksack onto the bed. "No, son, this is your room and your space. Now, the bathroom and shower is next to your room, but when Patsy, our daughter, comes, you'll have to share the bathroom. She works as a veterinary nurse in Manchester just now, so we won't be seeing her for a few months. Our son John is a trainer's assistant in Melbourne, Australia, so we don't see much of him either. Unpack your things and after we've had a bite I'll show you around outside; come down when you're ready," and with that he left, closing the door behind him.

Billy, standing in the middle of the room, looked about him. It was so quiet and peaceful. He sat down on the edge of the bed and waited for several minutes, trying to pluck up courage to go back downstairs.

David sat down at the table, Grace standing over the range frying bacon. "He doesn't talk much, does he?"

"Give him a chance, love, it's a lot for him to take in." David took a sip from his large mug of tea. "I think we're going to get on fine."

Grace buttered three bread rolls and slipped a double layer of bacon into each of them. "Go and fetch him; he might be too shy to come down."

Billy ate his bacon roll in silence as David explained that he'd been enrolled into the local secondary school, which was currently enjoying its Easter holidays, and that he'd be starting there the week after next. "It's small for a main school, and not at all like London. The headmaster is looking forward to meeting you."

I bet, thought Billy. *What's he on about?*

After their snack, which Billy thought was the best bacon roll he'd ever had, David led him out into the yard. "We have twenty stables here, Billy; the horses are out to grass and are brought in for the night, fed and brushed down. We only have nine in at the moment, and each have to be mucked out each morning, fed and ridden. Come on, I'll show you; they're in the paddocks over here."

Leaning on the post and rail fence, David pointed at each gelding,* naming them in turn: which ones had won, which had broken* down and had been unable to race again, which were kind and gentle in their box and which one had to be careful of.

Billy seemed enthralled. "Why do you put them in a box?*" he asked.

"No, son, we mean their stable; for some reason, in racing we use the term box."

"And you said they were geldings, why's that?"

"A gelding is a horse that's been cut, and by that we mean neutered. A full horse* can be difficult to handle, and if they haven't shown to be top class they're mostly gelded when they're three years old. My goodness, you're talking to me and I can see you're interested."

"Never seen a horse before except in books," Billy said. Then, continuing, he asked why the two in the next paddock were separated from the others. David explained he'd bought them as foals last October, and they would be going to the yearling sales in another six months. "Why are you going to sell them?"

"Because we hope to make a profit, and that helps to make what we do here worthwhile. When we take them to the sales, you can come too." Billy began to think things might be a lot better here than what he'd expected; somehow he felt slightly different inside, a feeling he hadn't experienced before. His attention returned to the geldings.

"Are you going to sell these too?"

"Yes, lad, we ride them every day, retraining them to be gentle and calm, and make them into nice riding horses. When you feel ready, you can be a help to us. We'll teach you to ride, if that's what you would like to do, and how to look after them, but only when or if you want to, Billy. Celine will be here any minute; you can go and help her bring them in if you want."

They walked back to the yard; Celine was already making up the hay nets. She stopped, looked up, and broke into a wide smile. "Billy? Is that you? I've been really looking forward to you coming home; it's been ages, and here you are." She put her arms round him and gave him a hug. No one had ever hugged him before except his mum.

He didn't know how to react; he didn't have to. "Like to help me fill these nets?" she asked, offering him an empty net.

David seemed concerned. "That OK with you, son?"

Billy nodded, still not too sure what it entailed. Celine showed him how, and he took to the task with vigour. When full and bursting with hay, they took them to each of the nine boxes and hung them up on the rings provided.

Celine showed him how to tie them up with a slip knot. Billy couldn't reach but managed the last one on his own by standing on a bucket.

David was making up the feeds and Grace had come out to help. "The boy seems quite interested," he said. "I'm pleasantly surprised. He actually wanted to know about what we do here. I think it's going to work out, but it's early days."

"Well," she said, "I think he's really sweet; I'm so pleased we've finally got him here. I know we can give him the very best start in life... As long as it's what he wants and it's not too late."

Horses brought in, fed and watered, and two bowls of nuts and mix for the yearlings, David called Billy over. "Grace is taking these feed bowls to the paddock... Here, take one, there's a good lad." Grace picked hers up, and they walked from the yard. Before they were even in sight, the two youngsters could be heard snorting and screeching with excitement, well aware of their approaching feed. Once Billy and Grace reached the post and rail fence, the two yearlings were cantering around, bucking and cavorting. It seemed quite frightening to Billy, but as Grace opened the gate he followed her in at a safe distance.

"Put yours over there." She pointed several yards away from her. Both yearlings crowded her, each trying to get to the feeding bowl. "Quickly, Billy," she shouted. He scuttled away from her and put his feed down. Both yearlings ran towards him. He stood his ground. One of them started to feed; the other returned to Celine's bowl. "Well done," she said. "They're all the same whether young or old. Can't wait to get to it."

Closing the gate behind them, Billy asked how old a yearling is. Which might seem a silly question. Celine smiled and, as they walked back to the yard, she explained.

"Whether a foal is born any time between January and May, in racing it becomes a yearling on January the first. And then, the following year, a two-year-old and so on. Yearlings are normally broken in and ridden away around November. Some then are ready to race the following season as a two-year-old. Most, though, are not raced until much later on, and just given a couple of runs as an education, ready to run as a three-year-old."

All done up for the night, Celine thanked him for his help, and said that she'd look forward to working with him. Billy couldn't help feeling a sense of pride. Him working, and learning of things he'd never imagined, and, for the first time ever, he felt he had something he could look forward to. Waving Celine goodnight as she rode out of the yard on her bike, he walked back into the house.

Later, whilst having his first home-cooked supper ever of cottage pie, Grace said she'd take him to Newmarket tomorrow morning to get him fitted out. Billy wasn't quite sure what she meant. "New outfit for school, and some casual wear; we might even get you some jods in case you want to get on a horse."

David interrupted. "Bit early for that," he said. "Don't look so worried, son. We can teach you to ride but only when you ask and want to. Now, about bedtime. We normally go to bed around 10.30, so you can decide to go up any time before that. You have your own telly in your room, and all we ask is no telly after 10pm. However, we get up early here so we'll wake you up at six. We just have a cup of coffee then go out to give the horses a brush over and a feed, then ride out our first lot. We then have a proper breakfast at nine... Do you have anything you'd like to ask us?"

Billy thought for a moment, then asked what jods were, and that he'd like to help and learn. "And what should I call you?" he asked.

"Well, that's a good question. We don't want you to call us Mr and Mrs Clayton, and I don't think it would be right to call us David or Grace... How about Uncle and Auntie?"

NINE

And so it was. Billy fell into a regular routine between helping in the yard and school.

Three weeks had passed, he was learning to ride, school was OK and the local social worker who had taken over from Marjorie had visited just the once. Seemingly satisfied that he was happy and that his foster parents were happy too, maybe she'd decided to leave well alone.

His mother had called as they'd promised she would and she told Billy they'd found her a one-bedroom flat, and that she was doing fine. Realising that he was enjoying life, and being well looked after, she'd sounded a bit off. Perhaps he shouldn't have told her he'd never ever want to return to London. All the same, he'd been pleased she'd bothered to call, promised to keep in touch, and he now had her phone number.

The school had rung David to say that Billy was trying hard and were pleased with him. He was still a little behind, but catching up fast. David was so pleased that, to show his appreciation to the boy, he decided to get him up on a horse. Picking out the quietest and most gentle in the yard, he'd tacked it up, hoisted the boy up into the saddle and led them out to the sand school. Attaching the lunge rein* to the snaffle* ring, he had the horse walking around him in a tight circle, gradually extending it out to the full length of the long rein. "Gather up your reins, lad, loop them over the wither* as I showed you. Now, feel the horse gait.*"

Within the week, still on the lunge, he was rising to the trot, and eventually a hack canter.* The next day Billy rode out of the yard with David walking beside him and into the sand school. After walking round three times, he trotted, then cantered around until told to pull up back to a walk to cool the horse off. Riding back to the yard, he slid off and led the horse into the stable. He'd never known what a feeling of pride was, but it hit him hard. It was just the most wonderful feeling he'd ever had. David undid the girth, lifted the saddle off and slipped the bridle into his other hand, and said what Billy could hardly believe. "Tomorrow, son, you ride out first lot with me and Celine."

–

The weeks passed and a new routine had been established. On school days Billy was hacking out each morning at 7am with David, Celine and sometimes Grace too. Weekends he was allowed, under instruction from David, to school the horses in the sand arena. Horses came and went; only one of the original nine was left, him proving difficult, refusing to reduce his enthusiasm as a racehorse to the level required for the average competence of an intended purchaser. David continued to work him alone with guile and patience.

It was around this time, in August, that the routine changed. David had started paying more attention to the yearlings. Billy watched as he and Celine walked them around the paddock on leading reins and for the first time in bridles. They would walk fifty yards, stop, make them stand quietly, then run their hands down the front legs, feeling the horse's tendons. As they came alongside, Billy asked what was happening.

David stopped. Celine pulled up behind him. "Sorry, son, should have explained. These two are going to the Tattersalls yearling sale on 15 October... Before they go through the ring, people will ask us to take them out of their box, ask for them to be trotted up* and likely want to feel their legs in case of injury. We can't risk these youngsters playing up, putting buyers off. They have to start learning to behave as we want them to." Billy nodded and as they moved on he hoped that when the day came he would be allowed, school or no school, to go to the sales with them.

That evening at supper David said he needed to explain something that had been on his mind for some time. "Well," he said, "two things, actually. When is your birthday?"

Billy said he thought it was 13 May and he was fourteen now.

"Oh, Billy." Grace was shocked. "We missed your birthday. Why didn't you tell us?"

Billy told her that, apart from wanting to be old enough to leave school at the time, he'd never thought much about it.

"I only found out yesterday, Billy," David continued. "And we have a confession to make: we're getting paid for giving you a home here. So, in missing your birthday, this is what we're going to do. We will open a bank account for you with an opening sum of one hundred pounds, and once a month and every month Grace and I will transfer another fifty pounds into it, that is, until you leave school. When you decide what it is you want to do, whether in the horse business or whatever else, we will support you all the way. So, if or when you feel you'd like to talk things through, please ask." Grace was also listening intently, and nodding her approval.

Billy didn't know how to respond. Tears filled his eyes; he got up from the table and ran upstairs, threw himself on the bed and sobbed. Why was everybody being so nice to him?

Even at school the girls and even the boys wanted to make friends; he didn't deserve such kindness. Did he? How could he reply to his foster parents' generosity? Billy thought on: by working hard at school and helping David and Grace whenever he could and making that extra effort, however hard. He pulled himself off the bed, went into the bathroom and washed the tears from his eyes. Sheepishly, he went back downstairs, walked straight over to Grace and wrapped his arms around her, burying his head into her shoulder.

Billy turned to see David coming around to his side of the table, then felt his arms wrapping around them into a group hug; each had a tear in their eye. The moment would never be lost. The moment that bonded Billy into this family, not as a foster child but as one of theirs.

TEN

At the start of the autumn term Billy was surprised to find he'd been moved up a class; it not only came as a surprise to him but also to local social services, so much so that they had apparently informed Finsbury Park how well their boy was doing and recommended that the appointment should be permanent as it was a perfect coupling.

Just a few weeks to go before the yearling sale. Billy had looked up the date and 15 October was on a Saturday. Yet again, Billy thought luck was working for him; surely bad things would follow. That's how things were, surely... wasn't it?

The yearlings were being brought in at night now; they were taught to understand that there was nothing to be wary of, man or woman. That they would be treated kindly, and given tasty food so different from the grass they grazed on during the day. The odd growl or sharp snap made them come to hand if they played up or tugged at their leading rein if their high spirits were triggered. They were, after all, just youngsters, and young things like to play. But thoroughbred yearlings are destined to become professional athletes and they would soon have to understand that.

Two weeks before the sale, the post had included a blue plastic envelope containing the Tattersalls catalogues. David took them straight into the room in the back that was used as their office, and locked himself away until teatime feeds. Working his way through the catalogues, studying the breeding detailed on each horse to be sold, he listed those of interest by jotting down their lot numbers.

Now no one else was allowed to prepare the yearlings feed; special supplements were to be added to increase bone growth, to strengthen up the hooves for being shod and for them to put on condition and show their health through shiny coats. Every horse has individual needs, and David knew his horses inside and out. David and Grace Clayton were known for producing their horses to the sale ring in top condition; their livelihood depended on it.

When the day's jobs were done, David beckoned Billy to follow him into the house.

They sat down at the kitchen table. David had the book in his hand. "This is the catalogue listing every colt and filly in the sale a week on Saturday. I'd like you to go through it."

He opened it up for Billy to see. "You asked me, when you first came, what a yearling was. Well, apart from being technically a year old, if it's male it is known as a colt; a female as a filly. When they turn four, the colt now is known as a horse and the filly becomes a mare.* Of course, if the colt has been gelded, or, as we say, cut,* it stays a gelding whatever its age. As you will see, including ours, there are 740 yearlings listed; we must arrive at a set time and if ours are not sold leave by a set time… Study this, son, and anything you don't understand, ask me. Whether or not we get a good price for ours, I may buy another two foals to replace them, but the foal sale's not for another five weeks."

Billy asked what a good price would be and how much he was expecting.

"Good question, Billy. I want you to understand our business, so I'll tell you. The dark bay cost me 4,500 guineas, and the bay colt 7,000 guineas. Add to that the cost of keeping them for the year – say, £80 each a week. So we need to add 4,000 to the purchase price of each of them. So, that's £8,225 for the dark bay and £11,400 the other one. A guinea, by the way, is an old money term for one pound, five pence. The five pence per pound goes to Tattersalls as their commission. Remember, those figures are break even, so anything over is our profit and anything under is lost money. We're in there, lots 431 and 432." Billy took the catalogue and went up to his room to read through it and to try to understand it. Little did he realise the importance of the knowledge within a sale catalogue and how that knowledge would serve him in later years.

ELEVEN

They were up earlier than usual on that Saturday morning, the horses were fed at 5.30 and half an hour later a proper shampoo and wash-down, dried off and then brushed over. The farrier had trimmed their hooves down the night before as they had never needed to be shod, but now it was Billy's job to oil each hoof. Once finished, he stood back and admired how their coats glistened. David came into the box. He ran his hand over the back of the yearling and then down each leg. "Well, Billy," he said, "we've reared these two youngsters and produced two good-looking prospects. The dark bay is by a promising young stallion, 'Sky Moon', who came second in the Irish Derby, and the bay is by 'Sing Again', who's already proved he can sire plenty of winners. But the mares of both of these two have never done very much, just four moderate wins between them and a handful of winners from their progeny.* We, I'm afraid, are in the bargain basement category. We could see some go through for hundreds of thousands, but one can sometimes strike lucky. Mind you, it's never happened for us, I'm afraid."

—

Billy, of course, had been shown around Newmarket. Grace had taken him early morning to see the horses galloping up the all-weather surface on Bury side, then to the racecourse side to watch them do fast work, and then seeing the two-year-olds being familiarised with being put through the starting gates. She'd also taken him to see Tattersalls' sale rooms, which to Billy's eye were so far from what he'd imagined it to be.

Even though the place had been empty and quiet, it somehow had an atmosphere that excited him, leaving him with a sense that he, little Billy as he was, was nevertheless becoming part of all this. Another time, later in the day this time, Grace had taken him for a tour of the National Stud, which he had found no less interesting.

He and David, normally on a Saturday afternoon, watched the racing on TV. David seemed to have a huge knowledge of the trainers and jockeys that were household names to fans of the sport. Billy was aware, now, of when the horse was on the bridle,* how a jockey rode a finish, and jockeys rode with just a toe* in the iron, and lots more.

David was never short of saying that, however long one worked with horses, there was always something new to learn.

No sitting in the snug watching the racing this Saturday. They loaded the two yearlings into the horse box at 10.30. It was the second day of the sale and they were scheduled to arrive not before eleven. As they'd walked the yearlings in and out of the horse box each day this week, they were led in without an ounce of resistance. Grace in the front, with David, Celine and Billy in the back with the horses, they drove off. Just fifteen minutes later, they turned into Tattersalls Drive and checked in. The two young horses were unloaded.

"We're in the Somerville paddocks," David explained. "It's a good spot just behind the sale ring." Attaching leading reins to the halters, he handed them to Celine and Grace. Billy carried the bridles and grooming kit, David the rugs, and together they walked and led up the sloping pathway, turned left behind the sales ring, and looked for the numbered boxes consigned to them.

"What are we looking for?" asked Celine, searching the numbers on the stable doors. "517 and 518: they're just behind this row."

Billy was amazed: so many different named paddocks, hundreds of boxes.

Prospective buyers, probably trainers, or agents watching selected yearlings being trotted up* by their grooms, just so much going on. "Here they are." David slipped open the bolts and held the door open for Celine and then Grace to lead their horses in. Then, David with the rugs and Billy following close behind, they took their gear to leave in the room provided for the grooms, just yards away. Each then took an armful of hay that was provided outside, and returned, to shake out into a corner in each of their boxes.

"We should be called to the pre-parade* ring around 3pm." David, turning to Billy, explained that it takes an average three to four minutes on entering the sales ring for a horse to be auctioned, whether bought or not. The exact time, though, usually depended on how many lots had been withdrawn. "So we have to keep a watch as the lot numbers go through as we might be called much earlier. All we have to do now is to wait and hope someone interested enough comes to look at our boys." He checked his watch... 11.40. "There's a cafe down there, Billy." He pointed way down the slope to the left. "If you want something to drink or a sandwich, you can bring us back a coffee."

It was a little worrying. Several people had come to look over the yearlings close by, but no one had approached them. Billy had just arrived with coffees and it must have been at least an hour later when two men and a lady walked towards them, stopped and asked to look into each of the boxes. They chose to see only the least expensive of the two, the Sky Moon yearling.

They seemed to know David, and, as they chatted with him, Celine slipped the bridle on and led the yearling outside. She turned it to the right and, pushing it forward and back, made it stand, straight and balanced equally on its four feet. After stepping away, the three of them viewed the horse square on, then one of the men came up to the horse and ran his hand along its back, then each of the front legs in turn, feeling the tendons from the knee to the foot, tendons that were as cold as they should be. He then lifted the front leg forward and bent the knee tight up against itself, let it down gently and then did the same to the other. He then asked for it to be trotted up. Celine walked the horse twenty-five or so yards away from them, as the three interested parties watched from behind, viewing the yearling's quarters.* Then, turning the horse around, she ran alongside him as he trotted back towards them. The yearling, apart from a couple of bucks, trotted straight and true: no close brushing of the hinds* or dishing* of the front legs.

The trio thanked Celine and, when about to leave, David suggested that they should also have a look at the bay colt,* which was by a new and as-yet unproven sire who had come third in the 1,000 Guineas at Newmarket and second in the Irish Derby two years ago.

Somewhat reluctantly, they agreed, and the whole process was repeated.

"Well at least someone's seen them," said Grace. She turned to Billy. "And that was Edward Henley, the trainer, and Lady Angela Worlinton, one of his owners. I think she knows as much about the breeding side of things as he does. The other man was Henley's head lad."

TWELVE

Three other interested people came to look at the Sky Moon dark bay* colt; no one showed interest in the more expensive of the two, the bay colt by Sing Along. Billy asked David why. "You never know," David answered. "The Sky Moon's two-year-old daughter won a race at Windsor last night, first time out, and I must admit he is the more mature of the two. We'll soon see; it's difficult to judge. Most people in this business like to keep their preferences to themselves. That's why they never appear too interested, but they're often the ones more likely to make a bid."

It was time to make a move; after a final brush over, Grace and Celine led the two up to the pre-parade ring. David and Billy followed. Billy had another question bothering him; although he hadn't wanted to disturb David, who was obviously up tight and anxious, he asked anyway. "Why haven't the yearlings got names?"

Although far away deep in thought, David put his hand on Billy's shoulder. "When someone buys a yearling, they have to register with Weatherbys the name they want for their horse. If accepted, that name will go into the stud book and be used for the horse's life and beyond. We must make sure we get those names later so we can follow their progress and see how they do, if anything."

Grace and Celine had been walking the pre-parade area for ten minutes when they were called in to the parade ring, from where the horses were being called inside, one at a time.

David and Billy watched from the rails. A smartly dressed man, who seemed to Billy quite old, came up and shook hands with David. "Good to see you," he said. "How are you? And Grace? Your two look quite promising. The dark bay especially. Seems an honest type." He then noticed Billy. "And who's this little lad? Looks like he'll make a good lightweight, eh?"

"My nephew," David answered after a short pause. "He already looks good on a horse."

"Well, if he'd like to ride out for me in his holidays," said the man. "Just give me a call… So nice to see you again, David; I was sorry you handed in your licence.* Always thought you had a gift for it… and good luck with your two." They shook hands again and, patting Billy on the head, he walked off. David picked up Billy's thoughts. "That was Henry Brothington. He's one of our leading trainers, top class. He's won many group races over the years. I used to work for him before I took out my own licence to train. He was very generous in that he recommended several good owners to me, which helped me get started."

Just then David noticed Grace with the Sky Moon colt being brought into the restricted enclosure and held there as the next to go in. Several onlookers took a last close look of him. The main doors opened and Grace led him inside. David took hold of Billy's arm. "Come on, son, this is us." They hurried inside and stepped up onto the raised stand to the left, most used by bidders not too worried about being seen. The tiered seats were three-quarters full all three sides of the arena. The auctioneer stood on a raised dais in front of them. A large electronic sign above showed the price reached by the yearling now being walked out the opposite end to which it had entered. A circular white sticker placed on its quarters by the yard man proved it had been sold. Prices on the screen showed in currencies of guineas, euros, dollars and yen. The colt had sold for 10,500 guineas.

As the yearling walked out, Grace walked the Sky Moon colt into the ring and around its tight circle. The auctioneer gave a summary of its breeding and that the sire, Sky Moon, was a new and exciting prospect with his first crop, that it had won three group twos and come second in the Irish Derby.

He continued. "Now... where shall we start with this fine-looking youngster? He looks so like the sire, don't you think? A huge opportunity to take this one home. Do we have twenty thousand?" He looked around the arena and to the several smartly dressed young people employed to point out bidders. He paused. "Do we have ten thousand, then? All right, surely five thousand. No? What about three thousand to start us off?" A bid was pointed out to him. "Thank you, sir."

Billy looked up at David and could see he was very much on edge. There was a pause. "Three thousand, five hundred... four thousand. Thank you, madam."

Several of the employees were now trying to get the auctioneer's attention. The bidding continued to increase by five hundred at a time. It reached ten thousand. Now each bid rose by a thousand. It slowed at eighteen. The auctioneer brought the gavel to his shoulder. A long pause, then, picking out the other bidder, and a further long look around the room, he had one last attempt. "Don't lose him now, sir."

The gentleman bidder on the far side shook his head and the hammer fell. "Sold. Eighteen thousand guineas. Thank you, sir." He turned to the assistant behind him and muttered the name of the successful bidder, well known to him as a top agent.

The Sky Moon colt had his ticket slapped onto his quarters; the exit doors opened and he was led out... Celine was already inside with the bay. David drew a sigh of relief. "This one cost the most; we'll be lucky to get as much with this one."

Billy felt so pleased for him; the tension had eased somewhat. The situation excited him, yet he still nursed a concern. "Where will they take him now he's sold?" he asked, as they watched Celine lead their yearling around in front of them.

"Grace will take him back to his box, and the new owner will probably call round to have a word."

The auctioneer was back on the mike, extolling the "Sing Again" yearling, telling the onlookers that he was out of the mare whose two-year-old had just the previous evening won a class 5 at Windsor.

Bidding was slow at first, only starting at the minimum price permitted of eight hundred guineas.* David's frown returned. The profit he'd made on the Sky Moon colt could all be lost on this one. The auctioneer cajoled for bids, and then suddenly they took off thick and fast. They rose to the ten thousand mark in quick succession, then, rising by the thousand, reached thirty-five thousand guineas. Again there was a pause. The auctioneer looked around for another bidder. "Forty thousand pounds. Thank you, madam." He returned his attention back to the previous bidder, but saw he'd already left his seat. "Thank you, madam. A very nice yearling and yours for forty thousand guineas." The gavel, already raised, came down with a loud bang.

Celine led the bay colt out as the next yearling was brought in.

David was trying very hard not to show how this had moved him, and Billy felt so proud to be standing next to him. A feeling, perhaps only for the second time in his life, made him believe that perhaps he wasn't just "Little Billy the No-Hoper" any longer.

And anyway, in Newmarket there were so many small people, grown-ups not much taller than himself. After all, this was the centre of the UK horse-racing industry and it paid to be small. Is that why that trainer called him a lightweight? Could it be that he could make it as a jockey, perhaps? Now that was a thought. David interrupted his dreams. "Come on, son, let's go to the paddock, take all our stuff back to the horse box, and I'll treat us all to a slap-up meal in the Tattersalls restaurant."

Grace and Celine were waiting for them with the rugs, grooming kit, bridles and buckets, all stacked neatly, ready for a quick departure. Grace gave David a huge hug, and Celine kissed him on the cheek. What a result! A gross profit of around thirty-six thousand pounds.

With yearlings watered and in case they were left overnight, a large amount of hay piled up into the corner of each box, they were ready to go. Celine asked whether they should leave the halters on.

"Some people leave them, some don't, but it's good manners to leave them on. It always makes me annoyed if they don't and it's very mean not to. Let's dump all this into the van and if you like we'll all go up together and have something to eat."

THIRTEEN

After the excitement of the previous day, when sitting down to their bacon and egg breakfast, David asked Billy if he'd enjoyed the experience. Yes, he'd had the best time and said that he'd not copped that David had actually been a trainer. David nodded, saying how hard it was for small trainers with fewer than twenty horses to make ends meet. "We had a few difficult years, lad, and I handed back my licence before we would have become bankrupt; it was even harder for Grace than for me. Anyway, we changed course, and it seemed to work for us. Yesterday, though, was the best result we could have ever hoped for."

Billy took a last sip of tea, as Grace cleared their plates. Before leaving the table he asked what he'd been thinking about most of the night.

"What did that trainer you talked to mean?" he asked. "When he said I'd make a good lightweight."

David smiled. "He meant you'd have a good chance of making it as an apprentice. If the lowest weight in a handicapped race is, say, 8st 12lb, as an apprentice one can claim 7lb off that, so that takes the weight to be carried down to 8st 5. The saddle weighs another 3lb so you yourself fully dressed would have to weigh in at not more than 8st 3lb."

Billy thought a second and then asked what if he weighed less than that. David explained that one then has a weight* cloth that carries lead up to the required amount, and the weight cloth is then placed under the saddle.

"Are you thinking, Billy, that you'd like to become a jockey in a few years? Because, if you do, we're well placed here to help you to do that. Mind you, it's tough, and not many make a success of it. I wouldn't suggest it, though, not until you've taken your GCSEs. Not until you're seventeen, anyway." David pushed his chair back and as Billy followed him outside he told Billy to think very hard about it, and that they would talk it over again in a few months.

Sunday was the easy day of the week: the horses were fed and allowed out in the paddock and not brought in until four o'clock teatime. Being a Sunday, it was Celine's day off, so Billy helped David, but only because he wanted to. It was a tidy-up of the yard day, of mending part of the post and railed fencing, of picking up the week's residue of horse dung in the paddocks. So much to do, hard work, but Billy just enjoyed being with David and doing whatever he could to help.

—

The fifteenth of November was already here; the time had passed so quickly, and here they were back at Tattersalls again for the foal sale. David had studied the catalogue and picked out six foals of interest. Partly chosen to his budget, partly on their breeding and of how they looked. No crooked legs or wild eyes. Those poor little things, taken from their mothers just a few weeks ago.

He'd explained his choices to Billy. Just six out of 900. "We're not buying the six, of course," he said. "We only want to replace the two yearlings we sold three weeks ago. We did so well with the yearlings I'm looking to splash out and go for something out of a mare that's got some black type* behind her. Do you know what I mean by black type?"

Billy shook his head. David thumbed through the catalogue to lot number 169, one of his six choices, and pointed out the name of the foal's mother and her pedigree. It showed she had produced six foals of racing age, four of which were winners, and, of those four, two stood out, highlighted in black type.

"Do you see now? These individuals have either won a group race or placed in a group race. The top echelon of achievement. These are the sort that make the best prices so we might not be able to afford him. Let's go see this one first; it's going to be a long slog."

They managed to buy lot 169. He seemed a confident little sort, seemingly not fazed by being handled and looked over eight or nine times by other interested parties. The auctioneer had dropped his hammer at twelve thousand guineas and had thanked David by name. Billy was impressed.

They had no luck or chance on any of the remaining five. Two of them had faults in their confirmation and the other the two had gone for something over thirty thousand.

So, once they were outbid on the remaining foal, they hurried outside to look for their second purchase. David had said several times before that it wasn't fair to have a foal on its own. It had to have another to play with and to gallop around the paddock with, and that one can often tell how good they're going to be just by watching them.

They hadn't researched anything else, so now they had to take a chance. Looking over the rails to those being led around the pre-sale ring, so many of them looked the same to Billy. David was quiet and concentrating on the task. Suddenly a black foal passing in front of them put in three little bucks and gave a short high-pitched screech. It had a little white blaze on its forehead and one white sock on its near fore. Something stirred through Billy's inside, something he couldn't later explain. He pulled at David's sleeve. "What about that one?"

David turned over five further pages of the catalogue to lot 189. "Well," he said. "You've got an eye for picking that one out... it's nicely bred, but we don't normally go for fillies. We'll go back in and see how much she goes for."

The little black filly went for twenty-two thousand guineas, and when the hammer went down it was David's bid. Billy had that warm glow flow through his body again. He himself had picked this one out, and David had gone with it, and here he was leading her down to the horse box.

David had followed with the little colt and, loading the two of them to each side of the central partition, they drove home.

It was still only mid-afternoon, and, as they pulled into the yard, Grace and Celine were there waiting to drool over the two newcomers. David led his out first. "Like it, like it a lot," Grace said. "Is that the one by Predominance?" Celine took it from him.

Billy walked out with the filly. Grace took a step back to get a better view. "My oh my, what a little corker." She paused, then said, "Already thinks a lot of itself. It's got such a presence." Grace walked around to look at it from behind. "Oh! ... It's a filly. My word, that's a change. How come you picked her out?"

David grinned. "Nothing to do with me," he said. "It was Billy. Billy picked her out." Celine and Grace looked at the boy; he blushed, red in the cheeks. Grace gave him a hug.

The four of them walked the foals up to the empty paddock, took off the halters and let them go. Both foals took off at the gallop, bucking and squealing with the sheer joy of being free again. It was at least another six or seven minutes before they settled and started to graze. Whilst the others returned to the yard, Billy stayed where he was. With one foot on the lower rail of the gate, and resting his arms overt the top, he watched this little black foal with legs that seemed far too long for her body, and thought what a huge responsibility it was in choosing her. Little did he understand that David had recognised something in her breeding that others had missed.

FOURTEEN

Over the weeks since he'd moved into his new surroundings with David and Grace, Billy had regularly made contact with his mother, having rung her every Tuesday at 5.30.

She was doing well in her new flat. Now eating properly, she had put on weight getting a daily hot meal from meals on wheels, all arranged by social services. She'd also said she was on the waiting list for an operation on her lower back, as the sciatica pain was still troubling her, and was only able to move around by the relief of prescribed painkillers. She kept asking when he was coming back.

Every week he dreaded that question. It wasn't her decision anyway. He was still under the control of Finsbury Park Social Services. In his mind he didn't want to remind her of this; if she decided to contact them, they might decide she could have him back.

He still loved his mum, but he'd never agree to lose this new life he had come to enjoy so much. The possibility of it being taken away haunted him.

After several weeks of worry, he'd decided to talk it over with David and Grace, but hadn't yet found the courage.

One afternoon after school, he went as usual to watch the foals in the paddock. They'd grown: no longer the fragile little things with shaky legs. Still beautiful, though, but in a different way: each now had a personality of its own. Every day whilst still light, he was there, walking up to them, putting hands on, stroking and talking to them. Of course, it was the filly who got most of his attention, and she responded; often she would come up to the fence when she saw him coming.

A month later after evening stables he'd walked into the house to find David sat at the table waiting for him. He indicated that Billy sit down opposite him and offered him a mug of tea. The kettle was already on the boil. He passed the mug and sat down himself. Billy took a sip, and felt that something ominous was about to engulf him. "Billy," he said. "I think it's time we had a serious talk."

David started by asking how his mum was doing. "Tell me about her. You've been very quiet about her; all we know is that she's not well enough to look after you."

Billy explained that years ago she'd been a dancer and had had an accident that had damaged her back and she'd been in a lot of pain ever since. Just recently she'd had the operation she'd been waiting ages for, and was now in her new one-bed flat and doing well.

"And what about your father?" he asked. Billy blushed slightly, wondering where this could be heading.

"Don't know who he is. Never met him, not ever seen him. Don't even know his name."

"Would you like to find him?"

"No."

"Billy, you realise that we are only fostering you. We have no control as to where they decide you should be. We don't want to lose you; it would devastate Grace, and I can't imagine you not being with us. It's just that the Finsbury Park people want to review your placement here."

Billy frowned; his lips trembled. David reached across and placed a hand on his shoulder. "I'm sure it won't come to that, son; the local social services woman is coming over here at five tomorrow for a preliminary chat. She'll make an initial report on how things are going, then, sometime later, after she's submitted her report to the London people, we may have to go… No, no, not for you to be left there, just to have them assess what they think is best for you."

Grace had appeared and had started to prepare supper. She struggled not to interrupt, but was all ears and very much involved.

"Don't I have the choice?" asked Billy. "Surely I'm the one who can choose what's best for me, and that's here."

"No, Billy, you don't have that right. Not until you're eighteen."

"It's just so unfair. If they take me back to London, I'll just run away again. As long as you still want me, I'll never leave this place, and never want to leave you… or the foals."

The next day, at a quarter to five, Billy, all cleaned up and tidy, was already waiting.

She was ten minutes late. Shaking David and Grace's hand, she said hello in a kindly, caring way to Billy. She seemed quite young to him and rather pretty.

Sitting around the kitchen table, David small-talked with the young woman, who said her name was June. Grace brought them mugs of tea and sat down too. June immediately took over. She first asked David how he thought the relationship had formed between the three of them and how everyone was coping… David, with Grace adding to it, told her how things were, and of how they loved Billy sharing their home. Of how Billy loved the horses and was riding most days and was thinking of becoming an apprentice jockey.

Immediately having said that, he regretted it. June responded immediately.

"Well," she said, "of course we would probably agree to that here, but I don't know whether they would when asked in London…" There was a deadly silence. "What do you think, Billy?"

"Uncle and Auntie have made me believe in myself. No one bullies me at my school here. I love working with the horses. It's all made me feel different. I now know what I want to do, and it's Mr and Mrs Clayton who will help me achieve it, which is something no one in London, including my mother, knows about."

June had listened intently. She was as surprised as David and Grace at the confidence of the boy, who only a few months ago could barely utter a word. She smiled at him. "Well spoken, Billy. My. You've come a long way in a very short time. I'll see what I can do and will be positive in my report, but you know we have to get through to the complete panel. It's them in the Finsbury Park office who have the ultimate decision. Have a word with your mother. If she's happy for you living up here it could be a big influence on the way forward. They may well insist that you don't leave school until you've taken your exams." Pushing her chair back, she addressed David and Grace, complimenting them on providing such a rewarding environment for the lad. She shook hands with everyone and was shown out.

Billy got up to go to his room. David stopped him, and asked him to sit back down again. "We were very proud of how you stood up for yourself, and feel so pleased that you're happy here. But we have to be very careful on how we make a good case in persuading them what's best for you is being here with us." David continued, and explained why he had previously mentioned Billy's father. "If we found your dad, and explained all this to him, perhaps we could get him on our side to support us. Who knows, if that were the case it might just turn the scales in our favour."

Billy turned the idea over for a few seconds. "If you think it might help us, but I don't want a father, never have. Anyway, how can we find him? Mum doesn't even know his name."

"There is one way. We could get you a DNA test, and if your dad had ever been tested, and they had a match, they'd tell us, and depending on his circumstances we could decide whether to make contact or not. What do you think?"

Billy reluctantly agreed. Any help was worth a try. Even so, the whole situation had made him lose that feeling of being content and safe. He tried to put his worries out of his mind, but the worrying kept coming back, particularly at night.

—

Several weeks passed by. Nothing was heard from either local social services or London. David had googled to find out how to get a DNA test, and had ordered it.

Following the instructions, he had swabbed Billy's mouth and returned the sample. A week later he received an email to say no match had been found but, as the sample was now registered with them, their systems would automatically recognise a match if one was found at any time in the future. They would then immediately dispatch the relevant details. Billy thought David was disappointed, but he for his own reasons was not sorry.

Christmas came and passed by. It was by far the best Billy had ever experienced.

It was also his first chance to meet Patsy, David and Grace's daughter. She'd come down from Manchester with a week off work with the vets.

She was so kind and welcoming to Billy, and, even though it was Christmas Day, they still had work to do. Patsy had helped and they had ridden out together. It had been a crisp and bright sunny day; everything had just felt so good, it had lifted his spirits, away from his deep concerns. In one way, though, he wanted to get it all over with, to get things sorted one way or another.

David had seemed confident that, in the end, all would go their way, whilst Grace had kept very quiet but was obviously deeply upset that these people should ever think of taking Billy from them.

A week after New Year's Day David took a call from June from the local office, saying she had received a reply from London and asking could she drop round to explain the situation. Just two days later, she was again sat at the kitchen table. A little small talk ensued and then out it came.

David and Grace had to bring Billy back to London to put their case to the panel, and a decision would be taken later as to Billy's future. They had to first take him to the hospital for another scan to see if his lungs had improved. His mother would also be called in person so that all interested parties would have their say so that the panel could make a considered judgement. David asked June how she thought it would go. "Who knows," she said. "Depends what sort of day they've had. But generally they get it right, and what's right for Billy is to leave him with you. They'll let us know the date within the next couple of weeks. By the way, it's all expenses paid, so keep your receipts."

FIFTEEN

Horses were bought or given, trained on, then sold on, always fitting the horse to the capabilities of the rider. It was Billy's favourite job as he was the one who now rode around paddock showing the prospective buyers the walk, trot and canter. Pulling up, standing still when asked. "My goodness," was the hoped-for thought of the onlooker.

After all, if a fourteen-year-old child could ride this good-looking horse in all his paces so competently, then surely it's not only a good-looking horse but a sensible sort as well.

Deal done with, a small haggle, and a healthy cheque at the end of it.

—

It was an awful day, rainy, cold and grey. They had got soaked riding out and as soon as they'd dried the horses off they went inside for a complete change of clothes and a hot mug of tea. As they sat at the table, the post dropped through the letterbox. David went to pick up the three envelopes. Throwing two of them aside onto the worktop, he sat down and opened the one remaining. Billy, seeing David's reaction, knew immediately it must from them.

"Right, this is it. You have an appointment Wednesday week at 10.15 for your scan, and then the three of us at their offices at 11.30.

That gives us another ten days to prepare our case." Billy looked crestfallen. David gave him a hug. "Don't be upset, lad. We'll put up a fight for you, anyway… it might not be as bad as we think."

The appointments were confirmed by email and David replied that they would attend as requested. He also rang Billy's headmaster and, after explaining their situation, asked if he would be good enough to write a letter affirming Billy's progress. He said he would be delighted to help. There was one thing he had added that worried David somewhat and that was that Billy still didn't mix with the others and was what he called a bit of a loner. Nearly all his class had their own phones and were regular users of social media, to which he added that it was something he and his staff had tried their best to contain, but it was a losing battle.

That evening David asked Billy why he was not interested in having his own smartphone. "Because," Billy said, "it's so stupid; it's all they think about. Walking around staring at their screens. I'm just not interested. I just want to get home to what I have here."

"Well, that's nice to hear, but it's no bad thing, lad. If you ever become a jockey, social media's not on. There are a lot of bad people out there who try to get details, particularly of young apprentices. They offer big money for tips, and even for stopping a horse from winning. Yes, jockeys need to have a phone to take engagements from their agent but should keep well away from using and giving out their details on social media. Now, have you talked things over with your mum?"

Billy hadn't, and, having missed making his regular call to her last Tuesday, felt he needed to think hard on what to say. Walking over to the bottom paddock, he called out to his black foal, officially now, from January the first, a yearling. She stopped grazing, looked up towards him, then trotted over. Billy stroked her head as her companion followed at a slow walk behind in the adjoining paddock.

The filly and the colt had been separated a few days before school holidays. The paddock they were now in was divided into two by a double-fenced, six-foot walkway, the filly in one half, with Patsy's retired childhood pony mare as company, now seventeen years old. The colt had David's twelve-year-old gelding in the other half as its companion, the gelding used as a lead horse.* Although separated, the two yearlings, who'd become firm friends, could now see each other over the rails but not run about together. They were growing up, and hormones would soon kick in, a huge problem if left out together. With the filly on one side and the colt on the other, Billy chatted away to each of them. No way could he ever envisage being away from all this. Letting out a huge double sigh, he knew this was his life he wanted, and, by the grace of God, no one had the right to take that away from him.

—

It was first day back to school and, catching the school bus, he sat on his own, lost in deep thoughts, oblivious to the chatter and chaos of those around him. Stopping at its next regular pickup point in Exning, another five pupils got in. Billy, looking out from his window seat, attention drawn by a string of horses walking past, became aware that someone had sat alongside him.

"Hello, Billy," she said. "Mind if I sit here?" He mumbled back at her, and returned to see the last horse passing out of view. "That's Peter Gibbons's string," she said. "He's my dad. I often ride out for him." Nothing else passed between them until they stood up to get out. "You're a quiet one," she said. "I like that." She skipped away to join her friends.

He wasn't really interested, but knew her name was Kate and that she was in the "A" form, one above him. His thoughts soon returned to his own problems, deciding he would call his mother later this evening, and then to his own surprise wondered if he would see the girl on the bus home.

She wasn't. He'd saved the seat for her, which had soon been taken by a loudmouth.

Once home, he helped Celine do the feeds and anything else he could find to do, anything to delay calling his mum.

—

The phone was ringing. He held on, then just as he was about to put the phone down she answered. "Billy? Is that you? I was worried about you. Are you OK?"

"Sorry I didn't call last week, Mum. I just forgot, what with all this going on."

"I know, love. Please don't be upset with me for wanting you back."

"Mum, please, you know I don't want to leave here. Mr and Mrs Clayton are looking after me fine and I love the horses. There's nothing for me in London."

"Billy, I love you. Don't you love me no more? I haven't seen you now for months. I miss you so much."

"Mum, I love you too. Of course I do, but please don't let them take me away from here. Social services want you to come to the meeting on Wednesday. I'll see you then."

"Yes, they've already been in touch… I don't know; let's just find out what they have to say. I can't stand the thought of those people taking my place as your mother."

"That can't happen, Mum, no one can change that, but if they come and take me back I'll just run away again like before."

"Well," she said, "I'll think about it. Now be a good boy and try to accept whatever they decide." She put the phone down, he still hanging on with a feeling of utter despair.

The following day, the secretary had come into his form and, with the teacher's permission, handed an envelope to Billy. It was addressed to Mr David Clayton. She told Billy he would be excused school attendance on Wednesday, and to hand the letter, which was from the headmaster, to Mr Clayton.

On the bus on the way home, the girl Kate was sitting by the window with a vacant seat next to her. Billy wondered what to do. He was about to pass to the end of the bus when she patted the empty seat for him to sit next to her. Billy was embarrassed, blushed, and cursed himself for it. He sat down. "You look worried," she said. "Can we be friends?"

"Your name's Kate," he said. "Mine is Brent." Kate was surprised.

"I asked one of your form and they said it was Billy."

"I'm going to be a jockey, and Brent is what I'll be known by."

Billy wondered where that had come from. He hadn't thought about it; it had just come out. Suddenly he felt good about himself, now he knew what he had long hoped for: the chance that someday his name would be well known in the racing world, not as Little Billy but as Brent, his surname only. He looked at Kate. She wasn't that pretty but there was something about her he liked, but he couldn't fathom what it was.

"Good on you," she replied. "You certainly know what to aim for in life. I shall call you Brent; it can be our secret." Billy, for the third time in his life, felt ten feet tall.

SIXTEEN

They left home by taxi at 7.15am to Cambridge and caught the eight o'clock express, arriving at King's Cross at 9.15. It worked out so much easier than when they'd travelled up before by car. Walking through the station they transferred directly on to the Underground Piccadilly Line and just four stops later arrived Finsbury Park.

Hailing a cab wasn't that easy, but after a few minutes they were picked up and arrived at the hospital just after ten. Not kept waiting long, Billy was taken into the X-ray department on time, whilst Grace and David waited in the hospital cafe. Billy was in and out within fifteen minutes. David, meantime, had made a call to Celine to check all was OK, which it was, as the relief groom had come in at 7.30 as arranged.

Hurrying out, they jumped into one of the several taxis lined up outside the front entrance, and arrived at the Town Hall a few minutes later, slightly stressed and yet relieved that although it had seemed it would be a complicated journey, he'd got them there bang on time.

Shown up to the second floor, they were asked to wait in reception. "Unless they ask," David said to Billy, "don't say anything about you riding our horses, or that you might want to be a jockey. If needs be, we can discuss it with them sometime in the future. Don't let's complicate things. All we want from them at this point right now is to keep you with us."

As he spoke, the door opened and the three of them were ushered into the conference room. A huge highly polished table faced them. Four men, three middle-aged and one much younger, and four ladies of mixed age, sat behind it. The only face recognisable to Billy was that of Marjorie, who beckoned them to sit down on three chairs placed at a distance facing the table. The meeting was opened by the lady seated at the centre, who thanked them for coming all this way. She went on to explain how the meeting was to be conducted. "We would first like to see Mr and Mrs Clayton alone, then Lucy, Billy's mother, and lastly you, Billy, so would you mind stepping outside until we call you back in?" Downcast and not saying a word, he left the room.

Expecting to see his mother, he was surprised that she wasn't there. He asked the receptionist, who said Miss Brent had not yet arrived and she'd telephoned her to check but no answer. Billy had a glimmer of hope: if she didn't turn up, perhaps it could work in his favour, but then he worried that something bad had happened to her.

–

The panel addressing their attention to David and Grace first thanked them for their excellent fostering of young Billy. The boy was obviously thriving under their care.

David then read the letter from the school's headmaster, which stated that Billy was a respectful and polite pupil, well liked by all members of staff. Perhaps sometimes a little too quiet. It had been noticed that he did not fully mix or socialise with his classmates but the boy had caught up with his studies.

The chairperson thanked them, and went on to explain that the problem, if it were a problem, was that the boy's mother wanted him back with her, and due to financial cutbacks within the department pressure was that the cost of foster care was a factor with the council. However, they would have Miss Brent in next and evaluate her situation.

David then made the case for keeping the boy, and of how much the child had come on, and how they now loved him and how he was now part of their family. He looked at Grace, next to him. "It would be such a huge loss in our life. My wife would be devastated and I would lose someone I now consider a son."

The members of the panel each nodded, moved by David's genuine plea of care over any financial gain. The chairperson thanked him, and added that they had received the results of the boy's lung scan, which showed the shadows had now cleared and the lungs were now completely fine and healthy. "Please leave us now and ask Miss Brent to come in. We will see you both again before you go."

Miss Brent did not go in as she'd still not arrived. The receptionist informed the panel, eyebrows were raised, and they asked for Billy instead. Billy's pulse was racing; nervous as he was, he would tell them, and tell him he did. Everything. His love of Uncle and Auntie Clayton, his love of the horses, how he enjoyed school where no one bullied him like they had in London. "I love my mum," he said. "I looked after her on my own since I was nine years old. No fun, no birthdays, no Christmas. But it was worth it; there was no other help, just me and Mum. Of course I love her, always will, whatever, but now I have the chance of making a life for myself. Please don't take me away. If you do I'll just run away like I did last time."

"Now don't you threaten us, young man. A child's place is with its mother, as long as the mother is fit and capable. We will judge and consider all sides of this dilemma. Now leave us, and if your mother's arrived, please ask her to come in. If not, we will have a word with your foster parents before you leave. Thank you, young man; we are impressed with what you've all achieved together in so short a time. You are old for your years, Billy; perhaps we should remember that."

Billy got up to go. Marjorie gave a smile and half raised her thumb so that the others couldn't see. Billy did.

No, Lucy was not there and now unlikely to show. David and Grace returned and sat down. It was brief and direct. They would decide over the next seven days which way to go and how to proceed. They would make contact with the boy's mother and assess whether she was fit and able to provide care for and control a fourteen-year-old teenager.

The receptionist kindly phoned for a minicab and, as they waited, Billy asked if they could call in to see his mother. It wasn't too far away. David, although not too keen on the idea, tried to phone to make sure she was home. No reply. Somewhat relieved, he suggested Billy call her later to see if she'd like to come up to the farm for the day.

"We could pick her up from Cambridge. If she realised she could pop up to see us now and again, it might be just enough to satisfy her, rather than wanting you living there. If she agrees, you'll have to cover the cost yourself. You could book her train ticket online." He looked at Billy with a twinkle in his eye. "I'm sure you have a healthy balance in your account by now." Billy thought it a good idea; he felt very grown up and would be only too happy to pay for her himself if she agreed to come.

In the taxi, the Underground and the express from King's Cross, they talked over how the meeting had gone. The fact that Lucy had not turned up might well be in their favour.

What with the headmaster's letter and the recommendation in the report from the local social services office, it surely had to go their way, but there was no real way of understanding how the system worked. If it came down to the bare fact of a financial cost-cutting exercise, David and Grace had already decided they would be happy to forgo their monthly foster fees, desperate as they were at the possibility of losing him.

Arriving back home at ten to six, David and Billy made sure the yearlings and horses were all safe and fed and that those stabled had fresh hay nets. Pleased that everything looked spick and span, they went inside and enjoyed a favourite chicken curry that Grace had left to defrost before they'd left that morning.

SEVENTEEN

Billy never thought it would really happen. Knowing very well that his mother might agree to come but would then at the last minute change her mind. He phoned her first, asking why she'd not turned up for the meeting. She said that she thought by not turning up it would be more likely that social services would decide to leave him where he was.

"I just didn't know what I'd say," she said. "Or what I really wanted. I was petrified at being grilled by those people. I'm sorry, love." Billy told her it was OK and then quickly thought again, suggesting instead that perhaps he could come down to London for the day sometime in the school holidays. "That would be nice," she said. "Give me plenty of warning as to when. You know I don't like surprises. By the way, what do you think of Newmarket?"

Surprised that she asked, he told her how he loved the open heath and watching the horses on the gallops, and that he often got the bus and spent time there. And then came an even greater surprise. She told him she had spent a week there years ago when her dance group were booked at the Newmarket Cabaret Club. "And I went to the races. We had a great time. I loved it."

"Well, then," he said. "Now you can understand why I love being up here. Anyway, I'll call as usual next Tuesday. Bye, Mum."

"Bye, love."

Billy gathered perhaps she might now understand what he would be missing if forced back to London. He felt things might well be going his way.

—

It was to become the custom that he sat next to Kate most times to and from school. Sometimes the seat was already taken. When that happened they usually waited for the other to step down from the bus and walked together into school. When he spotted the string of horses in Exning again, she reminded him they were her dad's. Billy's interest was obvious. "Do you ride out for him?"

"I thought you'd never ask," she said. "I ride out most mornings. We've only twenty-seven horses in at the moment. Dad's just one of us small trainers trying to eke out a living; it's not easy. We're struggling to survive, actually. Would you like to ride out with us?"

"I'll ask my uncle. It's time I started to learn the other side of what we do at home. We try to calm ours down, you freak them out."

"I wouldn't say that to my dad, if I were you. No way. We don't want to freak them out. The skill is to find a balance between their feed, the right amount of exercise and getting them to settle in their work."

Billy realised he'd been stupid. He apologised and thanked her. "What time do you pull out?"

"First lot at seven and second lot at 8.30."

"What lot do you think would be best for your dad?"

She chuckled at this. "Dad never turns down a freebie. Both lots, probably. If it's OK with your uncle, be at ours Saturday by 6.45."

Billy's heart quickened at the thought; he had a sudden feeling of excitement, and couldn't wait to get home quick enough to ask if they'd let him off his normal Saturday morning task of schooling their own horses.

Before she got off the bus, Kate tore off a piece from her notebook, scribbled their address and phone number, and told him to ring to confirm he was coming.

"Billy, why don't you have a phone of your own?"

"Because I only have my mum to keep in touch with, and I don't like speaking to anyone else. It's so uncool."

"Well," she replied, "I think that's the coolest thing anyone has ever said to me. But I'd be a bit upset if you wouldn't want to chat with me if you had one."

Billy knew it was happening: he'd started to blush, and he looked down into his seat to hide it. The bus had reached Exning; with a friendly smile, she patted his shoulder and left him with a short ride to Fordham.

—

The next morning at 6.30, he and David carried the yearling's feed out to the paddock. They stopped a few minutes to watch them. "Your filly won't make a two-year-old, you know: she's growing too fast and will need all her strength to do that, but I think the bay might."

Billy was puzzled, and with a worried frown asked why the filly wouldn't make a two-year-old. "Is she going to die because she's growing too fast?"

"No, son. Some horses are sufficient in their growth to race as a two-year-old. They may do very well, but if raced too hard they don't often make it at three. By the way, I know you spend a lot of time with the filly, but she's not a pet, you know; she'll be sold on before October, so prepare yourself for that and don't allow yourself to get too emotionally involved, will you?"

Billy thought for a moment. "I'd still want to know who the owner was. Perhaps I might even get the chance to ride her out one day."

"Perhaps," he answered. "Stranger things do happen, but I wouldn't think too much about it. By the way, I've thought it through overnight and, yes, you can ride out with Peter Gibbons. It would be a good grounding for you. I'm afraid Peter is having a hard time of it. He only had five winners last year and one can't live off that. And about your filly: we'll follow her career if she has one and will keep in touch. Who knows, one day your dream may even come true."

It was still only Wednesday, and time seemed to go so slowly waiting for Saturday. On the way to school, Kate had told him her dad had asked whether Billy rode at home, and that she'd said he could ride anything, however difficult.

Billy was a little disturbed by this. "Blimey, I don't know about that. Don't let him put me on a nutter."

"It'll be OK," she said. "Dad said if you're coming in for first lot you'd just as well ride second lot too." She laughed and told him not to worry as she'd be there too.

—

Worried that he would oversleep, Billy had been clock watching from three o'clock.

He got up at five, bleary-eyed and feeling very tired. By the time he got downstairs and made himself a mug of tea and a piece of toast and marmalade, he was feeling excitement creeping up on him. To calm himself down, he walked out to the paddock and called to the filly. She came up to him, expecting her feed. He gave her a carrot and put his arm around her neck and stroked her ears. The sun was just rising in a glorious red glow, everything so calm and peaceful. Billy felt an inner happiness replacing his previous nerves. He very quietly spoke to himself and to the filly. He told her he was off to learn how to handle a racehorse, which she would soon have to learn about too. He told her that one day they would come together as a team and achieve great things. Then to himself he whispered, "Do I really believe all this? Possibly not, but I'll try my best to make it happen." He gave her a hug and made his way back to the yard.

Jumping on the old bike, shared between anyone who needed it, he set off for Exning and twenty minutes later rode into Harraton House Stables. The boxes were in two lines facing each other. There wasn't a lot going on, just one middle-aged man filling water buckets.

"Morning, son, I'm Jack, head lad. The boss told me you was coming in. How's David? Ain't seen him for yonks. Now, give me a hand with these." He handed Billy two full buckets, and told him to put them into the stables opposite. Billy struggled with the sheer weight of them. By the time he'd managed to put them in the left-hand corner of each box, two lads and two girls had arrived. They seemed friendly enough, and none of them seemed to wonder what he was doing here. They just said hello and got stuck in to brushing their designated horse over and tacking up.

Jack was coming out of what must have been the tack room,* carrying a saddle and bridle. He beckoned Billy to follow him into a box on the far end.

"The boss said you're to ride this four-year-old. He's nice and quiet and will look after you. Once we see how you cope, he may want you to ride one of the youngsters. You're a lightweight; not many of those about today. These lads here are all over nine and a half stone. In my day, no one riding on the flat would be over eight-seven."

As he spoke, he tacked up the mature gelding. "If you're riding out second lot, you'll have to brush the horse over and tack up yourself. If you can't reach, just stand on the bucket."

Peter had come into the yard. "Come on, you lot, time to pull out. Let's get it on."

As Billy pulled out of the box, he saw Kate opposite. She gave him a half wave.

Her dad gave her a leg up, then he walked over to Billy and as he legged him up onto the horse said a kindly hello. "Kate's told me all about you. Don't worry, this old fellow knows exactly what to do. I think you need to shorten up a couple of holes." Adjusting Billy's leathers,* he placed Billy's feet back into the stirrups. "How does that feel?"

Billy nodded. Used to schooling, he'd always been told to ride long. The legs against the horse's side gave aids to the horse to vary their paces. The more leg on a horse also helped the rider feel at one with their mount. It also made the rider feel more secure.

Peter told him when at the canter or gallop to stand up out of the saddle and to loop the reins over the wither. "Show me. That's good, but not so upright; get up the horse's neck," he added. "That's it... And let the horse pull against you, so just hold him there, and talk to him. Anyway, Jack will be on the lead horse, so follow him and I'll be right behind you."

The other riders had all mounted and started walking the circuit of the yard. Billy waited till Jack came by and pulled himself into the string, another circuit and Peter slipped in behind him. Kate, on a flashy chestnut, made up the last of a string of seven.

Pulling out of the yard onto Exeter Road, they turned left for a couple of hundred yards, then onto a gravelled horse walk. This led them to a short tunnel taking them under the busy A14 dual carriageway. The horses were completely undisturbed by this, and once through they came onto the heath racecourse side.

Still at the walk, they turned left and continued to the start of the six-furlong all-weather track. Billy felt butterflies in his stomach. Jack turned in the saddle. "OK, son? We turn in here. Don't shorten your reins until you kick off. Then gather them up as quickly as you can. Keep two lengths behind me." Jack turned onto the all-weather surface. Billy followed. He didn't have to ask his mount to do anything; it was all too quick, straight into a half-speed gallop. Trying to gather up his reins, he took a little too long and was mighty close to Jack, but quickly managed to regain control.

Feeling the full power of the animal beneath him came as a surprise; arms aching and quickly tiring, he needed to do something. That something came as an immediate impulse. Thrusting his feet forward, he used his own weight against the pull. It seemed to work, and before he felt entirely sure of what he needed to do, Jack had started to pull up. Billy gave an extra tug, then gave back an inch of rein; the horse slowed to a canter, a trot, then a walk. Peter came upsides.

"Now you can understand why I shortened your irons. I think you should come up another two holes. I saw you used your weight against his hold. You did fine. We're now going over to the wood chip down the centre, back to where we just came from. What we did just now was to loosen them up; we'll increase the pace this time."

Billy nodded, mouth set tight and firm, somewhat tense but excited.

As Jack turned towards the wood chip, he called back to Billy, saying to leave four lengths between them and he'd lift his arm when he was about to pull up.

Billy was tempted to shorten his rein before they set off, but quickly changed his mind as the horse gave a half-leap forward. He remembered David telling him that the racehorse took off as one shortened the rein and stopped when one loosened it. But no time to start messing about: he was already on the track and had shortened up his rein twice as quickly as before. The feel of power, speed and partial control was, to Billy, a life-changing experience. But that came later; his full concentration was in keeping a four-length distance between him and Joe. He played the strength of the horse with his hands and his weight. They were in full gallop now and it was somewhat easier. He felt more comfortable. It seemed just seconds before Joe raised his arm. Billy loosened his grip and signalled for the horse to slow with what he'd been taught, to voice a gentle and extended "woo hoo".

As good as he was, the horse slowed, smoothly coming back to hand and still four lengths behind Joe. Billy sat back into the saddle, breathing a long sigh of relief. Kate came up alongside him. "So," she teased, "still want to be a jockey?"

With her dad just behind them, Billy was embarrassed in case he'd heard. "Early days," he replied. "I know it won't be easy. But I'll get there. This is the start, and if what I think is meant to be, it will happen for me. And that I now know."

EIGHTEEN

David and Grace sat at the kitchen table, each with a bacon roll and a mug of tea. They sat deep in thought, not a word between them. David broke the silence. "Am I being ridiculous? I feel a touch jealous with the lad having his first taste of riding across the heath with someone else other than me. You know, it's times like this I miss it. I miss the thrill of it all, and now I miss our lad. I'm so proud of him."

"I know," said Grace, "but we have to let him go his own way. We know how determined he is. Mind you, I worry about him. He seems to have no friends other than Kate Gibbons. And look how he keeps his bedroom. It's spotless and so tidy. Remember the state of Patsy and John's rooms? Stuff all over the place. I think there's a certain compulsiveness about it, but let's just be happy for him; it's been so lovely having him here. Isn't it time we heard from social services? You'd think they'd have made their decision by now. It's such a worry to all of us. I just—"

Billy interrupted her mid-sentence as he came into the room, all smiles.

"How did it go?"

"A bit scary at first. I hardly had time to sort things out, but I didn't get run away with I managed."

"Did you have a canter, then?" asked David.

"Yes, on the all-weather track, then a gallop down the wood chip. I'd got the hang of it a bit more by then. I rode a two-year-old out second lot, but we just went for a hack past Sir Malcolm's estate and trotted round one of his big fields. So different to the older horse. They're so sensitive and light; I loved it… Thanks for letting me off work this morning. Mr Gibbons asked if I wanted to come again next Saturday. I said I'd first ask if it's OK with you."

David nodded. "We were thinking of how you were doing all morning. Perhaps I might come down with you next week, and watch."

–

It must have been a good three weeks later that June called and asked when she could pop up for a chat, as she had received an email containing a copy of the Finsbury Park Department's ruling. Grace held her breath, wanting to know the result. June said it was rather explicit and she'd rather talk them through it in person. Grace told her the sooner the better and asked whether it was possible for her to come up this evening, around five.

Grace put down the phone and ran out into the yard to find David. He could see she was in a state and knew immediately something was wrong.

"June's just phoned. She's received the committee's findings."

"And?"

"She wouldn't tell me. She's coming here at five to talk us through it."

"Doesn't sound too good, does it? I'd rather have been told over the phone and it had been just us alone. At least we'll now have a decision; it's been hanging on far too long. Better prepare Billy as soon as he gets home."

June arrived and thanked them for seeing her at such short notice. Pleasantries were exchanged as they sat around the kitchen table. Billy, white-faced, stood leaning against the Aga. The young woman placed the file in front of her. She looked at each one of them. "It's bad news and good news. The bad news is that they haven't finalised a decision." June opened the file and started to read the official report. "The committee came to an original decision that Billy should return to his mother, Lucy Brent. Ms Brent was contacted and medically examined. It was found that, although she is now pain-free after her operation, she has very poor balance and has great difficulty in walking. The committee amended their opinion that, as of now, she would not be capable of exercising the care and control to the degree of requirement. Therefore for the foreseeable future it is decided that the boy continues under the foster care of Mr and Mrs David Clayton. Further, it is the committee's opinion that the boy has made remarkable progress within the year, and find that David Clayton and his wife, Grace, have been excellent in the extreme. The issue will be open to further consideration should the situation change, which might then enable a final reassessment.'"

June looked up. "I think, with Billy nearing his fifteenth birthday, by the time they think to review this case again, he'll be near the age of consent and then it would be Billy's choice rather than theirs. So I would say this is definitely good news."

She turned to Billy. "I presume you still want to be here and not in London?"

He nodded; the colour had returned to his little face, but he couldn't hide the tears.

So now they could all try and forget what might or could have caused a heart-breaking separation. Yes, it wasn't a final resolution, but the immediate status quo was very much to their liking.

—

The months flew by. Billy now regularly rode out for Peter Gibbons on Saturdays, and three times in the week during his Easter holidays. He not only rode the normal routine canter and half-speed gallop but once a week was also now riding work, which was a full-speed gallop on turf on the many marked-out gallops on the racecourse side. On occasions, just for a change, they would ride over to Bury side. With most of the top trainers being located in this area, it was a completely different experience; it was so busy, a complete contrast to the open spaces closer to home.

—

On Billy's fifteenth birthday, 13 May, David and Grace took him to the Wheat Sheaf pub for supper. They asked him if he'd like to ask one of his friends along.

Thanking them, he said he'd rather not. Grace suggested he might like to ask Kate. Billy rolled his eyes… Enough said.

He'd bought a cheapish smartphone a couple of days before as a present for himself and had been surprised to be given a smart pair of breeches* and leather riding boots* from David and Grace. David explained that one should be able to pick out the apprentice from the other lads in any yard by being the most smartly turned out: polished boots, clean, and tidy. Billy had been very taken by their generosity. He was still phoning his mother regularly on a Tuesday. She sounded fine. She told him she had met a very nice man friend who made her feel safe and that she seldom felt as lonely as she used to. This person, she said, was very supportive and if she ever needed help with anything he was there for her. Billy at first was not too sure about this, but as time went on, and she still spoke of this man, he realised that perhaps it would last this time, and it was good to know that someone apart from himself was caring for her.

It was a long, hot summer and time to start training the two yearlings to cope with the traumas of the sale ring. Billy tried to close his mind to the thought that he would lose the trusting young filly he'd come to love unconditionally. Most evenings after school he'd continued his habit of sitting on the fence and telling her of his thoughts and ambitions. Billy had no need to burden anyone else with his worries or concerns about his future; the filly was always there waiting for him. But for the summer only: what then might her future be?

NINETEEN

Keeping up to date with the produce* of the mothers of both yearlings they were preparing for the October sales showed promising results. The first foal of the filly's mother had not run as a two-year-old but now at three had won his maiden race in June, a class 4 handicap race. Three weeks later, he'd come second in a £28,000 listed race.

The mother of their colt had her two-year-old's first run a week ago as a two-year-old maiden coming third out of a field of fourteen.

David had explained how the three-year-old's performance, being a full brother to Billy's filly, would now have considerably enhanced her value as the mare of both horses would now have the result recorded in black type in all future catalogues, something buyers and agents always looked out for.

"Let's hope the two-year-old, a half-brother to our yearling, can get a win before sales week. I see he's entered in a group 3, 'The Classic Stakes', at Goodwood for two-year-olds. They must think very highly of him putting him straight into a group 3, a race worth thirty-five thousand pounds to the winner." Chuckling, he added, "If he won or placed in that we'd be laughing all the way to the bank." Billy asked if David would record the race for him. "Won't have to, son, we can watch it together: it's on next Saturday at 1.50."

—

It was the Saturday. Billy cycled home after riding out with the Gibbons string.

He'd noticed a growing atmosphere in the yard over the previous few weeks; there seemed no smiles, jokes or pleasure amongst the lads and lasses. He'd asked Kate what was bugging them. "We've only had one winner since the season started," she said. "That means no bonus for anyone. It's not Dad's fault; the horses are just not good enough. The most expensive horse we have cost a mere ten thousand, and that's bargain basement. We need at least ten winners this season to break even. I know Dad and Mum are very worried."

When he got in he told David what she'd said. "Half the trainers in the country," he replied, "are small yards with under twenty horses. Most have to enter lower-class races where the prize money is so poor that their ten per cent of a winner's prize money can't keep the trainer solvent. On the other hand, trainers with horses costing their owners huge amounts... ten per cent of £500,000 is another matter. A wealthy owner buying a classically bred horse sends it to one of the top trainers; unfortunately, those types of owner don't come to the likes of us." Having said his piece, which was obviously something he felt very strongly about, he got up from the table, switched on the television and sat down again in his comfy worn leather armchair.

The horses were already walking the parade ring.* "What's his name?" Billy asked.

"Sorel Point, that's him there, number six. We should be able to recognise those colours in the race: green with a pink croix de Lorraine and pink cap. Now I think I recognise the colours: they're Lady Worlinton's. Pass me the paper."

Billy passed over the racing page. David looked down the list of runners.

"Thought so: it's trained by Edward Henley. Remember them? They came to look over our two yearlings at last year's sale. Well, I never, if this wins I'm pretty sure they'll be very interested in our filly. There's a lot riding on this, lad, mark my words. Go an' call Grace; she's pottering about in the yard somewhere."

The three of them sat around the telly. The horses were cantering down to the start.

Suddenly the camera trained on Sorel Point. He looked the image of their filly, other than having a white blaze on his forehead. David commented how relaxed he seemed and had a smooth and efficient action.

They were now down at the start and moving behind the stalls. Sorel Point was drawn number seven of the twelve entries, a good draw for a straight run down the middle of the track. As he was being led in by the handlers, the colt went to refuse, stopping dead in his tracks. It only needed an extra push from behind and in he went. Then that awful wait as several of the other young horses played up and had to be coerced in.

Sorel Point, not expecting this delay, pawed the ground with his near fore. "All in," was called, the starter dropped his flag and the stalls sprung open. Most, including Sorel Point, came out upsides, three or four a fraction behind. They were off, a flat-out gallop with seven furlongs of green turf in front of them. For the first hundred yards they each maintained their position, then crossed over to the rails. Sorel Point was a little slow in the manoeuvre and other jockeys had now crossed in front of him.

"They've cut him up," David, his eyes glued to the screen, added. "He's got nowhere to get through. He'll have to take a pull and make his run from the outside." Billy watched, his heart pounding as these tactics were being played out just as David predicted. A furlong and a half from the finish, Sorel's jockey, with four horses in front of him, made his run for the line. With two cracks correctly placed on the horse's quarters, the jockey rode a finish with hands and heels. David Grace and Billy were jumping up and down, shouting the horse home.

Passing three of the horses in front of him, Sorel took the lead for three or four strides, then seemed to weaken yards from the winning post and was beaten into third place, no more than three lengths from the winner. David sat back into his armchair.

"Wow! Some race, that, eh, lad? He was just short of race fitness, but it was a great run. He'll still be recorded in black type as having placed in a group 3 race and another feather in the cap for our filly's mother. Sorel is her son, but by a different stallion."

Billy had felt the excitement of the race, and had ridden every second of it. He wondered: if he'd been on board, could he have gotten across to the inside a shade faster than the jockey had? But then, Gordon Stokes was one of the best in the country. Yes, Billy thought, perhaps he's not as good as he used to be, as he might be getting on a bit.

He asked David what he thought. "No," David replied. "It's just how the race developed; there's always an element of luck attached to most winning rides, as I'm sure you'll find out some day. Gordon is still a top man. A jockey comes to know when it's time to retire. One knows instinctively."

Billy left the room and walked out to the yearling's paddock. They were both already standing at the rails eyeing each other. As he passed, he went to stroke the colt's head, but it took off at a gallop. The filly stood her ground and let Billy fondle her ears and scratch under her chin. He told her about her half-brother's run, telling her if he'd been the one on top they could have won. Did he really believe it? No, Billy knew full well he had to learn and earn so much before he would ever get the chance of being put up in a classic group race. For sure, there would be many low-class races for very little prize money along the way, but someday, somehow, he felt his destiny was to make it, and to make it big.

—

Two days later, at 5.15pm, the house phone rang. Grace was in the kitchen, the boy outside, making up the evening feeds. Grace picked up the phone.

"Hello… Sorry, I didn't catch that. No, this is his wife, Grace Clayton. Yes, he's in the yard; I can call him in. Who shall I say it is?" Grace's eyes opened in disbelief.

"Yes, of course, please hold on a minute, I'll fetch him." Putting the phone down carefully, she ran out into the yard. "David, quickly… it's Lady Worlinton on the phone."

David dropped what he was doing. "Whatever could she want with me?" He hurried inside, Grace running after him, leaving Billy wondering what the fuss was about.

"Hello, David Clayton here... Yes. What can I do for you?"

"Forgive me for calling, Mr Clayton, but do you still have that Pollyanna filly you bought last October foal sales?"

"Yes."

"Did you know we were the underbidder?* After the sale, having thought things through, we realised we shouldn't have let her go. Her mother is doing rather well with her progeny* and, should I say it, rather well for us. Are you planning to sell her on?"

"Yes, My Lady, we will be entering her in the Tattersalls yearling sale in October."

"Would you think it presumptuous in asking whether we could pop up to see her?"

"Not at all; I'm here most days, but if you could make it late afternoon between five and six? It's just that I'd like my boy here as he is very involved with the filly. He was the one who picked her out. Do you know where we are?"

"Yes, I came to the yard and sold a four-year-old gelding to your father. He was such a nice man... We'll make it Thursday, then. I will of course have Edward Henley with me. If I don't call back, we'll be with you around five o'clock."

"We look forward to seeing you both, ma'am. Thank you."

David replaced the phone and looked at his wife, who'd been hovering around him, all ears. "Did you pick up on that, love? They're coming up on Thursday. Ha! Can you believe it? We outbid them! Us outbidding them, with all the resources they have."

"But what are you going to do?" Grace asked. "Do you think they want to buy the filly privately? And, if so, how will you know what she's worth?"

"Let's just wait and see, but quite honestly I don't think we would want to let her go for anything under a hundred grand."

Grace's eyes widened. "And what did we pay for her?"

"Twenty-two thousand."

"Things are looking up for us, David, my goodness. The things we could do to this place. Are you going to discuss this with our Billy?"

"That's why I've asked them to come up at five. I want him there and to be part of this, whatever we decide to do."

David went back outside to finish off settling the horses down for the night, and, walking up to the paddock with Billy, each carrying a bucket of feed for the yearlings, told him the unexpected news. Billy seemed to take it well, and commented that at least they would know the people who owned her and where the filly was, and asked whether David would let her go before the sales.

"If they come up with the sort of price I'm thinking of, then, yes, I think we should. I've only recently thought of her as the very valuable filly she now is, not just as a racehorse but as a quality stud mare, just the type owners of the top sires are looking to breed from."

TWENTY

Thursday morning at 5am they turned all the horses out into the free paddocks, and set about mucking out. They put down copious amounts of fresh straw into each of the first ten boxes house side, and filled water buckets to the brim. Lining up the wheelbarrows neatly, they washed down the yard and swept it spotless.

His help with the work done, Billy went off to school, full of anticipation but touched with concern and sadness.

David had explained the situation to Celine, and together they brought in the two yearlings, put them in adjoining boxes each with a huge hay net. Feeling satisfied that the yard was looking its best, they went into the kitchen for a mug of coffee.

Grace joined them as they sat around the table and talked things over. Celine thought, if Lady Worlinton wanted the filly that much, she should bid on it at the sale rooms, and that was the only way to find the true value of the horse.

"I don't know," said David. "I haven't a clue what she thinks. We don't know whether she might be coming to make us an offer, or maybe they just want to see the filly before anyone else does. Anyway, we'll soon find out. By the way, I've heard she gets very upset if one gets her name wrong. So please remember it's Lady Worlinton and not Worlington, as in the village up the road."

No clearer of their visitor's likely intention, they returned to the yard. Slipping a halter onto the colt, they brought him out of the box, tied him up, washed him down, then shampooed him. The colt seemed quite happy with this new experience, letting them towel him dry. Finally, Celine oiled his hooves and returned him to his box.

Now it was the filly's turn, and the whole process was repeated. She was somewhat more suspicious of what was being done to her than the colt was. But Celine was very patient, and, although it took twice the time, the filly was returned to her box, her black summer coat shining in the sunlight. Yes, the stables faced south, and David knew and used this difference to effect rather than using the stable row opposite. Sunlight caught the fineness of the coat of a healthy horse and gave it the look of extra quality. Once completed, they still had most of the day before them.

With the older horses already turned out, there was not much left to do. David told Celine she could go home, but to come back at four. Plenty of time before the visitors arrived, just in case of any unforeseen circumstances. David had learned the hard way never to take anything for granted and always to have a plan B.

—

Billy came out of the school gates and got onto the bus. His relationship with Kate had changed over the previous few months. They were still good friends but she had taken up a friendship with an older boy from the fifth form and he came to school on a moped, often picking her up or taking her home on it. At other times they still sat together on the bus, and he'd see her when riding out, and have a laugh on the ride back in. Somehow, though, the relationship was not quite as it had been. Billy wondered whether it was his fault, but couldn't think why, or quite why he felt a loss of something he didn't really understand.

On the short journey home, he could think of nothing else than what the outcome might be with his beloved filly. He couldn't make up his mind whether it was better she went to those people, or if she were sold at the sales in three months' time, but then she might be bought by someone far away, in which case he might never see her again.

Well, he'd find out soon enough, as this was his stop. Getting off, he gave a casual wave to those still on it, and walked the half mile back to Home Farm.

Celine was already in with the filly, combing its mane and trimming the tail.

Billy noticed the shine on the filly's coat, and had to force himself to leave without making a fuss of her. "I'll be out again in a few minutes; David said I have to put my boots and breeches on. Perhaps he wants them to think I'm the apprentice. Ha ha!"

"Well," she said, "you will be soon enough, won't you?"

"If they don't send me back to London I will. They still haven't made a final decision."

"They won't do that now; it's not that you're ten years old. Don't worry about it. You've got a great future here."

"Thanks, Celine, that's so nice of you to say that."

Feeling reassured, he went inside, gave Grace a hug, and went upstairs to change.

–

David kept looking at his watch. It was ten past five, and no sign of them. They all hovered around the yard looking for things to do. Twenty minutes later, the car drove into the drive, Lady Worlinton at the wheel, an elderly Edward Henley seated next to her.

By the time they'd got out, David had already walked over to them. Lady Worlinton extended her hand towards him. Unsure what he should do with it, he took a gentle hold and gave it a slight squeeze. "How nice to see you again, milady, and you, sir. Congratulations on your big win the other day."

The three of them walked into the yard. David noticed immediately that Henley was as much interested in assessing the yard and its facilities as the horses in it.

"I must say, Clayton, how much we trainers appreciate what you do here. It's always a concern to us as to what to do with our horses when they need to retire. I must say, we have a very high regard of you, and not only here in Newmarket."

"Thank you, sir. Now, I'd like to introduce you both to my staff… This is Celine, who schools our geldings and mares." Both nodded at Celine but did not deign to take her hand. "And this is my nephew, who rides work for Peter Gibbons and also rides with us."

Slightly more interest was aroused. Henley looked Billy up and down, and asked how old he was. Before David could reply, Billy spoke up and said he would soon be sixteen and applying for his licence. Henley made no response to this and rather abruptly said, "Well, then, let's see this filly Lady Worlinton seems to have so much interest in."

David led them to the two adjoining boxes the yearlings were in, and switched on the lights as he pulled open the stable door, then pushed and manoeuvred the filly to stand square on. Lady Worlinton and Henderson entered and had their first view of her.

"Well, Clayton," commented Henley, "I must say, your staff know how to turn a horse out looking its best. She's big. Look at the depth of her chest, and girth. There's a lot of quality here, Clayton." He approached the horse slowly and ran his hands over her, then opened her mouth, checking the teeth. Running his hand down each of her front legs, he looked up and said, "Good bone, I tell you now, but I'm sure you know it yourself, Clayton. She won't make a two-year-old. She'll need all her strength to compensate for her growth. I would suggest whoever trains her would just give her a couple of runs towards the back end of the season just to educate her for a three-year-old career. If she can win a few half-decent races she'll make a grand brood mare, and I think perhaps Lady Worlinton has that very much in her mind. Take her outside and trot her up for us, please."

David slipped a head collar on the filly and led her out into the yard. Handing her over to Celine, he suggested they take her to the grass track behind the stables as she'd not been shod yet, and if she trotted up on the hard surface of the concrete yard it might restrict her action.

As they all followed, the filly thought she was being taken back to the paddock and kept breaking out into a collected trot, snorting and arching her back. Rather than walking straight on towards the paddocks, Celine turned to the left and continued up the grassed path. David, Henley, Lady Worlinton and Billy waited, watching the horse's quarters, her gait and her antics from behind. Fifty metres on, Celine turned the filly and, running beside her, trotted her towards them. They'd only covered a few metres and the filly exploded. With a loud squeal she leaped in the air, came back onto her forelegs, dropped her head and lashed out with both hind legs in one almighty kick. She then broke into a canter, snorting and blowing with frustration. How Celine managed to hang on to her was impressive. Pulling up in front of them as if it was all part of a normal day's work, she gave out a big smile and loud chuckle.

Billy, though, thought it had made the filly look difficult and unruly. Without being asked, he grabbed the leading rein from Celine, turned the filly round and led her back again to the top of the path, talking to her quietly all the way. Before turning her, he breathed into her nostrils, stroked her face, ran his hand over her eyes, and trotted her back, calm and controlled. Henley and Lady Worlinton could now see her action as it should be.

No dishing of the forelegs, no brushing of the hocks,* just perfect.

Pulling up alongside them, Billy handed the leading rein back to Celine, then immediately felt embarrassed. No one said a word, until David explained that Billy had a special relationship with the yearling.

As they returned to the yard, Lady Worlinton patted Billy on the shoulder. He looked up at her. "Would you like to see our other yearling as well?" he asked. "He's a very nice sort."

David held back a smile. "Bring him out of the box, would you, Celine?"

Henley went through the routine once more, patted the horse, and knew its breeding off by heart, both of the mare and sire. Celine led it back into the stable, and David suggested whether Lady Worlinton and Henley would like a drink, or if they preferred tea or coffee. Billy thought correctly it didn't include him.

Grace had everything ready and waiting. The kettle boiled, and, knowing Henley liked a drink, an opened bottle of Chivas whisky and cut-glass tumblers stood on the sideboard. A plate of the poshest biscuits she could find graced the kitchen table.

As they came in, David introduced her. Sitting down at the table, both visitors and David had a whisky, Grace a cup of tea. After a minute or two of small talk, Henley thanked them for an enjoyable outing and said he liked the filly very much, and was very impressed with the boy. He continued, "Now, I don't know what value you put on the filly, David, but I know that Katherine thinks she will eventually make a fine brood mare. I think we need to talk it over and have a good think about where we go from here. Have you a figure in mind?"

David had dreaded this as he'd expected to receive their offer first. Taking in a deep breath, he came out with it in as much of a matter-of-fact way as he could. "I think we're looking at somewhere close to one hundred and twenty thousand. She's entered in Tattersalls Book 1* in October."

"Well, they obviously think she has value to put her in Book 1,* but thank you for that. Do you wish to add anything, Katherine?"

"Yes, I do, actually. If we managed to agree a sale, would you break her in for me? I was very impressed with your staff here and can see that the yearlings are very well looked after."

"I'm sure we could arrange that," David replied. "I know Billy would be thrilled; he's very attached to the filly, as you may have guessed."

They stood up to leave. Henley thanked them. Lady Worlinton shook Grace's hand, and, surprisingly, said she hoped to see her again soon. As David walked them to the car, Henley suggested if ever the boy wanted to ride out to give him a call, and then added, a little unkindly, "We'd put him on something with a little more talent than what he'll find at the Gibbonses'. With regard to our interest in your filly, we'll be in touch."

David opened the car door for Her Ladyship, and watched the car pull out of the drive. Calling out to Celine and Billy, he told them to come in for a briefing.

Sitting down at the table, Grace conjured up another mug of tea all round as Billy, with a worried frown, struggled to keep his mouth shut. David first centred on him.

"Billy, you grabbed the filly away from Celine. It's not up to you to make decisions like this on impulse. Yes. I know it worked out for the best, but I think it all shocked us, and then to cap it all you take it on yourself to invite them to look at the colt. It was my place to suggest that, not yours."

Celine butted in, saying Billy taking the filly from her hadn't upset her in any way.

"That be as it may, but I won't have my authority undermined. That said, let me tell you that nothing has been decided. I've told them how much we want for her and they'll let us know if they're still interested. The good news is that, if they do buy her, they'd like us to break her in."

Billy's interest created an immediate change in his demeanour. He had to ask, "When would we start?"

"Soon after Christmas. There's no hurry, as she won't go into training until around March or April. We'd break her in, ride her away, then turn her out again until she leaves us. That is, if they buy her, of course; if they don't, she's away to the sales."

That didn't seem such good news to Billy. "Perhaps if I go and ride out for them they'd be more likely to buy her."

David looked towards Grace and smiled. "No, Billy. You know, sometimes you astound me. No, it wouldn't make any difference. Do you honestly think they would be so enamoured with you that they'd change their minds and rush up here to buy her? I'm sorry, son, but you should know more than most people that life doesn't work like that. Sometimes we have huge disappointments and just have to get on and cope with it. Right, now let's get the yearlings back to their paddock and bring the others back in."

TWENTY-ONE

School broke up for the summer holidays and the end of the school year. Although he'd gained good experience in riding out with the Gibbons' string, Billy felt that, with them, he'd now come to a point where he'd learned all he was going to. With the six weeks of the school holidays stretching in front of him, the thought of continuing to ride out the four times a week, as was now expected, was going to be a bore. He felt he was being used and perhaps it was time to move on. After all, two top trainers had offered him the chance: Edward Henley the day before and Henry Brotherton, whom they'd met at the sales.

The problem, though, might be getting into Newmarket. It would be too much of a ride on that old bike. Thinking of David's words yesterday, Billy questioned himself. Was he getting above himself, too full of himself, overconfident and ambitious for his young age? He thought long and hard and came to the decision that, no, he wasn't. He had to push himself forward. Right or wrong, he promised himself he would never let go of the vision of where he wanted to be in the future. Yet, perhaps he'd overstepped the mark yesterday. He would in future try to control his natural impulsiveness.

Getting home, he changed into his working clothes and went into the yard to help with the feeds. Walking up to the paddock with David, they watched the two yearlings getting stuck into their feed bowls. Billy took a deep breath and asked if David could try and get him a trial ride out with Mr Henley or Mr Brotherton's yard, as he didn't want to continue with Peter Gibbons. David thought for a moment. "Yes, I can give them a call," he said, "but how would you get there? It's too far to cycle. I'll see what I can do, but I can't ring up Edward Henley just yet as he'll think I'm pushing him about the filly. Leave things as they are for the moment, and, if you don't want to carry on at Peter's, tell him when you go in tomorrow. When Henley calls me on their decision whether or not they want the filly, I'll ask him. By the way, did you apologise to Celine yesterday?" Billy said no, he hadn't; they'd just talked about it and had a laugh.

"Well, that may as well be," David looked Billy in the eye, "apologise to her anyway. I don't want her upset. OK?"

"Sorry, Uncle."

—

Next day, Billy cycled into Peter Gibbons's yard for what he hoped would be the last of his regular Saturday morning exercise of the small string of ever-diminishing horses. He wasn't looking forward to telling Peter but felt it had to be, and best to get it over with. No excuses, just tell him as it is. And this is what he did, and to his surprise Mr Gibbons was very nice about it and thanked him, and said that he'd been a great help and would be missed by all of them.

As they walked back after a half-speed gallop, Billy fell in to ride alongside Kate to tell her the news. She didn't take kindly to it; she shook her head and trotted away from him. That hurt; he just hoped she'd get over it and they'd catch up again together when back to school next term.

Later, whilst having supper and enjoying Grace's home-baked cottage pie, the phone rang. David made a grunt of disapproval, got up, and answered it.

"Hello, yes... Oh! Mr Henley, no, it's all right... Well, I'm pleased you liked her... No, I understand... No, I'm sorry, as of now I have to say no. I'd rather risk the sale ring. But thank you for your interest and our regards to Lady Worlinton. Yes... Yes, I hope so too." David replaced the phone. Grace and Billy knew before David had returned to the table that it was a no deal.

Grace was the first to speak. "He made you an offer, then?"

"Yes, seventy-five thousand."

"And you turned it down straight away? Why didn't you suggest a meeting and see if you could negotiate a figure somewhere in the middle? Really, David, I think you were a little hasty."

"People like Edward Henley are so sure of themselves they don't like to negotiate. It's not necessarily the end of it. They'll let us stew over it for a week or so, thinking we'll regret losing the deal, and may come back with an improved offer."

"Well, I'm sure you know best, love; let's hope you're right."

Billy had been listening and didn't know whether he was sad or sorry and, after reminding David that he'd forgotten to ask Henley if he could ride out for him, quickly realised that he shouldn't have done. David pushed his plate aside, got up and, showing his anger, walked to the door, saying, "Billy, you think the world revolves around you. Well, let me tell you, it doesn't. This is an important time for Grace and me so just button up your mouth."

Billy, shocked and sad, said nothing, and went up to his room to do his homework, something he had been taking much more seriously of late. Just recently he'd found out that the minimum age of getting a licence as an apprentice jockey was sixteen. Perhaps next year if he could take his GCSEs at the end of school year they might allow him to leave.

—

Left to themselves, David told Grace that the boy worried him. "He still seems to have no friends, he's obviously quite stressed, he worries about his mother, his future, and is a little too desperate to please. He always looks to find things to do in the yard, riding out with us as well as at the Gibbonses'. It's all too much. I love the lad, but perhaps we've put too much work and pressure on him and taken it for granted."

"I should have mentioned it before," Grace answered. "But I've been thinking the same. I worry too, especially as the one person whom he could talk to, other than us, was Kate Gibbons. When he came in earlier, he told me she was upset at him leaving and snubbed him."

David reached across and put his hand on hers. "I know he worries about his mum, although she does seem to be a lot better. It would be nice if she could come up for the day. Perhaps her new friend has a car and they could drive up. I'll suggest that to Billy tomorrow, and try to get him to slow down a little. I don't think we'll see him again this evening. Do you think I was too hard on him?"

"No, dear."

—

Sunday being easy day, the horses were fed, then turned out, two in each paddock, the yearlings and their old companions checked over and fed on their own. There were now only the four geldings left to work on, and two of those were almost ready to move on. Just a few days before, David had turned down the chance of taking on two others offered to him for free. He'd let this opportunity slip by and a little later wondered why. He talked this over with Grace, as he always did when things got to him.

Grace, in her quiet and considered wisdom, had the answer he already knew. They had been in the business of retraining retired racehorses now for eleven years. It was a business that just about paid Celine's wages and the bills and put food on the table.

"I'm tired of it," he said. "I think I'm going to concentrate more on buying and raising the foals. We could also buy a couple of well-bred yearlings, break them in and sell them in the breeze-ups in the summer. That would be a quicker turnover."

Grace thought for a moment. "Something to think about, love," she said. "Let's see how the yearlings sell; we can make our minds up then."

David felt the pressure he'd been carrying in his head for some weeks now just slip away; it was replaced with a sudden feeling of excitement. His mind was already made up.

With renewed enthusiasm, he called out to Billy and said he wanted to take the yearlings for a walk up the lane. Putting head collars on and leading reins, they walked them out of the drive. The two horses were sensible and quiet and were allowed to stop and take a tug at the lush greenery of the banks and hedgerows.

Under such a relaxing environment, David took the chance to have their concerns over Billy brought out into the open. "When I was your age," he said, "everything I wanted or needed to do had to happen or be done at that moment, and until it was done I felt stressed. If my books or papers on the desk weren't square on, I had to straighten them up in line with my pen. Everything had to be lined up straight and tidy. What was I doing? Giving myself stress. It came to the point where I became in need of some help. I needed to talk to someone. I was too worried to go to my dad, so I went to my grandpa, and once I started it all came pouring out, tears and all. He just listened to me sobbing away telling him all of my worries and troubles. He was so lovely; he put his arms around me and told me they weren't real troubles and worries because they were all put there by me, and by talking to him they weren't there anymore. Now, I've never told this to anyone but you, so please keep this our secret. I tell you now, Billy, it didn't cure me of how I was, but I learned to cope with it and stopped getting stressed by it. So what I'm telling you now is, if you worry about too many things at once, you'll not accomplish what you do want. So find someone you can talk it out to. I think you and me are very much the same, so I'm thinking you need to go with the flow more, talk it out with me or Grace or Celine, if you like, or with anyone. OK? Life has a way, you know, of giving one the answers and opportunities without one asking for it. It'll happen for you, son, just don't rush it."

Billy's eyes filled with tears. He started to sob and couldn't stop himself. David put his free arm around him and hugged him close.

Billy sniffed his sobs away and looked up at David. "I love you, Uncle. I'm sorry about how I've been. I love Auntie too. I've been so lucky to have found you both."

"We both love you too, but promise me that if you feel stressed and feel it's out of control, talk it out with someone. I would like it to be with me, but, if not, with someone you trust."

Billy wiped his tears away with his hand, smiled up at David and they carried on leading their yearlings along this leafy and beautiful country lane, deep in thought.

TWENTY-TWO

Later that evening David told Grace of his talk with Billy, and that the boy had agreed not to burden himself with so many worries and concerns. He suggested that they contact the boy's mother and see if she could come up for the day. Grace rummaged through her desk and handed him Lucy's number.

"They haven't seen each other in over eighteen months," she said. "Ring her now."

The number was ringing. For some reason he didn't quite understand, David felt uneasy and a little nervous. No answer... He was about to hang up and she answered.

"It's David Clayton, Lucy, Billy's foster parent... no, he's very well; we're so pleased and very proud of him. I know he calls you on Tuesdays, but we were thinking... would you like to come up for the day sometime? Do you have anyone who could drive you up here?"

She said yes, she did; her partner shared a car with his brother and she would speak to him, and perhaps drive up next Sunday if that was all right. He said it was, and she thanked him profusely, saying she'd confirm whether George could get the car when Billy rang her on Tuesday.

David told Grace, and they both agreed it was something they should have thought of ages ago, and the following morning they told Billy. Hardly jumping for joy, Billy thanked them but unemotionally said he'd really look forward to seeing her again. He would ring her on Tuesday, give her their address and how to find them, but thought she'd probably change her mind at the last minute anyway and disappoint him.

Billy, now in his school summer break and not riding out at the Gibbonses', fell back into riding the remaining geldings and preparing the yearlings for the coming sales. Even so, he had time to spare, and used it to revise his schoolwork.

His form master had given him two old GSCE exam papers, one on history and the other on English language, with the relevant textbooks. He also used his smartphone for cross references into either of the two subjects.

On the Tuesday he put through his regular call to Lucy, and was pleasantly surprised when she confirmed that she and George would be coming up on Sunday, and that they had checked it out and would be arriving about eleven. She checked the address she had, double-checked the postcode, and told him how excited she was at the chance to see her little boy again.

"I'm not little Billy anymore, Mum. I'm nearly grown up, and know who and what I want to be. I'm doing well at school, too."

"That's lovely, Billy. Perhaps you will see how much I've improved myself as well. I'm not that wreck I was when you were taken away from me. See you Sunday, then."

"Love you, Mum."

"Love you, son."

Billy didn't quite know how he felt about her coming. In one way he desperately wanted to see his mum again; on the other hand, he was worried how she'd get on with David and Grace, and then there was George. Billy tried to picture what he might look like: baggy trousers, flat cap, mucky shoes, and a lot older. He wondered how old his mum was now. She'd never let on her age. Billy quickly worked it out. If he was fifteen and she'd been nineteen when she had him, she'd be thirty-five now. Remembering his chat with David, he stopped worrying. What was it David told him? "Go with the flow." Billy liked that. He told himself to stop worrying about it, and did.

The days flew by and the Sunday visit loomed. On Saturday, the day before, the house phone rang. Grace answered. It was Edward Henley. Asking him to hold on a minute, she ran out to find David. He hurried back in.

After exchanging their hellos, Henley came straight out with it, saying that Lady Worlinton had thought hard about the filly and that they'd decided to increase the offer to a hundred thousand. There was a pause and then he asked whether David would come to his office on Monday morning as he had an idea that might be to David's advantage. "And bring the boy, he can ride out second lot and we can watch him together."

David asked what time they pulled out. "Nine-fifteen; get him here for 8.45. Is that OK with you?" It was, and what the idea might be was intriguing.

Grace was hovering, desperate to catch what was being said. David, with a grin, told her of the new offer, and Henley's mysterious mention of a proposition that might be of interest to them.

Grace was stunned. "Whatever could that be? How exciting. Perhaps it's about Billy."

"Could well be," answered David. "He's asked me to bring him to ride out second lot, and Henley and I will watch them on the heath."

David went back outside and told Billy the news. "You see how I told you?" he said. "Things that are meant to be just happen."

—

The sun came up, at first shining its pale light into the yard, gathering strength and warmth as the three of them had already fed, put out the geldings and mucked out.

Celine, who normally had Sundays off, had come in to help so they could finish early before breakfast.

There was an air of expectancy hanging over them, all fully realising the importance of this visit. David and Grace had smartened themselves up, and Billy was in his best jeans and favourite T-shirt.

He kept checking the time, feeling nervous but also tinged with excitement.

He'd already started to think they weren't coming, but at ten past eleven a fairly smart-looking Ford Escort appeared down the drive. It pulled up carefully onto the gravelled forecourt. The driver got out, walked around to the passenger side and opened the car door for Lucy.

Billy hardly recognised her, she looked so nice. She had a pretty summer dress on and her hair was longer and shiny. She just looked lovely.

Billy ran towards her, threw his arms around her and hugged tightly. Not wanting to let go, tears in his eyes, Lucy released his hold and held him away from her.

"My goodness," she exclaimed. "How you've grown, just look at you. Oh, Billy, how I've missed you. I really have. Now, I want you to meet George. George, this is my darling boy, Billy."

The man took Billy's hand in a firm grip. "So good to meet you and have the chance to thank you for how you looked after your mum all that time. She's told me so much about you."

Billy liked what he saw. George was nowhere near the man he'd imagined him to be. Yes, his hand was rough as a tradesman's but there was nothing wrong with that.

George was of medium height and had an almost handsome face and full head of hair. He seemed polite and friendly. He wore a nice summer jacket, grey flannel trousers and a crisp cream shirt.

Billy gave an inward sigh of relief as he ushered them into the house and introduced them to Grace and David. Grace busied herself offering them coffee, whilst David chattered on. He told them how pleased they were looking after Billy for her, how much they loved and cared for him, and how well he was doing at school.

Lucy was keen to learn about Billy's daily life here, and David filled her in with the daily routines but kept well away from the subject of Billy's ambition to become a jockey. It might have proved contentious.

Coffee and conversation were interrupted on cue when Celine came in and, once introduced, asked if they'd like to see the horses.

Everyone stood up and David suggested afterwards they'd all go out for lunch and have a quick tour of the National Stud if it would be something they'd like to do.

"Billy," he added, "will show you the young horse he picked out for us at the sales and Celine will show you the older horses we retrain here to be sold on in their retirement; when you're done, we'll all head on out."

Billy was in his element expounding his knowledge on the young filly and what her future was likely to be. She had, as usual, come up to the gate to be fussed and stroked.

The other yearling refused to come anywhere near them, so they moved on to the other paddocks for Celine to have her say on the work that needed to be done to retrain and prepare them for the next phase of their life, that previously they'd been encouraged to run their fastest, and how they now had to be brought back to listen to the rider's hands and legs to do what was asked. Once sold, they could be trained on for showjumping, eventing or hunting, or just as a quiet ladies' or gentlemen's hack.*

Celine was in her element, and had surprised Billy with her confidence. George asked a few pertinent questions, whilst Lucy beamed with the pleasure of just being there.

Continuing to glance to and from the horses to her son, her love for him, now with an added deep respect, filled her with pride and happiness. Fully aware of how selfish she'd been to him in the past, she promised herself there and then that she would move Heaven and Hell to help him achieve whatever he wanted or needed.

Walking back through the yard, Celine said she had to get home and that it had been so nice to meet them both. Full of smiles, she jumped on her bike and with a cheery wave rode off up the drive.

"What a lovely girl," said Lucy. "So nice and knowledgeable. How old would she be?" Billy didn't know but thought she might be about twenty.

David suggested they all go together in his car, so off they went, comfortable and at ease with each other. First, a nice Sunday roast at the Wheat Sheaf in Exning, then, as David drove up Hamilton

Road, he pointed out the yards and impressive houses of world-famous trainers, a brief look at the heath racecourse side, and finally they pulled up in front of the impressive double gates of the National Stud, now shut fast.

There was a brief moment of disappointment before the gates swung open automatically and they drove through and parked the car. David had pre-booked their tour, which was open to the general public.

Boarding a mini coach, they were driven to view the foals, the mares, the breeding enclosure, the beautiful paddocks and finally the Stud's four stallions. At each stop, they got off the coach and the guide explained the whole process of the breeding programme and history of the stud. It ended with a tour of the headstones of the famous horses that had been bred here.

George was enthralled by it all. Lucy, not as much: memories kept flooding back to her. She'd been here before as that young dancer enthralled by the flamboyant new boyfriend so full of himself, someone who seemed to have money to burn. Then there was the thrill of the races, the crowd, the excitement, for just that week feeling part of being part of something new and different.

She tried to picture his face; she remembered his lovely accent. Not English, for sure. French: that's it. He told her he was from Paris. It had been so romantic, and then he was gone. She never heard or saw him again. She'd never forgotten that short time they'd had together. His name, what was it? Yve. That was it; his first name was Yve. Funny, he'd never told her his surname, and she'd never had reason to ask.

Pulling herself back to reality, she tried to regain interest in what the guide was saying; feeling a tear welling up in her eye, she blinked it away.

"You OK, Mum?" Billy noticed she had a faraway look and had gone very quiet.

"Yes, love, I think a fly just hit me in the eye." She dabbed her eyes with a hankie. "All OK now, though."

It was a grand and very nice and heart-warming day. Once back at Home Farm, they shared a pot of tea between them, promised they'd all meet up again soon, and said their goodbyes. Billy walked his mother to the car and gave her a huge hug; she kissed his forehead. "You look so lovely, Mum," he said quietly. "I can stop worrying about you now." And in a whisper he told her how much he liked George. Holding the car door open as she got in, he gently pushed it shut. She blew him three kisses and turned away, and he watched the car until it disappeared out of sight.

TWENTY-THREE

Later that evening, having settled the horses down, Grace provided a light snack of cheese on toast. Sitting down with David and Billy, they talked over their day. "Well, that went better than I could have imagined," she said. "Billy, you never told us she was so young and pretty."

"I was surprised too," he answered. "I can't remember her ever looking like that. She could hardly walk, the pain was so bad. She was taking painkillers all day until she went into a kind of daze."

"What caused it? What happened to her?" David asked.

"She fell off the stage into the orchestra pit and broke her back; they thought she might never walk again. I'm so happy to see her like this, and I liked George too."

Grace's attention turned to David. "Did George tell you what he does?"

"He works with his brother. They have a plumbing business in Crouch End, wherever that is. I think he said it was quite near Lucy's. Anyway, let's now think about tomorrow. So, we're going to accept Henley's offer... Yes?" He was answered with silence. He smiled, got up and went to sit in his comfy chair. "And make sure your boots are polished, my boy. It's a big day for you too."

—

It was 8.30 when David turned left into Hamilton Road. They pulled up in front of the large pair of shiny teak gates, which opened automatically, and drove through to a designated parking area. A paved path then led them behind the large mock Tudor-style house to the yard behind it.

One hundred boxes formed a square; a walkway encircled it with a pristine lawn at its centre. All was a hive of activity. Lads and lasses moving in and out of the stables, some carrying tack, some already tacking up, some mucking out.

David asked a lad where they might find the boss and the office was pointed out to them. Billy started to walk across the grass before David stopped him. "I think perhaps Mr Henley doesn't like anyone walking on his lawn. Let's keep to the walkway just in case."

"Ah! Good morning, David." Henley acknowledged Billy with just a quick nod, and called one of the lads in. "Take this young person and tack up Hurry on Honey for him. The boy will ride with us this lot." Billy followed him out, feeling slightly nervous and rather vulnerable.

Henley offered David a coffee or a shot of whisky if he preferred. "Now, David, about this filly of yours… but before you answer I have a proposition to put to you. We'll talk this over when we get back." With that he got up and walked back into the yard. David followed.

The riders were already being legged up into the saddle by what appeared to be the head lad. Each rider then joined the others already circulating the yard at the walk.

Billy had been led into a box to find his horse already tacked up. The lad told him Hurry on Honey was a six-year-old mare. "What's she like?" Billy asked.

"Don't know nought about this one," he replied. "I only do the mucking out here. Can't even ride."

The lad led the horse out and legged Billy up. Being the last up, he slotted into the parade of at least twenty others. Edward Henley and David stood in the centre of grassed area, sizing up each horse as it passed. As Billy walked his horse by, Henley looked up at him. "All right, lad?"

Billy looked straight ahead. "Yes, boss."

"Horses away," shouted Henley. They continued around until the senior work rider came abreast of the walkway and led the string out.

"We're just going to do a half-speed gallop today up Long Hill side. So we'll take my car and meet them there." Henley strode off, leading David towards the car park.

Billy, meantime, wondered where they were heading to and what they were going to do. No one had told him or given him any information on the mare he was on. He wondered whether this was done on purpose to see how he coped.

Now they'd entered the horse walk adjacent to a busy road that led them to Bury Road, and onto the heath to the left-hand side of Warren Hill. He'd never ridden on any of the gallops Bury side before, only on racecourse side; there were so many more horses here.

Billy felt the mare tensing up and lengthened his reins, hoping to relax her. They had to wait as someone else's string was in front of them. Being held, some of the horses started playing up, setting off others, all eager to get going. It seemed the wait would never end, but within a couple of minutes their own lead horse set off with the others following, single file, each allowing a couple of lengths between them.

Billy had seven or eight behind him, and knew it was his job to keep his place and to hold Hurry on Honey to the same steady matching pace of those in front and behind.

The horse in front of him took off. Billy had no need to persuade his mount to follow on; it did so in one mighty leap forwards, straight into a gallop. Still on a long rein, Billy gathered them in, shortening the horse's ability to extend its neck into a flat-out gallop. He quickly caught on that they were meant to be in a controlled half-speed pace; his horse obviously thought differently. It was pulling the strength out of Billy's arms, and he wondered how much longer he could cope. Thrusting his legs forward, he lay back against the pull, and used his weight. Now the combined pull on the horse's mouth matched the pull of the horse. The horse settled, and maintained the controlled half-speed gallop, keeping the correct distance between the riders ahead and behind.

Billy thought it might be his dad and Henley watching as they flashed by, but full concentration was still needed on maintaining his position. His arms and legs ached, but now he could see riders were pulling up at the front. Billy let his weight off the pull, sat back, let the horse take back a length of rein, and gave out a soothing "woo hoo".

The horse slowed back to a trot and into his walk.

Billy's head was abuzz, a little red in the face but with a full smile. The string turned to walk back home. The head work rider held up his horse and waited until Billy came up alongside him. "She can take a strong hold, that one. You did good. It surprised me he put you up on that. Manage her OK, did you?"

"Just about," laughed Billy, now feeling elated. He then settled back into the saddle for the walk home, just being long enough to cool the horses down.

–

As the string approached from a distance, with David trying to detect Billy, Edward Henley confessed that he hadn't put Billy up on an easy ride. "She's as good as gold, really," he said, "but she can take hold on occasion. The thing is, she's a true pro and knows exactly when to pull up. So I know the lad won't get run away with. I do like to test them, so many of these kids are just too cocky and far too sure of themselves."

David nodded, thinking it would do no harm to let Billy realise the possible limitations of a fifteen-year-old. As these thoughts passed through his mind, the lead horse was head on, and now he could see Billy, feet as far forward as the stirrup leathers would allow, and his torso bent well down and into the horse's wither. More importantly, exactly two lengths behind the rider in front of him. *That's my boy,* thought David, not showing a hint of the pride he felt.

Henley turned and they started the stroll back to the car. "Sits into his horse well. How old did you say he is?"

David told him, "Fifteen going on twenty-five."

"Well," Henley added, "there's a slim chance we might make a jockey out of him but, as you well know, they have to have the dedication and give their all to it."

TWENTY-FOUR

Getting back to the yard, Henley ushered David into his office; the secretary already at her desk was introduced. An attractive blonde young woman in her thirties leaned across her desk and shook David's hand with a firm grip. Henley asked her to leave them. "I'll go and enjoy the garden, then," she said. "Nice to meet you, Mr Clayton."

Edward Henley poured them both a whisky into cut glass, and invited David to sit down with him into two well-worn leather armchairs. Both with a drink in their hand, Henley spoke of his idea.

"Now, David, many years ago your father once did me a very great favour that got me out of a fix. I never had the chance to return it, so, David, this is my offer to you, and the reasons for making it... I'm now approaching seventy, have been in this business for over thirty-five years, and I'm starting to find things a bit of a struggle, especially since my wife died four years ago. I've never had an assistant trainer here, so there's no one here ready to take over. For years now my wife and I have been close friends with Lady Worlinton, whose horses I've trained over those years. I'm now financially well provided for as she bought this property from me two years ago. She's only in her early fifties and has many years ahead of her as a principal owner of the six horses she has with us. She is fully aware and approves of what I'm about to offer you. Now, if I might get personal... Although I applaud what you do, David, it can't possibly give you much of a return. If I may ask, what do you make out of retraining these retired horses, not counting what you may or may not make from your risky foal purchases?"

David's thoughts were muddled, but Henley was being openly generous so perhaps he should be too. Hesitating, he said it would be between twenty and thirty thousand.

"Well, then," he said. "Let me tell you, I find it very draining spending so much time going through the catalogues of over two thousand yearlings in the October sales. I have orders from owners for twelve and I'd like you to pick me out ten colts and two fillies with plenty of black type, anywhere between fifty and a hundred thousand. We'll discuss your findings and perhaps add one or two of my own; I'd want you to go to the sales, check them out and bid accordingly. I would also like you to take the position here of assistant trainer, starting in January, which would give you chance to wind up things at home. Your place is only ten minutes away so you don't have to live on site here, and of course you could still carry on at home with your foals and yearling gambles. For all this I am prepared to offer you a salary of thirty-five thousand, plus one-quarter of the ten per cent we get from first-place prize money. I might add that last year we had eighty-three winners, producing six hundred and sixty thousand in prize money, which, with the quarter of our ten per cent, would have given you a further seventeen thousand or so. However, I am prepared to make it a condition that, should we not surpass this figure, we will guarantee you earn no less than a total of salary and prize money percentage of fifty thousand a year. Now, what do you say? Have you any questions?"

David leant back in his chair and took a first and large sip of his whisky. "Wow!" he exclaimed. "It's a lot to take in. Thank you very much, but I'd like first to talk it over with Grace."

"Of course you can, but the catalogues are due out any day, so start looking. Mostly we purchase from Books 1 and 2. But, now and again, I like to chance a bargain basement purchase of something that looks the part, perhaps from the second foal of a young mare. Always like to keep our options open. And with regard to your filly, do we agree on the one hundred grand?"

"Thank you, Mr Henley, yes we do." The two men got up and shook hands. "I'll talk things over it over with Grace, and come back to you later in the week."

"No need for the Mr; please call me Edward when we're together, Governor when we're not, and, by the way, I'd like you to break the filly in, then we'll turn her away and bring her back here in March. Are you OK with that?"

David said he was and that Billy would be thrilled, and thanked him for allowing the boy to ride out. Henley walked over to the desk and took a cheque from the out tray.

He handed it to David, who with a quick glance confirmed the one-hundred-thousand-pound signature of Lady Worlinton. "And, David… don't let the boy leave school to get his licence at sixteen. It's far too young for a lad to cope at that age, mixing with experienced jockeys screaming at him to let them through. I'd suggest he takes out a licence to ride as an amateur on his weekends and holidays. That way he could still be at school until he's seventeen and race with the non-professionals. Competitive lot, maybe, but they would mostly look out for him. It would be good experience before getting a full professional licence at seventeen."

David had been about to leave, but immediately stopped, listened, then reached to shake the man's hand and said it was something he'd been worrying about. "I think that's such good advice," he said, "and coming from you, Edward, I'm sure he'll see the sense of it. Thank you. I'll be in touch."

—

David found Billy outside talking to a smart-looking lad. He walked over to them.

"Good morning, sir," said the lad. They shook hands. "I'm Jason Scott."

"I guessed as much, I can spot the apprentice in any yard: polished boots! You'll be losing your claim soon, won't you? It's three pounds now, isn't it?"

Jason agreed and said his aim had always been to ride out* his claiming allowance rather than losing it by reaching the age limit of twenty-six. "I just need five more winners to reach my ninetieth, lose my claim and call myself a jockey."

David wished him the best of luck and walked Billy back to the car.

As they drove home David explained that, once an apprentice lost his right to claim a weight reduction on the horse's given handicap, it became much harder to get rides.

"Whether you're Jason Scott or top jockey Frank Osbourne, you get paid the same riding fee. That's when things get tough. By the way, Mr Henley was pleased with the way you rode. He's given us advice on how we proceed with your wish to leave school next year, but we'll talk things through later. He's also made me us an offer, which I'll talk over with Grace before making a decision. But I can tell you this: they've bought the filly and want to leave her with us to break her in, so we've got her for at least another six months." Billy sank into the back of the seat, closed his eyes and gave out a long and satisfied sigh of relief.

—

Grace was waiting at the front door as they arrived, worrying and desperate to know what Henley had in mind. Controlling her anxieties, she first asked how Billy had got on, and kissed David on the cheek. "Things went quite well, then," she said. "I can smell the whisky."

David reached into his pocket and waved the cheque in front of her, just beyond her reach. Laughing, he handed it over. She looked at it and gave him an extra big hug. "Billy did us proud too, I think Henley – or should I now refer to him as Edward? – was quite impressed, and came up with some sound advice. Come on, let's all sit down together, have a strong coffee and I'll explain what he's offering us, and the change of life decision we need to make for all of us."

David had wondered whether Billy should be party to all this, but decided to include him and, as he explained Henley's offer, including the financial details, Billy sat quietly, taking it all in. When David had finished, several seconds passed before anyone spoke as the enormity of the offer struck home.

Grace was the first to speak. "What would happen, then, if Henley became senile or, God forbid, he died?"

"I asked him that; he told me I'd have had plenty of time to get the confidence of the owners and I would take over. Lady Worlinton, who is party to the offer, would then transfer the lease of the yard to us. Just think, love: if we wanted to retire in ten or twelve years' time, what an opportunity it would be for our son John to come back, or even return earlier as my assistant trainer. Billy, have you any questions? This would affect you too."

"When I get my licence, would he take me on as the yard apprentice?"

"I don't know whether that would be the right move, son. With me as assistant trainer, the lads might give you a hard time, thinking you're there because of me and not by your own ability."

Billy felt somewhat miffed by this. "Well, I'd just have to prove them wrong, wouldn't I?"

"We'll have to see, but I've told you before, I would give you all the support you need, and with Edward Henley's influence behind us I'm sure we can get you placed with another Newmarket trainer of equal standing. Anyway, he's come up with an idea that I think we should consider." David then explained. "Next year in your summer holidays you apply for an amateur's licence and attend a two-day course at the British Racing School. You can then ride in condition races open to amateurs on weekends. That way you can stay on at school another year, get your GCSEs and then at seventeen leave school and reapply for your licence as an apprentice. Mr Henley thinks sixteen is too young for anyone of that age to cope with the cut and thrust of such a professional and competitive environment, and, quite honestly, I do too."

Billy was not too enamoured with the idea. David could sense his disappointment.

"Look, there's no hurry to make a decision on this yet, but Grace and I have to make ours, so we'll sleep on it, give it time to sink in, and hopefully make our own decision in the next couple of days. Yours can wait."

Billy gave a half smile of acknowledgement. "You told me to go with the flow," he said, "and it's just happening with me now I don't have to worry about my mum. It's working for you as well, isn't it?"

TWENTY-FIVE

Over the next two days, every spare waking hour, David and Grace thought through, talked and discussed the issues and how Henley's offer would affect their daily life and future.

Grace was not convinced of how the relationship between the two men would work. What authority would David have? What would his responsibilities be? She thought they needed a legal contract of employment detailing how the relationship should work.

Two days later, thinking they now had a clearer understanding of how they should proceed, they sat down together and drafted out a rough guide of what they envisaged such an agreement should include.

On a separate sheet, David made a summary of the key components of how they might ensure financial recompense should either he or Henley decide the partnership had become untenable.

Feeling satisfied that he'd covered everything, he made the call, and told Edward that on principle they agreed to accept his kind offer and asked whether they could meet up next week and draw up a draft agreement.

Henley seemed delighted and said he'd already discussed his intentions with his lawyer and that they would shortly be sending him a draft of a proposed contract, adding that Lady Worlinton would also be party to it with regard to the lease of the yard.

So, it was agreed that they meet up on Monday, in just four days' time, and they would start to work on the filly.

Later he spoke to Billy with the news. "We'll start lunging her every morning from now on and get her to realise there's more to life than being free and easy and grazing in the sun. We'll have you riding out on her within six weeks. However," he added, "the sales will be here before we know it, so we'd better crack on with the colt as well."

Billy had two weeks left of the school break and he got stuck into helping David breaking in* the two youngsters. David, in the meantime, had met up with Henley, and they'd agreed on the terms of employment.

The filly took to her task of being worked around the lunging ring, and Billy soon thought he could manage it himself after watching David.

Feeling unsure at first that he was fully in control, he soon settled down into the rhythm of it, regaining confidence, as did the filly. He quickly learned that, to keep her going forward, the long rein, and the flicking of the long tom* held in his left hand, had to be well behind the filly's action. The moment she got ahead of him she would come to a halt.

First getting her to trot round on a right rein, he got her to turn around and continue on the left. She moved sweetly, her coat shining in the sunlight. No saddle, no bridle, just attached to this long rein held in a young lad's hand.

Celine was in charge of lunging the colt, and getting him used to being lead around the yard and up and down the drive, getting him to stand still whilst she ran her hands over him and up and down his forelegs and tendons. With all this going on, David was finishing off schooling the three geldings still waiting to be sold on.

The days sped by and, two days before the start of the new term, the postman cycled down the drive as Grace was just coming out of the house. With a cheery good morning, he handed her the post. It consisted of three envelopes. The one that was addressed to David looked particularly interesting; the other two were addressed to them both. She went back inside and left them on the kitchen shelf. It was not until the evening, as they sat down for supper, that she remembered and handed them to David.

The first envelope he opened was a rates demand; he quickly put this aside.

Opening the second, addressed to them both, he busied himself with its contents.

Looking up, he smiled. "It's Billy's school report," he said, then returned to read it through. Billy, sitting opposite him, nervously awaited a reaction.

David handed it to Grace, and, noticing Billy's worried frown, told him that on the whole it was mostly good. After she'd read it, she looked across to Billy and read out the headmaster's summary. "So the headmaster says you've made great efforts in your work, and are a determined young person who applies himself to the best of your abilities. He adds that you are very deep within yourself, not readily mixing in with pupils of your own age. He notes that you have no interest in social media, which, in itself, is no bad thing. But says he sometimes regrets that social media is something of the normality and chief interest of the children of today. He says Billy is a likeable lad, polite and well behaved, and he considers you to be a credit to David and me. Finally, he says, in his opinion, determined as you are, you will make a success in whatever job or profession you choose as long as it's not academic. Signed Ralph Richardson. Headmaster."

Grace got up, came round the table and put her arms around him. "That's a very nice report, Billy," she said. "We're very proud of you."

Billy remained unimpressed. "What's it mean I can't be an academic?"

David tried not to laugh. "It means, son, you're not likely to become a scientist."

"That's all right, then. I suppose some of the kids that sit in the front row are academic and I know that's what teachers want, but it's not for me, not ever."

Grace returned to finishing off preparing their supper, and David's attention turned to the remaining important-looking envelope. Opening it carefully, he removed the contents, and started to read; his face changed to a look of surprise and then of concern.

He got up carrying the letter and started to leave the room. Grace sensed something had upset him and asked what it was. He shook his head and headed to their office. Grace turned off the oven and followed him out.

"What is it, love? Is it from Henley? I thought everything was settled."

David shook his head and passed her the letter. "No, it's not from him, it's from the DNA lab; remember, we sent them Billy's sample hoping to find his dad and they replied that no match was found."

"So what now?" Grace asked.

"They have a match of a male and want our permission to inform the person."

"Oh my God." Grace put her hands to her forehead. "Do they say who he is?"

"It's almost unbelievable... It's the French jockey Yve de Montagnes. It all ties up: we know Lucy was in Newmarket around at that time. What a coincidence, one can hardly believe it. Can you?"

"The name rings a bell," said Lucy. "Is he still riding?"

"Too right he is; he's won two Arc de Triomphes and comes over here once or twice a year if a French horse is entered in one of our group 1s. I'd reckon he'd be around forty now but still at the top of his game."

"What are we going to do? Are you going to tell Billy? Will the DNA people contact this man?"

"We'll keep this to ourselves for the moment, and they've asked if we want to make the contact, so the ball is in our court for the time being. I'll email them tomorrow and tell them to leave things as they are just now and we'll be in touch."

With the knowledge of all this swirling through their heads, they returned to the kitchen. Billy, thinking something was up, asked if there was a problem. Grace told him it was just a shock to have received another tax assessment but they would sort it out with their accountant tomorrow. With that, she put the food on the table and it was eaten in silence, which to Billy was very strange. He went up to bed later feeling something had been left unsaid.

—

No one slept very well that night. Learning the identity of Billy's father lay heavily on their minds, whilst Billy felt sure something had come up that might well affect him too, possibly social services causing another upset.

Coming down to the kitchen early, somewhat bleary-eyed, David decided to clear the air and face whatever problems it might bring. The lad deserved to know.

"What Grace and I told you last night was not what was in that letter. It was from the DNA company; it was to tell us they've found a match."

Billy put his hands over his face and looked down at the floor. Peeking up again, he let out a double sigh. David held the boy by the shoulders and asked if he wanted to know where and who his father was. "Does he live near here?" he asked in a whisper.

"No, son, he's French and lives near Paris."

"Then I don't want to know. Please, Uncle, don't tell him where I am; he might want to take me away from you. You're my dad now. I love you and Auntie."

Unable to hold back his tears, he sobbed and tried to hide into David's arms. Grace came and joined them, forming a group hug. David broke the moment. "No one's going to take you away from us, lad. I've already sent them an email telling them not to make contact unless we come back to them. This could become a positive thing, you know, and if needed it might get us free of social services if they tried to take you back to London again. I'm sure this person would look out for you. Just let's forget about it for now, and, when or if you ever feel ready to let him know he has a son, we can make contact." Billy wiped the tears with the back of his hand and managed a smile. "And Billy." David squeezed his hand. "Now you're nearly grown up, and if you feel happy with it, you can call us by David and Grace."

Once Billy had gone outside to help Celine and feed the yearlings, David talked things over with Grace. "I'm glad we've got that out of the way for now," he said. "I'm going to find out all I can about this guy. I'll google him later: the more we know about him now, the easier it'll be to decide at a later date what might be best for the lad. If he asks, though, and if he wants to know, I'll have more to tell."

TWENTY-SIX

Monday morning Billy got on the school bus, hoping to see Kate. Since leaving the Gibbonses' yard, and with the school break, he'd not seen her. Disappointed, he took a seat next to a lad he'd not seen before. The boy seemed to want to strike up a conversation, saying his family had recently come down from the north as his father had taken a job in Morris Wellby's yard in Newmarket. "I've been riding out with them last week," he said. "Can't believe the facilities you have down here." Billy was immediately interested, and opened up not only about his own riding experiences but mostly about his filly at home. The boy said his name was Paul; he was nearly sixteen and hoped, if not in the same class, they should meet up after school. Getting off the bus, they walked into the school gates together and into assembly.

Billy found he'd been moved up to the fourth form. He found his way there and quickly sat down, reserving his normal place one row from the back. Sometime later, Paul came in, taking up the only remaining seat at the front.

–

With only three weeks to go before the sales, the two yearlings were brought in, and each had now become accustomed to wearing a bridle with the mouth accepting a bit or when led out a chifney.*

Both had been loaded into the yard's own motorised horse box, driven around the lane, back again and then offloaded. Already used to it now, they even seemed to enjoy it. The colt continued being lunged by Celine, then led out along the lane to cool down. Billy, meantime, lunged the filly before and then again after school. She was now working at the trot and if asked to break into a collective canter gave her customary squeal and a couple of mighty fly kicks before settling. She was also getting used to her walks with the colt, and, being so interested in the new surroundings, generally behaved herself.

So much had happened over the last few weeks. With David scheduled to start work at Millgate Stables at the beginning of January it was important to find owners for the three remaining geldings. They were now ready to be moved on, and adverts had already been placed in the September issue of *Horse and Hound*. Things were changing.

Everything had been explained to Celine. Once David had taken up his new job, she would become head girl responsible for the foals yet to be bought, and for the first time two possible yearlings. Old Joe could come in part time when needed, and Celine's wage would be increased accordingly, and she was well pleased.

Within a few days of school, Billy had established a surprising friendship with Paul, and had asked him over at the weekend to see the filly and to ride out with them on one of the geldings.

The following week two enquiries were received and both had made appointments, one for the Saturday morning and the other at two in the afternoon.

David asked Billy to ride all three so they could each be judged independently. He did, of course, and did it well.

Performing first at a walk, a walk into a collected canter, finishing with a controlled gallop up both sides of the long paddock, then bringing back to a walk and a halt, standing quietly and still for thirty seconds at the gate. The first was a lady and she picked out the third horse ridden, the grey. Not Billy's choice, but he kept that to himself. He jumped off, and David, who had been watching, asked if she would like to take a short ride out with himself; she agreed and said that she'd love to.

Taking the reins from Billy, they walked the horses back into the yard. Celine held the grey as the lady got up into the saddle from the mounting block, whilst David mounted by jumping from the ground, throwing his leg over the horse's quarters and sitting himself deep into the saddle. It wasn't just the lady who was impressed; Billy was mightily surprised. He'd thought of David as being old, but the man had just shown he could still do something Billy would later learn was one of the many things those hoping to become an apprentice had to do: mount a horse from a standing position unassisted.

The two of them rode off, and when they returned fifteen minutes later Celine and Billy took the horses from them and David and the lady went into the house. It took no longer than ten minutes before they returned, she full of smiles and promising to come back with her horse box tomorrow to pick up the grey. Job done, deal made, cheque in hand.

Everything was repeated after lunch, but this lady was very knowledgeable.

Running her hands over the chestnut horse, she checked for any tenderness in its back by bridging her fingers and pressing hard either side of the backbone. Satisfied, she then picked up alternate forelegs and bent the knee back as far as it would go. Finally, running a hand down each of its forelegs, she checked for splints* or any bowing of the tendons. Then, standing away from the animal, she studied its overall conformation.

"Nice horse," she said. "Now give me a leg up." David obliged, and she then proceeded to ride it through its paces around the paddock. David felt very pleased with himself and with the horse, which only six months ago had run over hurdles, falling at the last. She asked its name. David told her it was called Jackson.

"I'm not interested in the other," she said. "This one's a very nice horse. Now, how much did you say?" David was taken aback by her straightforward approach.

"He was advertised at six thousand, five hundred."

"I'll take him off your hands for six," she offered. David shook her hand and they walked into the house, where she wrote out the cheque, refusing Grace's offer of tea.

Within minutes they loaded the horse into her trailer and they were gone.

"Well, that went well. Wish they were all as easy and nice as that. Thanks, you two; only one to go now. I might enter him into the autumn sales in case we don't find a buyer before November."

"Why did she bend the forelegs like that?" Billy asked, always keen to learn.

"She was checking for a chipped knee. It mostly happens to yearlings and two-year-olds, not very often in a mature horse, though. She rode him well, didn't she?"

–

With less riding to do, David starting his new job in January and Celine being given control of the yard, Grace might have felt somewhat left out. She didn't; she loved the idea of having, at last, some time of her own and, with her own ideas and plans, she was happy; for the time being, though, she was keeping them to herself.

The following Monday the catalogues arrived from Tattersalls. Books 1, 2 and 3. A total of two thousand and thirty-three yearlings to pass through the sale ring over a six-day marathon. David spent the whole day listing a selection of lots that might have the breeding and black type promise to prove value within Edward Henley's guide budget.

This of course didn't include those that might be of interest to himself personally.

These three books were of the top quality, some likely to fetch well over five hundred thousand. No, David would wait for the November yearling sale, where if one could spot a bargain of something nicely bred he could perhaps find a couple within his own budget of under twenty thousand.

When Billy got home from school, David handed over Book 2

and suggested he go through it and pick out six lots that might be of interest and to see if any of his selections might match up with his own. Billy excitingly grabbed the catalogue and ran up to his room and was not seen until called down to supper.

David asked how he'd got on with his selections. "I'm only halfway through," he said. "I'll finish off after we've eaten."

"Me too," answered David. "I've still got Book 3 to finish. It's quite an exhausting job. Be glad to finish with it. Try and get back early tomorrow: I want to move on with the filly. We'll long rein* her together tomorrow and then you can carry on with it yourself over the next couple of weeks."

The following day, when Billy got home, David was already in the paddock. The filly was attached from her bridle to twelve feet of rein with David holding her from behind. He was talking to her kindly, asking her to walk on, and with a slight tension on the left rein encouraged her to turn to the left. Billy watched as she walked on calmly and then made a right turn. They were now at the gate. David handed Billy the reins.

Slightly unsure whether he was fully in control at first, Billy gave a small shake of the rein and asked her to walk on.

David watched from the gate as they made a complete circuit of the paddock. "Just do a couple more turns and then walk her back to the yard, I'll leave you to it." With that, David walked away.

Billy was not completely sure whether the filly might take flight. What if she suddenly decided to take off? She'd always had an unpredictable side to her. Cautiously, he turned her through the gate and they walked calmly back into the yard, where David was waiting for them. He unclipped the reins and put the filly into her stable. "We'll do that again over the next few days," he said, "and over the weekend we'll walk her round the lane. Well done: for the first time, she's had to accept that someone other than herself is in control of what she's allowed to do."

TWENTY-SEVEN

David took the *Racing Post* just on Mondays and Saturdays. Where once it had been bought by everyone in the yard, the lads or lasses could no longer afford it; for them it had priced itself out of the market. Even for David it seemed a luxury. He could afford it but the cost of it still bothered him. Once he'd read through the entries, the results, comments and articles, he passed it on to Billy, who would take to his bedroom. There was a lot to learn here, a lot he didn't understand. The many times this bothered him, he would take the paper downstairs and ask David to explain.

On the bus to and from school, Billy and his new friend Paul would talk horses. What was running and where, which apprentices were getting the most rides, and, amongst many other facts, which trainers were most likely to use an apprentice's weight allowance, to gain advantage for a win. This happened mostly on low-quality class 6 events, held mostly on the all-weather tracks.

Sometimes they talked about the girls, those in their class and the girls in the yards. Billy wasn't riding out anywhere at this time, so didn't have much to say on the matter, but Paul seemed to have plenty to say. Billy told him of his previous friendship with Kate and how she'd dropped him when he'd stopped riding out for her dad. "She's in the fifth form now," he said. "Been going out with that Greg Matthews from upper sixth for a good few weeks now."

Paul thought for a moment. "I'm not getting involved with no girls, nor should you. Best wait till we're famous."

Billy laughed. "I'm not going to wait till I'm an old man of thirty, but I know what you mean. Anyway, I'm going back to Mr Henley's with David at the weekend. Hope I'm put up on something decent this time."

–

That same evening David told Billy they needed to have a talk. Those very words meant something serious was on his mind. They sat down together. *What,* thought Billy, *could it possibly be now?* So many things had happened in so short a time, most of it good or exciting, but perhaps this time their luck was running out.

"Have you thought," said David, "about the idea of staying on at school, just for a year, and applying for your a licence to ride as an amateur at weekends?"

"No, not really," answered Billy.

"Well, it's time you did. Whether you leave or not, to get a licence to ride amateur or professional you have to pass not only their accepted degree of fitness but pass the required test of strength as well. Your riding ability is good enough, but we can't risk you failing the other. So, I've spoken with your headmaster and he's agreed you can use the gym, and, not only that, he said he'd get a Mr McIntosh to give you instruction on getting you fit and strong. Is that OK with you?"

Billy was amazed that his headmaster knew of his ambitions, and was being so positive and helpful. And what's more, he liked the sports director, Mr McIntosh, with whom he'd talked about their shared interest in racing.

Billy thanked David and said it was great and he would work hard to get himself fit and strong, but he still wanted to leave school at the end of the next summer term.

"We'll have to see about that," David answered, stroking his chin. "I'll see what Mr Henley thinks when I see him on Monday. By the way, it's not till twelve so no chance for you to ride out. Now, can I see the yearlings you've selected and whether they match my own?"

Billy ran upstairs and brought down the catalogue Book 3. He'd marked down the pages of his selections in red. There were twelve markings. David looked at each one in turn, making no comment until Billy's last choice, that of lot 1937.

"You've chosen some of the best-bred yearlings here; it shows me you now have some understanding of what's looked for by the top agents representing the big players of our industry. Most of these, though, will sell for two or three times over our budget of a hundred thousand. Two lots of yours – lots 1818 and 1870 – I also have. Yes, we'll watch most of these go through the ring, but we've little chance of getting them. Let me show you my other choices, and why with those we may have a chance."

–

David met up with Henley as arranged; they agreed on a selection of twenty-four yearlings they would bid on, and out of those hoped to secure their target of twelve. Their total budget would be one million, two hundred thousand guineas. On top of this would be the five per cent due to Tattersalls, plus the twenty per cent VAT, which would be reclaimed later. It was a mind-blowing expense to David; the huge responsibility of this and what was to come would be something he would just have to get used to.

Something else was weighing heavily on his mind. He'd found a host of information on the Frenchman, and kept asking himself whether it was fair or even right to keep it all from Billy. He had, of course, talked it over with Grace – several times, in fact – but she'd insisted it was his decision, refusing to commit herself one way or the other.

David found himself torn, as the saying goes, "between a rock and a hard place", well aware that whatever decision he made could trouble Billy adversely. So, realising that, whatever decision he took, the outcome could be construed either way, he decided to tell him all he knew.

Not wanting Billy to have to go to school coping with all this, David waited until the Saturday. He suggested that Billy long rein the filly around the lane for the first time and, to give the filly a lead, he would ride the old horse.

The filly behaved herself and the whole exercise went without a hitch. On getting back to the yard, they took off the bridles and tack, put on head collars, walked them out to the paddock together and let them loose. The filly gave out a squeal, fly bucked in delight, galloped twice round the paddock, then with three loud snorts she settled down to graze. David's old horse took one look at her antics, gave a snort and took no further notice.

"She does like to show off a bit," David said. "It's just so lovely to watch; for me, it helps to make up for the bad bits we have to put up with sometimes… Having said that, Billy, I have some shattering news for you."

Billy looked up to him; a shudder passed through his whole body. David put his hands on Billy's shoulders, and looked him in the eye. "It's about your father," he said quietly. "His name is Yve de Montagnes. He's French, and he's one of France's leading jockeys."

Billy's mouth dropped open in shock. He bit his lip and for the moment was at a loss of comprehension; he shook his head in disbelief. After a brief pause, David continued to relate the information he'd gathered. "Your birth father," he said, "was champion jockey in France for four consecutive years from 1996 until 2000. He's now thirty-nine. He's still retained as first jockey to Guy Mattice, who is a trainer of multiple group 1s and trains from Chantilly near Paris. He's married to the famous French actress Jeunette Jeneaux. They have one child now, age three. And, if this isn't enough of a coincidence, we found out he was brought up in a boy's home and has never known his parents… Look, I'm sorry, Billy, I've racked my brains whether to tell you all this but in the end I decided that it was only right to let you know now, instead of you finding out later."

"Does he know about me?" Billy asked, his heart pumping but white-faced in shock.

"No, son, it would be the DNA people to speak to him first.

They'd tell him about you and then it would be up to him if he wanted to make contact. So nothing's going to happen unless we ask them to proceed. I think it's important that we now know who he is. It's OK if you just want to leave it for the moment, but it may well be something that could help you with your career later."

"I don't want any help from him. You see, I'll be as good as him. I'll ride more winners then he has; this only proves it was meant to be. Somehow my future's all planned out for me."

"Well, let's hope so," David said, greatly relieved. "You've a lot to think about, and, if you need to talk about it, any time, don't bottle it up: you know where to come."

Billy had recovered; colour had returned to his face. He smiled, now feeling rather proud. "You know how you told me to pick out horses that had loads of black type in their breeding? It's the same with us, isn't it?"

"Yes, I suppose it is," David answered. "Why do you ask me that?"

"Because, if my dad is a champion jockey, my name should be in black type too."

David chuckled. "That never occurred to me before, son, but I suppose in a way you're right. The genes of a champion are passed on to his children, but a lot also depends on the mother. It would make a difference if she were a champion too, so, yes, it's the same. A greater proportion of genes passed in the breeding of the foal come from the mare. As for the sire, nearly all have to be good enough to produce winners, but, if the mare has produced winners as well, the chances are greatly enhanced. A sire* is only as good as the quality of the mares he gets."

The load of apprehension had been lifted from David's shoulders. Billy had taken it well. Things for the time being would be left as they were. The two – surrogate father, and loving "son" – walked back to the house and later sat down together and watched the racing on TV. It was Newmarket's Cambridgeshire meeting, featuring one of the season's biggest handicap races over a mile and one furlong.* The race they were most interested in, however, was the three o'clock group 1 over a mile for two-year-olds worth

£124,762, and Sorel Point was entered. The full brother to Billy's filly, trained by Edward Henley, owned by Lady Worlinton with stable jockey Gordon Stokes up. Amazingly there were only eight horses entered. The favourite was Jacobs Creek at 5/2 and Sorel was 12/1 outsider. The going was good – good to soft, and he was drawn stall 5.

The bell went in the parade ring, and jockeys were given a leg up. Sorel was on his toes, prancing and cantering on the spot, giving his handler a hard time. Gordon Stokes seemed unconcerned and sat still and calm. The horse glistened, the sun catching its quarters. David was quick to notice. "He's sweating up," he said. "It's not that warm." Billy asked why and what it meant. "It means," David explained, "the horse is already anticipating what's about to happen, and he's overexcited or worrying about it. It takes a lot out of them; it's not a good sign. There are a few that sweat up who are OK with it, but I wouldn't put money on any horse that does."

The camera followed the runners cantering down to the start; Gordon Stokes was having a hard time holding him. Sorel, throwing up his head and swinging it from side to side and fighting the bit, was trying get away from him. Gordon used all his skill and technique to calm the horse and managed to arrive at the start still intact.

The horses were now being led into the stalls. Being two-year-olds, several were difficult and reluctant to load; Sorel was no exception. Goading, pulling and pushing him from behind, the stall handlers managed by physical strength to finally get him in.

"All in," was called. The starter shouted, "Ready," and dropped the raised flag. The stalls sprung open with a loud clatter and the eight young and volatile youngsters flew out at the gallop.

With such a small entry, the riders kept together in a tight bunch for the first furlong and then spread out with a couple of lengths between them. Two horses eased ahead of the pack; Sorel was struggling to match the pace and was now a length behind.

They stayed as they were and then, two furlongs from home, Gordon made his move and changed his hands on the rein to get Sorel to retake hold of the bit. They started to make ground on to the leading pack. A small gap opened between the horse on the inside rail and Gordon took the gamble; Sorel was brave enough to take it and they sailed through.

Now, with just two horses in front of them, Gordon gave Sorel one crack of the whip. Sorel responded, and caught up to the leading pair and for a few strides took the lead. Now, with only a furlong left to run, David and Billy were on their feet, jumping up and down with excitement, shouting Sorel home.

The other two jockeys, taken by surprise, started to ride a finish still four lengths ahead of the chasing pack. Sorel had given all he had and was starting to tire. With two more cracks from Gordon, the horse was unable to quicken for a second time and was overtaken. They finished a tired fourth.

David was the first to speak. "He ran a good race; he just didn't stay the trip. Next year he'll be stronger and get the mile, but right now he'd probably needs to be dropped back to seven furlongs. I think going for a group 1 at this stage was a bit too much to hope for. He's a good horse, though, make no mistake."

Billy showed his disappointment. "Do you think Gordon Stokes rode a good race too, or is he too old now?"

"Billy, I don't like you putting a down on Stokes. He's still a good jockey; he couldn't have won: the horse was just not mature enough. Perhaps it'll now make you understand how hard it is to win a group race, or any race, actually. Some owners have horses for years and never get a win. This business is very competitive, and on the flat it's the money that counts. One has to be hard and at the end of each season get rid of the no-hopers and replace them with new stock every year."

Billy asked something that had been on his mind for some time. "The filly, we've only ever called her that. Why can't we give her a name? I'd like to give her a name. Can we call her Sunshine?"

"You must have noticed," David replied, "none of the yearlings in the sales are named. The new owner names it and that becomes the official name that's listed in the stud book. When they're settled into a yard, though, lads sometimes give it a nickname of their own but as soon as the official name is registered in its passport, then that becomes its name for life. We can call her Sunshine whilst she's here, if you like, but it's not up to us to suggest a name for her once she leaves us."

TWENTY-EIGHT

It was a Friday, third day of the four-day sale, again just up the road at Tattersalls.

The Clayton yearling lot 1097 was estimated to go through the ring at 5.25. The yearling had been beautifully turned out by Celine, and by the time Billy along with his mate Paul turned up on their bikes they still had plenty of time to watch the action inside, both competing with each other on how much they thought each yearling would go for.

David, of course, had already been there most of the day, bidding on some well-bred lots for the Henley yard. Over the two previous days he'd bid on eighteen, been outbid on ten and managed to secure eight. Another two had been knocked down to him earlier in the day and he now needed just another two to fulfil his quota.

Then he would still need another two for himself, but not in this sale, which had the best-bred stock on offer. He knew from past experience that his best chance of finding a bargain would be the following sale in November, especially when buyers in this sale would be unlikely to attend, having already filled their order books.

Celine was now leading their colt around the outside ring along with twenty others, having judged the timing well. People crowded around the white-railed paddock, assessing each passing horse in turn. Sometimes a handler was signalled to take the horse to the far side and into an inspection area and asked to trot it up and then be checked over. But now lot 1097 was led into the gated enclosure ready to take its turn, its future unknown.

The huge doors opened and Celine walked the colt into the sale ring. Bought as a foal a year ago for twelve thousand guineas, plus its keep, feed and care, the next four or five minutes would determine whether the selling price against its total cost would be a profit or loss.

Lot 1097 was knocked down for nine thousand guineas. Celine walked the colt to the exit, a white ticket was slapped onto its quarters, the exit doors opened and Celine walked him out and back to its stable, where it would be left to the responsibility of the new owner.

On the way home, David driving them back in the empty horse box, they talked over their disappointment. David had always been fully aware of the risk of this business; he was philosophical about it. You won some and you lost some, and anyway, overall he'd come out on the right side with what they'd achieved with the filly.

–

With the Wednesday edition of the *Racing Post,* Billy eagerly read a report and comments on the biggest race held in France, and near on the most valuable race in the world, La Prix de l'Arc de Triomphe. It was to be contested on Sunday.

With eight French horses entered, plus three from the UK, four from Ireland, one from Germany and two from Japan, it brought together a field of eighteen. Billy turned the page, and there it was: a full list of the runners, their name, previous form, their racing colours, total prize money each had won, age, and something that made Billy gasp; he looked up from the page and wiped a tear from his eye, for there it was: the name of the jockey riding Tempest, horse number six, was that of Yve de Montagnes.

Billy hurtled downstairs with the paper hanging open at the page; David was sitting, having a mug of tea, Grace sweeping the flagstone floor. They both looked up startled as Billy's panicky rush caused him to trip on the bottom step, just saving himself from a nasty fall. Recovering his balance, Billy put the paper onto the table, open at the page.

"He's riding in that big race in France, look."

"I did notice it," said David. "You left the paper on the table; I read it myself and wanted you to discover it for yourself. We can watch it on TV at 3pm on Sunday. If we tape it, and they feature Yve in the parade ring, or cantering down to the start, we could freeze frame it and capture the picture of him on your camera."

Billy managed to calm himself. He apologised, and said he thought it a brilliant idea. Sheepishly, he carefully folded the paper, and took it back up to his room.

Looking through the pages, he read everything over again, soaking up every detail about the race, the horses, trainers and jockeys. He stared at that name; it held him transfixed and to think that, in just four days' time, it was possible he might catch a glimpse for the very first time of what his father actually looked like.

–

Billy had now been long reining the filly for some weeks, and with Celine lunging her each day she was beginning to muscle up and fill out. David had kept a close eye on her progress and now thought that she was ready for the next step in her education.

Early next morning, David asked Billy to bring the filly in from the paddock. Once in her box, David, with a bridle in his hand, gently slipped the bit into her mouth and the bridle over her ears. He then walked her around the box four times and as he did he told Billy to empty the water bucket outside, bring it back in and turn it upside down. "Now," he said, "I want you to stand on it... now place your hands over her wither and ease your chest and tummy over her with both legs hanging down this side. Let her accept your weight, be very slow in your movements... and if she accepts you, I'll walk her around the box again. Talk to her, Billy... talk to her... Now, gently does it."

Billy eased his body over her, talking softly and slowly as he'd talked to her so often in the paddock. Now, hanging half on and half off her, he could feel her tremble beneath him. She threw her head about but David held her. Billy continued talking to her, soothing her, and after a minute or so could feel her becoming less tense. David told him to hang on and walked them three times around the box.

They stopped and Billy slid off. They repeated this sequence three times and all went well, the filly accepting it as something she just had to put up with. "That went well." David looked pleased. "Tomorrow morning we'll slip a saddle on her back and a loose girth, and after school we'll have you on her back."

The next morning before school, the whole process was repeated, the filly accepting Billy as he hung over her back, and, as promised, after school the moment of all this effort was about to unfold.

Holding the bridle, David slipped it over her ears and then eased a thick saddle pad gently over her withers. Used to having a rug put on her, she barely noticed, nor did she seem concerned when David eased the saddle onto it with the girth hanging down her offside.* Moving to the other side, he reached under her belly for the hanging girth and attached it loosely to the saddle straps. The filly reacted with two quick kicks from behind, but Billy held her tight. David then took over from him and walked her around the box twice. "Now," he said, "I'm going to leg you up in one quick movement. Come down on her as gently as you can; be ready for a buck or two."

Billy swallowed, not too sure of what to expect. He bent his left leg, David took hold and, aided by Billy's jump, lifted him upwards. Billy swung his right leg over the horse and eased himself down into the saddle. The filly tried to get away but David held tight. She gave three quick little bucks, but nothing big enough to unseat Billy.

"Take hold of the reins and just let her feel you on the bit. I'm going to walk you round the box."

Four turns and no resistance. David told Billy to slide off her, and they repeated this another three times. Putting Billy up again a fourth time, David opened the stable door and led them around the yard with Billy still aboard, gingerly holding a loose rein.

Up the drive, turning and back again, Billy got off, made much of her and led her back into the stable, removed the tack and gave her her evening feed.

This would be all be done again over the next few days, tightening up the girth a notch each day so in three or four days' time she would be ready and hopefully settled enough to be ridden away.*

–

Today was Sunday, and the Prix de l'Arc de Triomphe. David, Grace and Billy sat around the TV to watch the race, which was also set to record every moment, Billy with his phone set readied to camera mode.

There was the first half an hour of the proceedings in which the chances each of the favoured horses were discussed and interviews given. Tempest was given the odds of 12/1 against and was not featured. The interviewer moved on, and as jockeys were about to mount the cameras caught sight of Tempest giving his handler a hard time.

Hurrying across, they just had a few moments to introduce its jockey, Yve de Montagnes.

Billy's heart leaped, forcing himself not to use his camera with a reminder from David they were recording it. Even so, he had to force himself to wait for the playback. There he was, Yve de Montagnes in full focus talking as best he could to ITV's interviewer David Blakeny.

He spoke in broken pigeon English with a heavy French accent. Billy judged him to be about five foot six in height, with a swarthy southern complexion, his face heavily lined and weather-beaten, showing signs of age. Billy liked what he saw. The man looked the part and possessed the charisma of a man who had enjoyed great success and it showed.

The race was run, the second favourite won, and Yve on Tempest came sixth and therefore took no further part in the discussions of the race. David rewound the recording and froze Yve's profile for Billy to take a picture, and then another of a shot of Yve and Tempest cantering down to the start. Now he had pictures of his dad on his phone, to look at and wonder at leisure. He thanked David and asked them what they thought.

David said he could see a likeness, and Grace that she thought he was very nice-looking, and came over as very likeable when being interviewed. Billy studied the picture of them cantering down and asked why jockeys rode with only their toe in the irons. "To tell you the truth," answered David, "I don't really know, but, after noticing the American jockeys riding on the toe,* all ours have taken up with it. I think it might allow the rider to get lower into the horse and further up its neck when riding a finish, but I'll find out for us."

From this day on, when mounted, Billy, with leathers pulled up yet another notch, rode with only the toe in the stirrup.

David had ordered the farrier to come and put shoes* on the filly. It would be her first time to be shod. Not an easy job with a nervous yearling, but Newmarket farriers were well used to taking their time and giving the horse the confidence that they wouldn't be hurt.

So, with the grounding done and the filly shod, Billy tacked her up at 5.30am and led her out. David was already mounted on his old lead horse. Celine gave Billy a leg up and, still holding the bridle, she led them twice around the yard close behind David. Celine stepped aside and, with Billy now in sole charge, they continued around once more, then, turning up the drive, they rode a circuit around the lanes.

The filly was nervous and on edge at first, but, following the lead horse, she slowly regained her confidence and, once back in the yard, Billy slid off her back, patted her and led her back into the stable, very pleased and relieved that all had gone well.

Ridden out for two weeks, she was then put away and turned out to grass.

TWENTY-NINE

Billy still phoned his mum, Lucy, every Tuesday and they were thinking of coming up again sometime before Christmas. She seemed very relaxed and happy, which made Billy feel happy too.

At school he'd asked his teacher if he could take two of his best GCSE subjects at the end of the school year in July and they'd agreed he'd prepare and try for a pass in geography and French.

As far as Billy was concerned, it was just a plan B in case he was stopped from leaving. He'd talked things over with David yet again, and David had made the suggestion that he should sit the two exams in July, and take a further two subjects and resits if needed the following December. He could then leave and go for his licence at the Racing School a year next January.

It all seemed so long and far away, when he felt eager and ready to leave now.

No, he wasn't riding out for anyone, but, as soon as David started work at Henley's in just two months' time, he would be riding out with them six days a week.

Waiting over eighteen months to leave school and get started seemed to him such an awful waste of time.

Four days a week after school he was spending time in the gym under the supervision of Mr McIntosh. He'd already developed muscle and upper-arm strength, and twice a week he ran to school and back. The kids in his class all thought him mad, but he was still seen by most as the coolest guy in the school as he was never seen with a phone; phones had begun to dominate the lives of so many of those around him.

The days flew by and new routines were being set now that the filly and the only unsold gelding were left, and he was no longer being ridden. David had entered him in the forthcoming sale of horses in and out of training. The foal sale, however, became the first priority, and the two foals David had hoped to get and bid for found their way back to the yard and let loose in the paddock.

The following week it was their seven-year-old retrained horse's turn to be auctioned off.

Not attracting bids, it looked like he'd leave the ring unsold, but the auctioneer was persistent and received a bid of eight hundred guineas,* the minimum bid, as anything under is not accepted. There'd been yet another pause and, just before the hammer dropped, someone signalled an interest and the horse finally went for fifteen hundred. David took it well: better get rid now than have the cost of its keep over what might be some considerable time.

So now, with only two foals and their filly to look after, David purposely took things easy in order to see how Celine coped on her own, as it was now just weeks away from the start of his new job of taking over the training of the young horses at Millgate.

October was always the month of sales that followed almost one after the other, the last being the final November yearling sale from 31 October to 2 November. This was going to be David's first foray into buying stock at this time of the year to sell on as two-year-olds in the breeze-ups* next May.

He, together with Billy, had gone through the catalogue and listed eight, mostly out of young untried mares or first-season sires. They started to worry after being underbidders on the first four on their list, but struck lucky on the fifth.

A strapping specimen by a group winner's first season as a sire and the second foal of a winning mare. They got him for fifteen thousand, and then, straight after bidding up to eighteen thousand, they secured a compact little chap that looked as if he would make his mark as a two-year-old.

Loading the two horses into the trailer, they took them home. Grace came out to greet them and together watched as the two yearlings were turned loose into the far paddock. It was a joy to watch as they bucked, fly kicked and galloped, sliding to a stop, rearing up on their hind legs and then galloping back the full length of the paddock.

–

Try as he might, Billy couldn't stop looking at the photos of his dad. He desperately wanted to share it all with someone else, but apart from David and Grace there was no one else. He couldn't worry his mum at this time, and, if he told anyone at school, they would find out he'd been – and was in fact still – under the care and control of social services. It was playing on his mind continually, and was becoming an obsession. He fought to maintain the decision of not wanting to make an approach to this man, but as the days and hours passed by he came to realise that he needed to face up to the fact that, underneath, he wanted to meet his dad more than anything he'd ever wanted before.

How should he go about it? He knew he should talk it over with David but every time he was about to broach the issue he backed off from it. Then the idea came to him to write a letter: it would be more personal than an email, and he didn't have an email address anyway and would never know if Yve ever received it. So, one evening alone in his room, he started to write.

Next day at school he asked his form master to check it over and later rewrote it in his very neat and precise hand. He re-read the revised copy, and was well pleased with his effort.

Dear Mr Montagnes,

My name in Billy Brent, and I know now that you met my mum Lucy in Newmarket sixteen years ago in 1994. I looked after her for four years when she was ill, but was taken into care when I was thirteen. She doesn't know I have found you. I now have wonderful foster parents who work with racehorses, and since I've been here, months before I found out about you, my only wish has been to become a jockey. My foster father thought I should look for my dad, and we sent my DNA to the people who look for a match, and found out that it was you. I enclose a copy of their letter confirming this. I know you are a famous jockey, which is really such a coincidence. I want to leave school next year and become an apprentice. My foster dad is taking a new job as assistant to Newmarket trainer Mr Edward Henley, starting in January. I know all this will be a shock to you, but if you accept me I should be very proud, and feel complete in myself for the first time ever. Please don't think me or my mum want anything from you, both of us at long last are settled and happy, and anyway, I'm fifteen now and I'm going to be nearly as well known and rich as you are as I am already a very good work rider.* My address is Billy Brent, C/O Mr Clayton, Home Farm, Fordham, Suffolk, CB8 323, UK. My mobile number is 0044 1639 0071 2652.

Billy Brent. x

Billy didn't know Yve's home address, but had looked him up on Google and found he was the retained jockey* of Claude Emery, trainer with a chateaux and yard of 140 boxes and every box filled with some of the top horses in Europe. Billy addressed the envelope to Yve de Montagnes, C/O Mr Claude Emery, Chateau des Eaux, Chantilly, 1073583, France, and wrote on the top: "Personal. Please Forward." Sliding the letter into the envelope, he hid it in his one of his books, which he now had in growing numbers.

The letter stayed hidden for ten days before he decided whether to send it. Then, on the Friday morning whilst running to school, he stopped at the local post office and stamped it. Taking it out to the post box, he held it in the slot, paused, still undecided, took a deep breath and let it fall into the box. Done, sent, now wait and see and, however things turned out, he felt it would resolve and settle his mind one way or the other.

THIRTY

With the filly, two very young foals, and two yearlings needing to be broken in and fit for the May breeze-ups, David realised that it would be too much for Celine to cope with on her own. They talked it over with her, and she said to leave it with her and that she knew of someone who may be just right for the job and quite happy with the minimum wage.

The girl who'd been working in Peter Gibbons's yard started work the following week. Celine had found out that the trainer was winding down his business after yet another disastrous season. The new help was a seventeen-year-old girl called Cindy, and over the weeks leading up to Christmas she had proved to be hard-working and punctual.

The two foals were cavorting about and doing well, as were the two yearlings. Until after the Christmas break they were rugged up and turned out during the day and brought in at night. As for the filly, she continued to enjoy Patsy's old pony for company and the freedom of their paddock. Having grown a full winter's coat, she was only rugged up in really cold weather, and brought in at night if gales heavy rain or storms persisted.

A week before Christmas, John arrived from Melbourne, meeting Billy for the first time. David and Grace were so happy to have their son back home, having not seen him now for two years. With Billy asking him so many questions about his horses, he was very patient and nice. The two started to get on so well, Billy felt of him as a brother.

The day after John had arrived, Patsy turned up from Manchester. Grace was beside herself with happiness. The family was now complete, and ready to enjoy Christmas Day together for the first time in ages.

There was still work to do, of course, but the minimum amount necessary, all horses got an extra dipper* with carrots added to the feed as a treat.

Grace did herself proud, producing a wonderful roast goose with all the trimmings for their Christmas dinner. Sensibly priced presents were exchanged, Billy buying them each a different brand of chocolates; he in exchange got a new hard hat, white racing breeches, and a pair of shiny black racing boots.* His eyes shone with pride then his feelings kicked in and they filled with tears of joy and gratitude to this wonderful family who'd taken him in and saved him from a life which would now be hard to imagine.

How could he ever thank them enough? He made a promise to himself there and then, that someday he would.

—

David, over the last few weeks, had been to and from Henley's, checking over each horse's breeding, age, form and future prospects. This took a huge amount of time and attention. Since breaking up for the school holidays, Billy usually tagged along and rode out whenever it coincided with the time they pulled out. Now, with only a few days to go before David started there full time, Billy looked forward to riding out first lot, every day before school.

Until then, he had time on his hands, time to spend with the filly and a bond had certainly developed between them. He would walk into the paddock, and wherever he went she would follow him. When he stopped he would talk to her. If he started to run, he would call her to trot on; she trotted behind him, and then, stopping, he would call "woo hoo" and she would stop. Billy hadn't shown anyone this, thinking it best to keep it to himself.

Normally, he realised there was seldom enough time to bond with a young racehorse in a busy yard. For the lads and lasses, having their three horses to muck out, brush over and ride out left little time for bonding. Yes, most of them got to love their charges, but the important part of their work was to get the job done. Particularly when sometimes asked or expected to take on a fourth.

Billy looked forward to being a regular part of this racing yard life but only until he was getting rides and being fully occupied as the apprentice.

Henley's current apprentice, Jason Scott, had only two more rides to lose his claim and become a fully fledged jockey, and was hoping to be retained as the yard's second jockey behind Gordon Stokes. Edward Henley would be looking for a seven-pound claimer* to replace him. This caused Billy some concern as it was unlikely to be him with his own licence, still many months away.

Since the school summer term had finished, Billy hadn't seen or heard anything of Kate, and now, with the news that their yard had closed down, he asked Cindy if she knew where she was. "She took her GCSEs and got seven passes," she said. "She's left school, and got the job as assistant racing secretary to Sir Toby Richardson… lucky cow."

Sir Toby Richardson, a trainer with many group 1 wins over his fifteen-year reign, was the envy of all. Kate had got lucky there. In a way, though, Billy was glad she was still to be involved in racing, and felt sure they were likely to cross paths again sometime in the future.

In the meantime, Cindy was proving to be an asset and a knowledgeable help to Celine, and all was being done to compensate for David's absence from the day-to-day running of the yard.

Every morning without fail, Billy looked for the arrival of the post, trying very hard not to let anyone notice. Each time the mail dropped from the letterbox or lay on the mat, he would pick it up and put it on the kitchen table, making sure that there was nothing addressed to him. Day followed day of disappointment, and by Christmas he was resigned to the fact that his letter would've been received with shock and resentment.

Billy tried to find the strength to tell himself that he could well manage without a famous father and a great future of his own was his for the taking, and he'd jolly well survive very well without him, thank you.

—

David and Grace had been asked to a drinks party do at Edward Henley's large Georgian house at Millgate Stables. Grace had been in a panic over what to wear as it was a black tie event but David had managed to convince her that the little black dress he'd bought her eight years ago and hardly ever worn would look great.

When she walked downstairs into the kitchen, Billy, seeing her with full make up on for the first time, was amazed at how young and pretty she looked. What with David looking so posh in his dinner suit, they made a fine-looking and successful couple off to an upper-crust New Year's Eve party.

Apologising for leaving Billy on his own, they left by taxi and he didn't see them till next day, the first day of the new year. Celine and Cindy had the day off so David and Billy did the horses themselves.

Today, January the first 2010, the filly automatically became a two-year-old, as did the two new arrivals, and the foals became yearlings. Every racehorse in the country and Europe born between January and May would add a year to their age, and the day was just regarded as any other day in the calendar for most yards, unless, of course, they had entries to run in one of the many race meetings.

John left Grace in tears as he left for Australia the following day, Patsy having left two days earlier, and, with David leaving the house at 5.30am to start his new job, the house seemed very cold and empty. David had explained to Billy that he needed the rest of the week to get settled in, but would take him in each morning on his way to work, to ride out first lot, but not until the following Monday.

THIRTY-ONE

Over the coming months of winter, a settled routine was established. David would take Billy in with him each morning, Billy would ride out first lot, then change back into his school uniform and catch the school bus on its last stop.

Although he continued in his class, he moved up to fifth form three times a week for his four GCSE subjects: history, geography, English and French.

Meantime, David and Henley decided that they'd split the seventy-four horses between them. David would take the two-year-olds, Henley the three-year-olds, and they'd split the older horses between them, these to be divided by ability. David would take those with fewer or no wins and Henley those having enough form to win again.

To be fair, Henley realised it to be very much in his favour so thought of the excellent idea of simply splitting the older horses equally between them, disregarding ability. It had also been decided that David would attend all race meetings where they had a runner, except for the high-value handicaps, listed races and group races.

Things had started well, and pre-season they ran several times on the all-weather tracks to sharpen up some of the early types before they ran on the turf. With six entries, they had three wins, two seconds and a third, giving hope of a successful year ahead.

Billy was still going to the gym after school, three days a week. He was fit and was still running; he'd put on a bit of weight but had muscled up considerably. No longer was he this puny little waif. Yes, he was still short for his age, but being short in Newmarket was something of a blessing. It mostly meant light in weight, much sought after and an important necessity within its world-famous racing facilities. There was always an opening for a lightweight and Billy was certainly that.

–

Billy's friend Paul had already left school and had been working for Morris Wellby; having attended the Racing School, he now had his licence. His own yard hadn't yet given him a chance of a ride and nor had anyone else.

Paul was already nine stone, and with his claim of 7lb had no chance of riding at eight stone in a handicap race of 8st 7lb, and therein lay his problem. The lad had no alternative other than make a move to a jumping yard in Lambourn, and hoped to use his claim over the jumps as a conditional jockey.*

Lambourn was in a hilly valley in Berkshire and as well known for the training of National Hunt horses as Newmarket was for the flat.*

Billy had met up with him before he left and Paul had seemed very depressed.

Apart from his home up north, he'd never been anywhere other than Newmarket, a busy, bustling town, and when told Lambourn was a lovely little village he was none too pleased. However, the weights over jumps ranged from ten stone to twelve stone, so there was still a chance he could make a success of it. Billy had bombarded Paul for every detail of his time at the Racing School. Paul told him that as he'd already been working in Morris Wellby's yard: his boss had rung them up and vouched for him. This enabled him able to skip the thirteen-week course geared mostly for those with little or no previous experience. So he'd only been there for the week, passing his knowledge and riding ability tests without a problem and being granted his dual licence over both the jumps and the flat.

This was news to Billy: if it only took a week and saving three months, it was a godsend. If he left school next summer he would still have a chance of a race or two well before the season ended.

Sad to be saying goodbye to his friend, and wishing him well, his spirits were lifted, making him more determined than ever to leave school at the end of the school year in July. He would need, of course, to persuade David that this was the best option. Then a new worry dawned: would social services allow him to leave?

Billy thought it through: even they may well accept that having the chance of an apprenticeship was what they normally aimed for; they would think he was taking the thirteen-week course, no different in their eyes, surely, than an apprenticeship in carpentry or bricklaying. His mind was set: that's what he'd aim for and that's what would happen.

When David returned home that evening, Billy talked it over with him but only received concerns, and future problems that might arise by leaving school at sixteen. It was mostly about the possibility if things didn't work out as a jockey. What would Billy do with no school qualifications behind him?

Billy had an immediate answer to that. "If I wasn't successful," he said, "I'd still find work with the horses. I could eventually join you as your assistant trainer, or with John when he comes back. I wouldn't need any GCSEs or A levels for that, now, would I?"

"Well, then," David said with a resigned sigh, "I'd better first contact June to come up and we'll discuss it, and see how she views it. At least she'll be more understanding than the people in London. If we get her on our side, she'll know how best to approach them far better than we will."

Five o'clock the following evening, June arrived and they sat down together and talked it over. As usual, she was very positive, and agreed she'd put forward the suggestion that Billy would sit his GCSEs in July and leave school at the end of summer term. She would inform them that Billy would be going to the British Racing School in Newmarket and take up an apprenticeship with Mr Edward Henley.

David was to ask that Henley book Billy a place first week in August and arrange that, based on his own recommendation, Billy be allowed to skip the basic thirteen-week course and be accepted for the one-week assessment to secure his provisional licence to ride as a 7lb claiming apprentice.

What with Paul having problems with his weight, Billy had now become conscious of his own, especially when Mr Henley had asked him to step on the scales in his office. His height was also measured.

The trainer wants to know a rider's weight as, when the horses are asked to extend themselves in a trial run, the horse carrying a rider of nine and a half stone would be at a disadvantage to someone riding at eight stone. The trainer has to take this into account if he's to judge the performance of the horse prior to a run. By knowing the rider's comparative weight, he may well make the correct decision on which horse is the better.

Billy now had his own weight etched into his mind. He'd weighed in at 7st 13lb and measured 5 ft 3. Mr Henley seemed pleased with that and asked how tall Billy's mum was. Billy didn't know, but told him she was about two inches taller than he was and that she was very thin. Politely he asked the reason why.

"Because," Henley said, "we think the mother has more influence on the height and weight of their offspring than the father." He chuckled. "Rather like our preference when looking for a well-bred horse, eh? We look more closely at the mare's pedigree than the sires." Billy could have told him he was small because his dad was a world-class jockey, and had been for fifteen years or so. But the secret remained with him; there would be the right time to divulge this sometime in the future and only when it could be used to his own advantage. Billy was getting smart.

—

On 15 February David, on a whim, had popped into Tattersalls, just to reunite with old friends in the business. Whilst chatting with a retired trainer he'd been friends with for over twenty years, he spotted a brood mare being led around the parade ring. He opened his catalogue to lot 432 and liked the pedigree. She'd been covered* on 5 May the previous year by an up-and-coming young sire so was due to foal the first week in April. She'd produced four winners out of seven foals of racing age, and was a winner herself.

There was something about her, a gut hunch, maybe, but David excused himself to his friend and went into the ring. It was a quarter past one and the place was almost empty as most of buyers had left for their lunch.

The mare was led into the ring; her name Sunset Girl. The bids were slow; the auctioneer struggled and was about to drop the hammer at 1,750 guineas when David did something he'd always told himself not to do: he acted on impulse, raised his hand, received a "thank you, sir", and the mare in foal was his for two thousand.

Having signed the paperwork, he fetched the car, drove to Home Farm and returned with the horse box.

Grace, who'd been out doing the weekly big shop, had arrived as David was unloading the mare. Finding it difficult to accept what he'd done, she berated him for not thinking things through. OK, it was nice to look forward to the foal being born but they'd then have to get the mare covered again; it would become a never-ending responsibility. David's only explanation was that it had cost the previous owners ten thousand pounds to cover the mare, plus her upkeep for the year, and by getting her for only two thousand guineas they'd get a valuable little foal for free!

When Billy got home and went to feed the filly. There stood the mare, calm, relaxed and grazing contentedly next to the filly's paddock. He could see she was in foal and wondered where she'd come from. He was soon to find out.

So now at Home Farm they had plenty to do. Two two-year-olds to look after, and ready to start their breaking-in process. Two yearlings at grass, the filly that would be leaving them in a couple of months, and now this mare with her foal due in a few weeks' time.

On cold or bad weather nights they all needed bringing in, and not forgetting Patsy's old pony and David's nine-year-old lead horse,

Celine and Cindy would have their hands full, but, with Billy's help in the evenings and Old Joe called in when things got too much for them, they thought they could manage.

–

Billy's mum and George hadn't come up before Christmas as promised but made it with excuses the third week in February. They'd met up in the Rutland Arms Hotel for coffee then moved on across the road and had a lovely lunch in the restaurant opposite and George was quick to pick up the tab. They then went back to Home Farm to say hello to Grace and David.

Taking them to the paddocks to show them the horses, he explained the plans they had for each one, but both Lucy and George took most interest in the mare and her hoped-for foal.

Now, all were pleased and comfortable that they'd bought the mare, and it was something else Billy could learn from witnessing the birthing process himself, but as of now he couldn't answer some of the questions Lucy asked.

Over the few hours they would spend together she'd wanted to know how he was doing at school, what his plans were for the future, and whether he had a girlfriend. So many questions about his life; too many for Billy's liking. He told her about leaving school in the summer and would start work for Mr Henley.

What he didn't tell them about was discovering her ex or anything about the man. Anyway, why should he have? He'd still not received a word or even an acknowledgement of his letter. For the moment, he was trying to forget all about him, and, by the time they'd said their goodbyes and drove out of the yard Billy was almost pleased to see them go. Of course, he loved his mother and was grateful to George for being with her, but they were just not his sort of people, and pretending they were just didn't come easy.

THIRTY-TWO

Going in with David six days a week, and riding out, Billy was beginning to come out of himself, and enjoying the camaraderie between the twenty lads and lasses employed there. On Saturdays, when he didn't have to rush off to school, he joined them in their break, before riding out second lot at nine.

Some of them smoked, some rolled their own, but most simply enjoyed a hot cup of tea and a biscuit or two. Two or three copies of the *Racing Post* were passed round; the day's runners were discussed, as well as who might win the feature race of the day.

For the first time in his life, Billy now felt part of all this, something he'd never felt at school. He'd now found a true confidence in himself rather than a made-up one, and somehow those feelings of loneliness and being so much into himself hopefully was a thing in the past, his future secure.

–

It was half term, and it was a time to help the girls at Home Farm, so a rest from riding out at Henley's became a week working twice as hard at home.

Old Joe was now on a part-time basis where he came in four days a week from nine till twelve. Billy enjoyed listening to the old man talk of how racing used to be. How things had changed from when a lad did just one or at the most two horses.

How each day at evening stables the horses had to be properly and fully groomed with its lad stood to attention alongside his horse waiting for the boss to inspect them both in every detail. Sometimes he'd be wearing a white glove and run the gloved hand over the horse, and woe betide the lad should any dirt or dust show up.

How the straw had to be laid perfectly over the floor and built up along the sides and straw rolled and weaved, then laid immaculately across the threshold.

How vets were seldom called as the trainer had more knowledge and understanding of what needed to be done if a horse looked off colour or was injured or lame.

How, if a horse got colic,* they used to take it out for a stirring gallop to ease it and get the bowels moving again.

Oh, and so much more. It was enthralling listening to the old man, and of how it used to be. Famous trainers and jockeys Billy had never heard of. Tales of horses who'd become world-famous sires; well, Billy at least knew some of those through looking through the sale catalogues, but it was all so fascinating.

Old Joe just loved talking to someone interested and eager to listen. It brought back memories of his youth. To his mind, this lad showed him respect and he'd not even mentioned, nor would he, that he'd won fifty races over hurdles and thirty over fences. Just because you're old, he thought, and no one knows what one's achieved in life, it's a bit sad to be just known as Old Joe, the part-timer.

Over the years Joe now possessed a rare collection of books written by trainers and jockeys now long gone. He offered to lend Billy them but only one at a time. Billy was thrilled and was already halfway through the first of many, learning the history of the sport and of how it had evolved.

—

It was now Friday towards the end of February, Billy got home from school and walked into an empty house. Grace was out, and Celine and Cindy were busy making up the feeds in the yard. Walking up to his room, he changed into his working clothes, ready to go out and help.

Billy walked down into the kitchen, and, heading for the door, he noticed a large parcel on the table. It was more of a box than a parcel and had four colourful USA stamps stuck above its address. Billy did a double take: it was addressed to him. "Mr Billy Brent, C/O Mr D. Clayton, Home Farm, Fordham, Suffolk, CB8 323, UK."

Picking it up, he felt the weight of it; he shook the box: no rattle. Billy couldn't comprehend what it might be or who was it from. He didn't know whether he should open it or wait till David or Grace came back.

Taking it up to his bedroom, he placed it gently onto the bed, stood and simply looked at it for a few seconds, then, taking a deep breath, he took hold and looked to find the best way to open it. He needed something to cut the cardboard folds so hurried down for Grace's kitchen scissors and a sharp knife. Cutting the folds to the lid, he put the knife down and carefully opened it. The contents were wrapped in bubble wrap, but he instantly recognised what it was.

Carefully, he took it out of the box, removed the wrap and gazed at it in awe.

A brand-new, shiny black racing saddle, and etched in gold on one side was a signature, a name... and the name read... Yve des Montagnes.

Billy sat down on the bed and held it in his hands, admiring its quality and detail. Laying it over his knee, he looked deeper into the box. There was something else. He removed it and turned it over, and to his wonder it was a photograph. It had a script title at its base that read, "Big Thunder, Winner of the Breeders Cup 2010 Yve des Montagnes up".* Billy could hardly believe what he was seeing: written in black ink, scrawled across the green turf beneath them, read:

"To my son Billy from his papa Yve"

Not only that but there was a two-page typed letter. Billy read it out to himself in a whisper.

Billy, I am in Keenland, Kentucky, I have been here since the Breeders Cup eight weeks ago. My wife and little girl will join us here for Christmas. I have been to the Kentucky yearling sales and have a couple more big rides, so we have no plans to come back to France before March. When I get back I will make contact with you so we can meet up sometime. I hope to get a couple of rides in the Classics in Newmarket and Ascot on my trainer's three-year-old who has shown us great promise. My wife is also looking forward to meeting you and your little sister is too. I haven't phoned as my English is not the best. My agent has translated this letter for me so I hope he's made a good job of it. I remember Lucy as such a lovely person. I tried to make contact with her but had no address and didn't know her surname.

I was called back to Paris to take the place of a jockey who was injured. It was a complete surprise and unexpected. I hope Lucy is well now, and that you seem to be very well looked after by your foster family. You have a father now, so get out there as soon as you can and start riding winners. I am sorry we have missed so many years when we could have been together. Jeunette and I have an apartment in Paris but during the season live in Chantilly in the annex attached to the Chateau des Eau.

As my agent is always in touch with me it's best if you use his address, which is Jacques Cartier, La Rue Motier, Chantilly, 1073585, France.

I hope you like the 3lb saddle.* These days I need my lightest; by using it I can still just about make the 9st 2. I shall probably retire in the next three or four years as I am thirty-eight.

Your papa with love… Yve.

Billy read the letter three times, and was going to once more when he heard Grace coming back in. Suddenly he realised he'd have to tell them he'd written and made contact. Would it upset them that he'd done so without discussing it with them first? However much he might want his birth father in his life, he in no way would want to risk losing his life here at Home Farm. He loved them both and was ever grateful for all they did for him and for the life opening up before him.

Putting the saddle back into the box, he took a last look at the photo and put it with the letter on top, closed the lid and slid it under the bed.

He stopped at the bottom of the stairs. Grace was putting the groceries away; she turned and, as mothers do, noticed straight away that something was troubling him. "You look a bit sheepish," she said. "Have a bad day at school, did we?"

Billy's mind raced. "Yes, they've moved me up into fifth form and now they want me to sit another subject. Religious studies. They don't expect me to pass any of them, let alone five."

"Never mind, dear; who knows, you might surprise yourself."

Billy, still looking rather glum, went outside to help bring the horses in and hand out their feeds.

Later, with David home and when sitting down for their evening meal, Billy took a deep breath and said he needed to tell them something he'd done, and he would be so sorry if what he had to say might upset them. Both David and Grace stopped eating. "Whatever it is, son? It's best you get it out; there's nothing that can't be fixed. Are you in trouble at school?"

Billy told them he'd written to Yve and had received a reply, and that Yve accepted he was the father and wanted to meet up later in the year.

"Why, that's wonderful news. You've every right of finding your birth father. Grace and I are very pleased for you."

Pushing his chair back, Billy ran upstairs and brought down the box. "And he sent me this."

Once Billy had gone outside, David and Grace talked things over. They wondered how it might concern their standing as foster parents if social services discovered that the boy had found his birth father, a father well able to provide for him. "I think once he starts work we would lose our fees anyway," David said. "Whatever happens, though, as long as he wants to, we don't want to lose him; he's part of the family now, and look what we have to thank him for. If he hadn't pointed out the filly to me, we would have lost the deal to Henley and I wouldn't have been offered my new job."

Grace cut in. "He's brought us nothing but good luck. I don't even want to think about it, hun, I couldn't bear it if we lost him. It's not that we need the money from social services now; what's it matter, as long as he's happy here? It's his home too."

"I agree," David added, "but I think I'll tell him we think it best if he keeps it to himself for now. If social services got involved, all his hopes could be put on ice."

The following week, David took a call from June. She had good news from London as they agreed Billy could leave school at the end of the school year as long as he attended the apprenticeship course at the Racing School and had a pre-arranged job to go to at the end of it.

Everything was falling into place; he was a very lucky lad.

—

The two-year-olds had already been backed and were being ridden out at the walk and trot, and this weekend were due for their first canter around the prepared track that circled the five paddocks. Billy was also using the track to prepare the filly for her move into training at Henley's. She was already giving him a nice steady hold as he talked and cajoled her in and out of her paces.

Whenever he came up to her or rode her, he called her Sunshine, and was sure she recognised it as a greeting. Even when it was decided, and her official name was registered in the stud book with Weatherbys,* she would always be known to him as his Sunshine.

THIRTY-THREE

Ten bales of straw were delivered on 2 April. Celine and Cindy spent the morning washing down the walls and floor and, when dry, laying down a thick bed of straw, turning it up around the walls on all sides of the one stable large enough to accommodate a brood mare and her foal.

Tension was growing in all of them. David had told them to keep their eyes open on the mare still in the paddock, and that, if she took herself as far away from the others as she possibly could, and seemed pretty miserable, to bring her straight in, as it was a sure sign she was ready to foal. He said they shouldn't panic, though, as most mares foal in the middle of the night.

This put them behind their normal routine and when David arrived home they were still at work, with Billy helping too. He went to look at the mare, and told them there were no signs and it wouldn't be happening tonight.

Neither had it happened a week later. Billy had broken up for the Easter holidays and, with the thought that he'd only have one more term at school, he was in a happy state.

Having just finished lunging the filly, he noticed the mare had gone to the far corner of the lower paddock, and was just standing there and not grazing. He quickly took the filly back to the yard and put into her stable, removed the tack and hurried back to check the mare. She had a distressed look about her, wild-eyed, and she kept turning her head, looking towards at her hindquarters.

Running back, he told Celine, who immediately used her phone to speak to David. She told him the mare was starting to show her first labour pains.

"She won't drop the foal yet," he said. "They're most likely preliminary pains and they'll pass in a few minutes. I think we're on course for her to foal tonight. Bring her in, but don't put her in the foaling stable yet as she'll only mess it up. Leave her in one of the other boxes until I get back; I'll come home early. If she gets too agitated, ring me and I'll come straight back."

Celine and Billy brought the mare in and put her in the empty stable next to the foaling box. They shut the bottom half of the stable door and watched, and to their relief the mare seemed more relaxed. Grace came out to see what the fuss was about. She looked into the box. "Don't think we'll be getting much sleep tonight; now, finish up, you two, and go home. I'll ring you later. Celine, we might need you. It could well be in the middle of the night so keep close to your phone."

Billy helped the girls tidy up and once they'd gone he checked the mare every half hour or so until David came home early.

Grace rang him again and told him she'd already rung the vet and warned him the mare had started her pains and was expected to drop the foal in the night; she asked whether, just in case of a problem, he would remain on call. Billy had listened to this and asked why the vet wouldn't come anyway. "Only if the foal's presentation isn't normal," she answered. "Its head should be foremost, resting on its fetlocks,* its two little legs sticking out in front of it. Things can be bit more difficult if its buttocks are foremost but any other than these I'd call the vet fast."

"What are the other things?" Billy asked.

"Its head could be bent back towards its rear. It can have one or two forelegs bent under it other than straight out under its chin. It can be lying on its back. So many complications, I don't want to think about it. Luckily, these problems only occur about five in every hundred."

"I shall be so scared," Billy said. "I can feel the butterflies in my stomach even now."

"Perhaps you'll feel better to know I worked on a stud farm for several years before I met David. I've helped with the birth of so many foals. It's usually a quick and simple procedure, but things can go wrong. That's why we always let the vet know he might be needed whatever the time of night. Now." She smiled. "Be a good lad and fetch that folding table from the store and set it up in front of the stable while I go and get the things we might need."

Billy rushed off, and by the time he got back and unfolded the table the mare was fidgeting and moving around, pawing the floor with her foreleg. Billy watched and worried; he could see she was upset and obviously uncomfortable. She started to stamp her front leg and then alternately her hind.

Grace returned with her equipment. She spread a white linen sheet over the table and started to lay out the other things. "Is she about to have it now?" Billy asked with a worried frown.

"No, not yet," she said, "but we'll keep a close watch."

Billy brought the mare out and led her into the box, ready prepared and waiting for her. The mare gave a snort of approval as she felt the depth of the sweet-smelling straw so different to the wood chip normally used as an economic necessity.

Back outside, Grace was laying out her equipment onto the table. A piece of thick cord with loops either end, two round-ended rods, each about sixteen inches long, a nail brush, a large pair of scissors, and a sharp knife, all set in a neat row.

"What are those things for?" Billy asked, looking more scared at the sight of them.

"Just let's say," she replied, "as long as one has the right tools for the job, anything's possible." Then, with exaggerated neatness, she laid out a bottle of olive oil, a jar of Vaseline, two bars of carbolic soap and a box of sulphonamide powder.

Finally, she went back into the house and returned with a porcelain wash bowl, an electric kettle and several old bath towels over her arm. She put them under the tabletop shelf. "Would you keep an eye on her whilst I go and get supper ready? After we've eaten, David will stay with her through the night and when her time comes he'll wake us. So, straight after supper, me and you straight up to our beds to try and get some sleep."

Once David arrived home an hour earlier than usual, he came straight over to check the mare. "I see Grace has got everything sorted. I don't think I'd have put her in the foaling box yet, but we won't disturb her now she's there. There's some hours to go yet."

With that said, they left the mare to herself and went back inside to find their supper on the table. After they'd eaten, David took one of the kitchen chairs and went back outside. Billy followed him out for a last look before going to bed at such an early time.

The mare had had nothing to eat since the morning feed so there was little likelihood of her fouling the clean bed they'd prepared for her. She was still standing but the intervals between her pains had shortened. Billy was reluctant to leave her, but David insisted he go and get some rest.

Instead of getting into bed half dressed, Billy opened his page and continued reading one of the books Old Joe had lent him. But after a little while, feeling sleepy, he slipped under the duvet, turned out the light and fell asleep.

Meanwhile, David was sitting on his chair with his coat wrapped around him, getting up to check whenever he heard the mare moving about. She'd been arching her back against her contractions and the pains that came with them. Fretting and concerned, she would lie down only to get up almost immediately.

Half an hour later, there seemed to be little or no further progress and she became more at ease with herself. Time dragged on. David was stiff and cold; it was a beautiful clear night, the full moon and the light from the two stables spilling out over the yard. Nothing much was happening so David went back into the house and made himself the biggest mug of strong dark coffee. The house was so quiet and peaceful it was hard to keep his eyes open.

Spending the long wait, he took out his notebook and made himself a list of all he needed to do the following day. It was something he was used to doing, as by writing things down he removed those worries from his mind and for the most part remained calm and relaxed in what it took in looking after the thirty-four horses, being his sole responsibility.

The coffee helped and he gave himself another half hour before going back out into the cold.

Looking into the box, he could see the straw had been strewn into a central heap; she was pawing the straw with her front leg and had gone down onto her knees. She tucked her back legs under her and rolled over on her side. She gave out a heart-rending groan as if to indicate it was all too much to bear. This time she stayed down.

David checked the time: 11.30. Going into the house, he woke Grace, and then Billy, hurried back out again, picked up the kettle, took it to the tack room and plugged it in. Billy arrived, closely followed by Grace.

"Billy, you can come in, but be ready to pass me anything we might need from the table. Grace and I will help the mare if she needs us."

Grace had already poured the kettle of hot water into the bowl. David rolled up his sleeves to the elbow and washed his hands and arms with carbolic soap.

Grace did likewise, then they both went into the stable.

Noticing the appearance of the as-yet barely visible bluish-red bag of waters showing from under her tail, David helped Billy to understand what was happening. "Don't be alarmed at what's about to happen, son; this is just the preclusion to the birth. It's all quite normal."

The bag extended from the mare like a balloon, and protruded three-quarters of its diameter. The mare moved her hind legs to counter another spasm. There was a sudden rushing sound as the bag burst, the escaping fluid pouring onto the straw.

Billy's heart missed a beat as the mare, alarmed at the noise behind her, sprang to her feet; she turned her head to her hindquarters, looking red-eyed and frightened.

Billy's heart went out to her; he wanted to go and stroke her face and make her feel he cared. As if in answer to his concern, she let out a groan, then, arching her back against another contraction, she pawed at the straw. Minutes later, she got herself down again but this time her hindquarters were too close to the wall, so David had to get her up again. Turning her, he made sure that as she lay down this time her hindquarters now faced the door.

Billy could now see things clearly and noticed a yellowish green membrane slowly protruding below her raised tail. It was smaller than her waters and a different shape. Grace looked up, sensing his concern. Reassuring him, she said that this was the caul and it would rupture as the waters had done. She explained that the caul covers the foal's forefeet, and completely surrounds the hoof, which prevents scratching. If the caul became pierced by the feet whilst in the womb, the foal would die, but it needed to burst now, and, if it did not, she would do it herself.

The protruding bag slid out at an increased rate, then stopped. Grace reached forward and dug her fingers into the middle of it, causing it to burst. A flow of mucus ran over her hands. Billy's heart leaped; he could now distinguish two tiny forelegs sticking out from under the mare's tale. Grace stepped over, came out and washed her hands. After drying them, she poured some olive oil onto the palm of her hand, and smeared it over both hands and arms. "I have to feel inside her to find out whether its head is resting between the forelegs where we hope they will be, so keep your fingers crossed."

Talking to the mare quietly, Grace gently eased her right hand between the foal's protruding forelegs and into the mare herself. She felt around for a few seconds, and extracted her hand. She turned towards David and Billy, beaming.

"Fabulous. I could feel its nose. I think it's all going to be OK. Its chin's resting on its fetlocks just as it should be. We have to wait now till its muzzle appears."

Billy breathed a sigh of relief. He felt exhausted, his knuckles white from clenching his fists, his heart pounding. Grace stood up and came out to sit down on David's chair.

They waited. Five minutes later the mare suffered another bout of severe contractions and suddenly the muzzle appeared. David, still in with the mare, asked Billy to pass him one of the clean hand towels from the table. Taking it, he wrapped it around the foal's forelegs and with a firm grip waited for the mare's next contraction. As it came, David pulled steadily, yet gently, against her. This he repeated with each of her next four, and on the fifth the foal's head appeared hung between its forelegs. Just three minutes later, the complete form of a perfectly developed foal lay wet and bedraggled on the straw bed.

Billy fought back the tears welling up inside him. Unable to control them, he turned his head and walked away a few yards.

Finding privacy, he sobbed uncontrollably for a few seconds, then, regaining his composure, dried his eyes.

Grace noticed his distress. "Don't be upset, darling," she said. "It's a little colt, perfect in every way." She put her arm around him.

Billy looked up to her and smiled. "I feel so stupid crying like this. You must think I'm such a baby; it's just I feel so relieved and happy."

"Come on," she said. "You can go in with her now: the worst is over."

The mare had now got to her feet and in doing so had severed the navel cord between herself and the foal. The supply of oxygen being cut off triggered an instantaneous reflex action; the foal started to breathe of its own accord.

As Billy entered the box he heard the foal cough and gurgle. It coughed again and brought up mucus and fluid from the back of its throat. Once out, its breathing became more regulated.

"Hold its back legs for me, Billy," David asked. "One in each hand, that's it, now a bit higher up." David lifted a few inches of the umbilical cord and looked for the sulphonamide. Grace took off the lid and passed it over.

Sprinkling a liberal amount over the complete area around the navel, David got off his knees and stood up.

The foal lay, eyes staring, still with part of the caul wrapped around him. David led Billy back outside and the three of them stood and watched to see if the mare would start cleaning the foal herself. A few seconds later, she hung her head down low and sniffed the wet and bedraggled inert object that lay before her.

The colt started to shiver; she sniffed it once more, then pushed it over on its side with her muzzle. She then started licking it, going from the foal's head to its feet, then turning it over so that no part of its body was left untouched. David explained that the mare was stimulating, warming and cleaning it, and above all reassuring it. "She's certainly a good mother and knows instinctively what to do, but she ought to as I think it's her sixth foal."

The mare had visibly calmed; she looked tired, but relaxed and content. So were the three onlookers. Tension had evaporated, replaced by smiles and pleasure.

The mare started to nudge the foal to and fro, trying to encourage him to stand. Each time he got up, the little fellow swayed on his spindly legs only to fall back again. Finally succeeding, with feet splayed wide apart, he stood of his own accord, big eyes blinking at this strange world so different to the warmth and darkness of his mother's womb; within a few minutes he was suckling heartily.

"That's it," said David. "Let's clear all this into the empty stable, and we'll tidy up in the morning." Putting everything back onto the table, they carried it into the adjoining stable and, turning off the lights, left the mother and son to themselves.

Back in the house, they sat down, each with a mug of tea, tired and relieved.

"Looks like a fine little chap," said Grace. "I think he'll be a chestnut and I love the white flash on his forehead and four white socks!"

"His sire, Rocking Louis, was a chestnut," David said. "Let's hope he's got some of his ability too. We'll check how they are in the morning, as we're not completely done with them yet. The milk the foal's suckling now has extra colostrum in it, which helps to open the foal's bowels and get rid of a pitch-like substance that blocks the bowel of all newly born mammals. If it doesn't clear of its own accord by morning, we'll have to give him an enema. The mare hasn't done with her efforts either, as she'll have a few more pains yet in order to get shot of the afterbirth. Both should have happened by morning. Now, let's all get to bed. Don't know about you two but I'm knackered. Don't get up early, Billy; try catch up on some sleep." The time was 3.15.

Billy still woke up bright and early, and, as he expected, Grace and David were already up. They walked together to check all was well. To their obvious relief, both were fine. The foal stopped suckling and turned its head towards them, then quickly returned to his feed. Billy looked at this thing of pure wonderment. It seemed to be all legs, its little body and powder puff tail all out of proportion to its height. The mare moved herself between him and the foal, hiding it from their view, but not before Billy had seen it take a few faltering steps.

David went into the box and checked the mare over. Everything had gone as it should have; all was done. He asked Grace to help him and they moved both mare and foal to the adjoining box, deep in fresh straw. They filled the water buckets, gave the mare her feed and threw a generous amount of hay into both corners.

Celine and Cindy arrived and, after spending several minutes transfixed by the sight of this darling addition, they mucked out the birthing box and washed down the floor.

In a few days, the mare and her foal would be turned out to grass and fed twice a day. Not a huge amount of extra work for them both, but, pushed as they already were, they looked forward to the breeze-ups, where they hoped the two older colts would be sold and off their hands.

THIRTY-FOUR

Billy returned to school and fifth-form studies for the GSCE exams, due in just two months' time. They now wanted him to try for maths as well. He struggled, and Grace could see he was just trying to do too much. She spoke to David and for the time being they tried to stop him helping the girls in the yard, only allowing him to ride the filly whenever he wanted. Billy wasn't too happy with this, and they agreed he could continue riding out with the lads at Henley's but only on Saturday mornings.

The subject returned of Billy seemingly having no close friends. They knew he'd kept in touch with Paul, still in Lambourn, but that was about it. However, becoming aware that he'd struck up acceptance from the lads and lasses in the yard and sometimes met up with them at the White Horse Inn settled the issue for the time being. His struggle early on to hold a horse into a steady canter or half-speed gallop had improved hugely. "Let the horse do the pulling rather than you," he was told. "With your rein bridged, lock your left knuckle and the rein into its wither and play the horse with your right rein, then give and take, just don't let the horse lengthen its neck." Billy tried this and it worked; he was also so much stronger now, and still continued with his fitness regime.

He was growing, too, and putting on a bit of weight due to the build-up of muscle and upper-body strength. His weight worried him so he asked the secretary if he could be remeasured and weighed.

The following Saturday he stepped on the scales. He was 8st 3 and had grown an inch to 5ft 4. This surprised him as he hoped that by the time he was eighteen and fully grown his height could improve to around 5ft 5 but his weight should be no more than 8st 5. He thought deep and hard about this and now realised he would have to keep a closer check on what he ate and how much he ate.

–

Having done so well in selling the filly to Lady Worlinton, David had given Celine a bonus of £150, for which she'd been surprised and grateful. David felt perhaps he should have rewarded Billy somehow, as he was the one who'd picked out the filly at the sale now over fifteen months ago.

This coming Tuesday was Billy's sixteenth birthday and, after speaking with Grace, he took the horse box into Cambridge and bought Billy their present.

Putting it into the back, he drove home and left it hidden there. But, before the day came, there was a nasty shock in store.

Billy, having come back from school and before going into the house, walked up to the paddocks to talk with the filly Sunshine. Surprised she wasn't there, he thought she must have been brought back in. With some urgency, he went back to the yard and checked, but she wasn't there. The only answer in his mind was that she'd broken out and galloped off somewhere.

Running into the house, he found Grace and, in a state of panic, told her the filly was missing. Grace stopped what she was doing, held him to her and told him that David had rung her from work, that Edward wanted the filly brought to Millgate straight away, as Lady Worlinton was coming to see her cantering on the track tomorrow morning, mistakenly thinking that the filly had been with Henley for some time and was already part of the full training regime. He'd explained it as a slight misunderstanding.

Billy was devastated. He had never had the chance to say goodbye to her or put her at ease. "But you'll see her when you go in on Saturdays." Grace understood his concern. "They might even let you ride her." Billy broke away from her and ran upstairs and threw himself on his bed.

Feeling something on his hand, he discovered two birthday cards, and his upset left him for a moment. The first was a card from his mum that George had also signed and the other was a larger card with four French stamps stuck to it.

The card had a picture of horses walking through a beautiful wooded path.

Under was the title *Early Morning Horse Walk Chantilly France.*

Staring at the black ink signature from Yve and written in broken English, Billy deciphered it and read it as:

> A happy birthday to my son Billy, I don't know the exact date of your birthday but I hope this finds you well. Jeunette and I returned to France last month so we are closer to you now. Jeunette starts filming next week, she sends you her love, and I have many rides. So we will both be busy for the rest of the season, then I'm off to Melbourne for three months. I hope we can meet up before that and sometime soon. Yve xx

Billy put the open cards on his bedside table and went back downstairs and told Grace rather proudly that his dad had remembered his birthday and apologised for being in a mood over the filly. She said she understood.

The next morning, Grace and David were already downstairs waiting and excited as Billy came down for breakfast. They wished him a happy birthday and gave him a hug. "We have something for you," David said, and they led him outside.

Opening the ramp of the horse box, he wheeled out the shiny red moped.

"This is from us both," he said. "Because you're just sixteen, it's only 50cc, but it'll get you about and give you some independence."

Billy was aghast and asked if he needed a licence. "I've booked you a test Monday week, your half term, at the DVLA Bury St

Edmunds." Billy straddled the saddle, beaming. It was the first time he'd ever owned something of worth, and this was now his very, very own. Putting the machine on its stand, he ran to hug them both.

"Practise up and down the drive," David told him, "and tight circles around the yard. We've got you an L plate and with a bit of luck you could pass first time and get a provisional licence."

Billy went off to school with so much to contemplate. Having "wheels" opened up so many new opportunities for him. The lads in the yard had invited him several times to join them, and sometimes with the girls, for nights out, but he hadn't wanted to ask David or Grace to drop him off or pick him up later, and, anyway, they might not approve of where or who he was meeting. Better still, he'd be able to go down on his own now whenever he wanted to see the filly. He could hardly wait to get back home from school to start up his moped and practise new moves.

—

Billy passed his test and now had a provisional licence. He started back at Millgate again, riding out three lots over half-term break and then just Saturday mornings whilst back at school. He was doing less at home, though, as Celine, Cindy and Joe were now working as a team and coping quite well, and best left to get on with it.

THIRTY-FIVE

Things had changed slightly two weeks before the breeze-ups. David and Billy rode the two colts down onto racecourse side at 6am, and met Henley's jockey, Gordon Stokes. David jumped off and legged him up and gave them his instructions.

"Take it easy down on the sand canter for about three furlongs, turn them onto the turf gallop and come back alongside the Rowley Mile. A steady half-speed gallop for the first two furlongs and then let them stride out full gallop for the final furlong, pulling up opposite the winning post. Neither of them has been tested before, let alone galloped, so let's see what they've got. You OK with that, Billy?" Billy nodded. "Just stay upsides* with Gordon."

This was what would be needed in two weeks' time for the buyers and those just curious, watching a hundred and eighty two-year-olds galloping past in turn at full speed, to be judged on their foreleg action* and athleticism.

Billy was slightly nervous, these colts, never having been extended out of a canter before, were as yet an unknown quantity.

Walking alongside Gordon they crossed over onto the sand track, and trotted a hundred yards before breaking into the canter. Billy's colt* took a keen hold but he held him, and they carried on upsides for the three furlongs. David was watching every move through his binoculars.

Pulling up to a walk, they carried on a hundred or so yards past the marker, turned and walked onto the turf gallop, Even though the animal beneath him was already excited and playing up, Billy made sure he kept a loose rein but readied himself for a quick shortening up. Gordon turned in the saddle. "Come up alongside me, son, and try to stay with me… OK, then." The two colts cantered on the spot for a second, then plunged forward straight into the gallop. Billy had a struggle to hold his in at half speed; Gordon's hands were still and his experience showed.

Billy's arms were being pulled from his armpits, but he held on, longing for the marker telling them to increase the pace to the maximum. Flashing past it, Billy let the bridged reins slip through his fingers, allowing the colt to stretch its neck and do what all thoroughbreds are bred for, and that's to gallop, to feel the wind in their ears, the beat of their hooves, the thrill of the speed. This was the first time Billy had ever had the chance to experience a full-on gallop.

Up on the colt's back, at this very second he felt a little unsure of the outcome, but he was still upsides of Gordon and had spotted the Rowley Mile wining post.

Gordon shouted at him, "Ride him out now; ride a finish on him." Having a second start on Billy, Gordon drew ahead a few yards. Billy bent himself way up the colt's neck and pushed, pumped and verbally encouraged the colt into a last extra effort.

Flat out now, they sped past David with Gordon just two lengths in front. Billy sat up in the saddle and played the reins, talking to the horse in a soothing tone. He was ahead of Gordon now, and by the time he regained complete control Gordon, so cool and relaxed, had pulled up fifty yards behind him.

Billy, flushed in the face from his effort, but with a smile on his face, trotted back to him.

"You did good, lad," Gordon croaked. "Considering he's carrying me, probably two stone heavier than you, I think we might have something special here. I'd advise anyone this chap's worth a punt, at a price, but either of these could be very useful. Come on, we'll walk back to David and see what he thought."

David had worried that Billy might not cope with a young untried colt's first bit of work* and could see that the lad was having a hard time of it, but he'd done what was asked, and pulled up safely. He liked what he saw; it had all gone according to plan, and as they came back to him he was pleased to have his opinion confirmed by Gordon.

Four days later, and two before the sale, the exercise was repeated, but this time they worked the gallop separately, one at a time. Billy went first, as Gordon had to control hold his overexcited mount until he saw Billy pulling up in the distance.

All went well, and, when they safely got home, the colts were turned out for the rest of the day and brought in for the night. While in the stable they were rigorously groomed twice a day, ridding the remains of their winter coat and revealing the fineness of their summer coat, which enhanced a view of their muscle development and, in its shine, their obvious fitness.

–

The day they'd all been working towards arrived. The colts were not due to breeze up until around twelve noon, plenty of time to get them shampooed, dried off and groomed, and their hooves oiled, looking mighty smart in their lightweight rugs. Billy and Celine loaded them into the horse box and David drove them down to the racecourse car park, where Gordon Stokes joined them. He was to ride both colts separated by only three lots, adjusted now to lots 40 and 43. They waited their turn.

As usual, things were running a little ahead of schedule and the call came through to David's phone that they needed to be readied in ten minutes at 11.53.

Unloading the first was the Swirling River colt. Celine held on to him as David legged up Gordon who, without a word, walked the horse to the sand and cantered up the three furlongs to the start. Seven minutes later, he was back and legged up on the Hot Summer colt, who, missing his companion, had been kicking up a fuss, kicking and jumping about in the box with high-pitched whinnies.

David asked Gordon how the first ride had gone. "Went a treat," was the only comment he got.

As Gordon began to ride off on the skittish colt, it now became reluctant to leave its companion. Gordon gave it one crack of his stick* and a firm kick with his heels. The colt reacted with a huge buck and plunged forward; Gordon just sat tight and off they went.

Celine had taken hold and loaded the returned horse into the box and tied up a hay net for it. David joined the crowd to watch his other horse at the gallop, and was very satisfied with the way it looked, nice low knee action, short in the back and plenty of speed. Well pleased, he returned to the horse box and waited for Gordon to bring it back.

Jumping off, Gordon slipped the irons up the leathers and turned to David, saying, "This one's got that something the other hasn't. He loved it, wants to give his all; he was on the bit the whole way. I rode his sire, Hot Summer, a couple of times and this colt should do him proud. I'll recommend him to the governor, if you like." With that he took off the saddle and stomped off without a word of thanks.

With all horses breezed up, buyers with orders to purchase had ticked off those that had caught their notice. The auction would be in two days' time, time to let the galloped horses relax and calm themselves before another wash and brush up.

—

The sale came and went. The Swirling River colt fetched twelve thousand guineas, a loss of three thousand, and the small compact Hot Summer colt reached thirty-seven thousand, a gross profit of nineteen thousand. David found out later that evening it had been bought by his boss, Henley, for a loyal owner David already knew. His name was JJ Johnson and it would be nice to have the chance now of being able to follow and be part of the horse's future progress.

No one could be upset that David having made a good profit on the deal as all prices of any racehorse when bought or sold could easily be researched by just putting the horse's name into the *Racing Post*'s search engine. It was there for all to see, all above board.

THIRTY-SIX

With the filly and the two colts now off their hands and just the foals to manage, Celine and Cindy could quite easily cope on their own and dear Old Joe was stood down. Celine, not wanting to lose Cindy as well, took it on herself to ring around the yards and within the week had taken in two horses to be retrained: a ten-year-old ex-hurdler and an eight-year-old off the flat. Neither horse had ever won a race. She made a clever deal whereby she got the horses for free but with the promise of a payment of £1,000 for each when sold on.

Rather worried what David might think of her impetuousness, she wasn't too sure, but he happily agreed and he gave her another £150 bonus on their success in the breeze-ups.

Billy, on the other hand, had been concerned over the filly. The girl who'd been given her to do had been riding her out now for three weeks and they were having issues. The filly was being reluctant to follow the string out in the mornings and had to be cajoled and coaxed to do so. She also took several tries of refusing to walk onto the track and was often left behind. As the girl was fully aware not ever to let a horse get the better of one, she had to wait until someone led her on and geed her off into a canter. At this stage of her training, she'd not yet been galloped.

David, who came each day, mostly on racecourse side, would watch and assess his two-year-old's progress, and was well aware he had a problem. He suspected the filly might well behave herself with a more experienced rider, so asked the help of the yard's head lad, ex-jockey Martin Stoddard.

Martin was legged up in the yard, and managed to get the filly to join the others before they pulled out, but as they did she put up a performance, but Martin coped.

Once on the heath, she again showed reluctance, and Martin gave her two cracks with his stick. Normally no one was allowed to carry a whip when exercising, but he'd previously agreed with David to do so.

The filly reacted by rearing up on her hind legs and then running backwards.

Martin had his feet out the irons and slipped off her back as she came down, just missing him with a fly kick. The filly crashed to the ground, struggled up and took off at a flat-out gallop riderless.

Thankfully not hurt, Martin picked himself up and ran back to David.

Jumping into the car, they raced off, following in the direction she was headed. She was out of sight now, but, seeing another string of horses coming onto the heath at the far end, one of the lads had somehow managed to grab hold of her.

David pulled up, jumped out, thanked the lad profusely and legged Martin back into the saddle. The filly, totally unconcerned, walked back to the yard as if nothing out of the ordinary had ever happened.

Later in the day, David had the chance to talk things over with Edward as to what action was needed to take over the problem filly. He suspected that Billy might have been allowed to get too closely involved with her over the many hours he'd spent with her, and that perhaps the filly might behave differently if he rode her.

Edward agreed it was worth a try but David explained that Billy was about to sit his GCSEs and couldn't be riding out other than a Saturday morning, so it was decided that Billy should ride her out first lot on Saturday to see if it made a difference.

—

Billy liked the girl who did the filly. She was older than him and before they were asked to be legged up he apologised for jogging her off, and explained that he loved the filly and had spent a lot of time with her. She was only too glad for him to give it a try, and Billy liked her all the more for it.

Once up he coaxed the filly into line, and had a slight struggle to leave the yard, but by the time they arrived on the heath she'd become more at ease. Billy talked to her, easing her between two other fillies in the middle of the string.

David watched from the viewing platform and held his breath, knowing full well that, when a filly or mare decided to rear up, they often collapsed backwards, and many times a rider had been severely injured, sometimes killed.

Billy was entirely confident in how he approached the problem, knowing any nervousness on his part would be picked up by her and cause her, and most horses, in fact, to freak out.

Riding onto the track with an extra length of rein, as the horse in front set off, he barely took hold of her, and let her decide to follow by a slight squeeze of his legs rather than heels.

Where did he find these skills? Perhaps they were in his genes. Of course they were: it just seemed to come naturally to him, an instinct heightened by his love of the animal under him.

The filly trotted for a few yards, then broke into a steady canter. Billy gently shortened up, taking a light hold. The filly held a steady pace, keeping the distance from the one in front of her.

As they approached the end of the six-furlong all-weather track, Billy cooed his voice – "Woo hoo" – at her three times and with a gentle touch on the bit she pulled up smoothly and happily. Keeping her place with the ten others in their walk back to the yard, she was calm and settled.

Jumping off, he undid the girth, took off the saddle and pad, led her back into her box, and took off the bridle. He carried it all back to the tack room and sat down in one of the old yet comfy tattered chairs next to the filly's groom, Angela.

"You did a good job there," she said. "We all thought she was going to have you off and teach you a lesson, but I'm pleased we were wrong. I think most of us will now see you have a natural talent, so well done."

Billy felt a warm glow of pride but kept his feelings hidden. "Don't know about that," he said. "It's just that I've spent nearly every day with her since we bought her as a foal, and she's been my best friend. What about you?" he asked. "Are you married?"

Thinking it might have been too personal a thing to ask, he blushed. She noticed and touched his hand, laughing. "It's all right, lovey. No, I'm not. My mum told me never to get involved with anyone in racing and of course I did: he works for Sir Toby Richardson."

The name rang loud in Billy's brain. "My friend from school works for him. Kate Gibbons. Do you know her?"

"Yes, we know Kate, a bit too stuck up for us. Listen, why don't you come up to the White Horse Inn after work? We meet there most weekdays for a drink and chatter. Chance to pick up or share a few tips and what's entered and where."

"Nice of you to ask," he replied, "but I'm only just sixteen and not allowed."

"Don't worry about that; you can still have a Coke. You come along, I'll look out for you. Come up on Monday: if the weather's good we'll be outside."

THIRTY-SEVEN

Billy thought long and hard on whether he should meet them at the pub.

Although previously he'd visions of meeting up with them, he'd not done so, and decided it was not the time to do so now. Best wait until he'd left school in just three weeks' time.

Instead he went up to his room and spent the time in revision of the books and notes in preparation of the fast-approaching exams.

His mum and George had come up again, and he never missed his call to her on Tuesdays. All was going well for them, with George's business flourishing.

On Saturdays, after riding out, Billy would stay on and go racing with David. They were having plenty of runners now, and the results of all the hard work over so many weeks proved either a disappointment or the sheer thrill of a winner.

Billy helped with the saddling of the horse and often led it around the pre-parade ring before the travelling head lad took over. Just being there, he felt part of it all, soaking up the atmosphere and excitement of seeing their horses run.

He particularly enjoyed the two-year-old maidens,* which he'd learned were races for horses that hadn't run or won before. They had to run three times in these races and were assessed by the handicapper on their performance and given a rating,* enabling entry into handicap races.* The higher the rating, the greater the perceived ability, an indication of how good the horse might be, and what grade of race to put it in.

The filly had her chip* implanted by the vet, and her name registered with Weatherbys. To Billy, she'd always be known by his pet name, Sunshine, but it was Her Ladyship's choice of name registered. From this day on the filly would be referred to and raced under her official name of Black Sunday.

Strange name for a filly, but he admitted the name gave something of her quirkiness and added to her character. Since riding her a few weeks back, she'd improved her behaviour to some degree, but continued to be somewhat untrustworthy. However, as she was only being brought on slowly, she would be given plenty of time to mature as she'd only have a couple of races back end* as an education for her three-year-old career.

–

Billy had just one more hurdle to get over before the excitement of leaving school and his admission to the British Racing School: GCSEs. Due to commence in a week's time, he was taking history, geography, religious studies and French, having discarded maths as a non-starter.

He didn't expect to pass any of them, but was determined to try his best, mostly to please David and Grace, as the results, good or bad, would reflect on them too.

So he worked his socks off each night and over the weekend, and by Monday he was well prepared to give the exams his complete attention and effort.

It was with some trepidation that he walked into the school hall, now arranged with desks set apart and a hush of expectancy in contrast to the usual noise and commotion of normal morning assembly. Billy was ten minutes early and chose to sit at a desk two rows from the back. Students were filtering in, their usual chat and clatter replaced with serious faces and silence.

The teacher supervising delivered the history exam papers on each desk, told them they had a maximum of two hours to complete the work and, having put the last papers on the last desk, she told them in a loud voice, "Your time starts from... now."

History from ten until twelve today, religious studies two until four, and tomorrow geography, with French in the afternoon.

–

Billy had no idea how he'd done. David and Grace seemed more interested than he was. When pressed, he told them he'd been able to understand most of it, had guessed some of it and tried to make the best of the rest, but was dreading the French oral, which was the final test at the end of the week. "I think I'll be able to manage a few sentences," he mumbled, "but my accent is worse than Yve's English."

–

Much to his surprise, Billy got through it, and the young French lady was so nice he thought perhaps he might not have failed after all. Now that was over, whether he'd passed anything or not; for himself it hardly mattered, but he hoped to have passed something of worth when David and Grace asked how he'd done.

Anyway, all the school stuff was almost over; after tomorrow he could get on with his life. It would be his last day at school, and the end of the school year. He could hardly wait and was tempted not to go in at all. Of course, being Billy, he put such thoughts out of his mind and went in on his moped.

The assembly hall was packed out with all the pupils from all the classes, together with their teachers, who sat on the stage behind the headmaster. Mr Richardson made his yearly speech, and then they presented school sport prizes.

Lastly he finished by making a short speech of the school's benefactor, Lord Frobisher, and said that he would now present the Frobisher Award for Outstanding Achievement.

"This person," he said, "has surmounted many problems in his life through no fault of his own. He came to this school two years ago and has been a pleasure to us all and we are very sorry to lose him. I know we all wish him great success in the future, wherever life might take him. Will he now come up and claim his well-earned prize? I am pleased and honoured to tell you… the winner is… W. Brent, who we all know as Billy."

A hush descended throughout the hall, followed by thunderous clapping.

Billy sat where he was, not quite realising it was him. Little Billy Brent, an achievement award! It took some seconds for it to sink in until the young person sitting next to him pushed him out of his chair.

Walking down the full length of the aisle with the whole school looking at him, he squared up his shoulders, looked neither to the left nor to his right and climbed the steps onto the stage. The headmaster shook his hand. "Well done, Billy," he said quietly. "I expect this is probably the first of many awards you may win in the future, so good luck and please come back to see us when you do."

With that, he handed Billy a framed certificate with his name embossed in gold leaf, and an envelope, which he would later discover contained a cheque for fifty pounds. Billy thanked him and returned to his seat as the clapping and whooping continued.

The headmaster then wished all those who were about to leave school his best wishes for their future, and reminded everyone that school would restart on the 10th of September.

Immediately, huge noise and pandemonium broke out as chairs were pushed aside, everyone standing up in the rush to be first out of the hall. Collecting their coats and belongings, they dispersed singly or in groups, to wherever they were meant to be or wanted to be.

Billy took his moped and went straight to Millgate Stables just in time to ride out third lot.

Chatting with Angela on their way to Bury side, she told him the filly was now in full training as they'd decided to enter her into a maiden and if she showed enough ability she would run in a listed race for two-year-olds at York in October.

Billy couldn't decide whether this was good news or whether he should be disappointed. He'd secretly hoped to be in a position to partner her for her first race next year as a three-year-old. There was no hope that he'd be given the ride now when her first race was only a few weeks away and he might only be able to obtain a six-month provisional licence.

Angela had been giving him an update whenever they had the chance on how the filly was behaving, and it was mostly good news apart from a few tantrums.

At least she hadn't reared up again, and more importantly they'd come to the conclusion that the filly reacted wildly against any use of the stick.

Billy had learned not to pester David about the workings of the yard or progress of the horses. He was just being professional, and would be seen to treat Billy as just another member of the staff. No favours, no special attention.

However, he did let on that the boss had deliberately not taken on another apprentice to replace Jason Scott, but was holding the position open for Billy as the yard's 7lb claimer.

David also related what Henley had said, which, in his own words, was: "I think your lad has a rare gift, and if he keeps his head things will happen for him, and we should use it to our advantage as well as his."

Hearing this meant more to Billy than winning his prize, and, although David had originally thought it better that Billy be apprenticed to some other yard, the fact that Edward had said he wanted him settled the matter.

It wasn't until later on that evening that Billy told David and Grace rather sheepishly that he'd been awarded the school prize. Grace stopped setting the table and David put down his *Racing Post*. "Billy, that's fantastic," he exclaimed. "Where is it? Weren't you going to show us?" Grace was already hugging Billy. He broke away, laughing, ran upstairs and brought down the framed parchment. Inspecting it closely, it impressed them both.

"It's beautiful," Grace said. "Do you want to hang it your room? Or can we put it up in the hall."

"In the hall," David answered for her. "We are so proud of you,

Billy; whatever you achieve in the future and when you leave us, I want that hanging there reminding us of the many memories of our time with you."

"And they gave me a cheque for fifty pounds," chirped Billy. "It's lucky I have a bank account."

Billy had been thinking long and hard about something but hadn't raised it as he thought it might upset them, but realised now might be the time to bring it up.

"Do you think I should get a passport?" he asked. "Cos if Yve ever asked me over for a few days I'd need one, wouldn't I?"

"Good idea, son," David said. "I'll get an application form for you."

THIRTY-EIGHT

Two days later Billy turned up for his assessment and interview at the Racing School at 10am. Edward Henley had already submitted his recommendation, and the interview was deemed unnecessary. He was taken straight into the gym and introduced to the fitness instructor. There were several other boys and two girls already being tested on various equipment.

Points were given on the ability to achieve the required performance on each exercise. Billy waited his turn and used the time to watch those already performing and comprehend how and what he would be asked to do.

His turn came soon enough. First the ball held against the wall by his back and keeping it there whilst doing squats for four minutes. Next, lying on his back and raising his legs for four minutes, no resting, and straight into standing on a wobble board, and doing squats for four minutes. Straight into a press up and hold for ninety seconds, then sitting in a rowing position and pushing forward the elastic resistance cords with every beat of the metronome for two minutes. Onto the watt resistance bike, maintaining the 100-watt input at resistance level 2 for four minutes, and, finally, holding the plank position on the floor for four minutes.

Billy, of course, having prepared himself for several months, managed every test but it was pretty tough, and now all that was left was to await his turn on the mechanical horse, on which he was asked to ride at the gallop for three and a half minutes, and that part of it was fun. Total time of workload: forty-five minutes.

Making his way to the canteen with the others, they waited for their results, which took an hour. He had no doubt in his mind that he'd passed but the wait was still nerve-racking. The fitness guy came in and read out the results. Out of the twelve lads, two had failed, including the poor kid who'd fallen off the mechanical horse, which had cruelly caused some laughter; both the girls had also got through.

The losers were told to get fitter and to try again, and those who'd passed and lived close by to report the following day at eight o'clock to start the course proper.

They would be accommodated within the complex for not one but a full two weeks, told to arrive in working clothes suitable for stable work and for riding out, plus casual wear to change into for evenings.

Those who'd come from more distant areas than Newmarket had already settled in; the others dispersed back to their homes or yards.

–

David had given him a fatherly hug before leaving for work and Grace fussed over him and helped him pack. It would be over two years since he'd come into their lives and this was the first time he'd be away from home. Close to tears, she waved her goodbyes as he drove off on his moped.

On arrival, Billy was shown to his room and the lady who led him upstairs pointed out the boys' showers and toilets at the end of the corridor.

It was small single room, spotlessly clean, bright and fresh. A single bed ready made up, a small fitted wardrobe and corner table were frugal, but all that was needed. He was told to come down to the canteen at 8.45 to sign in and join the others for a tour of the whole complex.

Once signed in, they all followed their guide, who explained everything in detail as they were shown around the facilities both inside and out. Billy was amazed at the size and scope of it all: the raised seating of the lecture hall, the gym, the equipment, the stables all filled with horses bedded on straw, the horses looking resplendent, coats shining. Finally, the post and railed all-weather track on which they would have to prove themselves. Billy felt very proud to be given his chance here and felt grateful to the people who'd designed and built this facility for the benefit of someone such as him.

—

The two weeks seemed to flash by; they were lectured on the main injuries that can happen to the horse in training, particularly ailments to two-year-olds, and what to do and look for if your horse goes lame. They were taught the protocol in the weighing room on a race day, of weighing in* and weighing out.

The rights and financial rewards to which an apprentice is legally entitled, and claiming allowances were explained. The number of wins needed in losing those allowances, from the initial 7lb to 5lb to 3lb to nil, were discussed at length. That an apprentice had to ride ninety winners to lose that final 3lb allowance before becoming a fully fledged jockey. How trainers use apprentices to gain a weight advantage in handicaps, and how, once the claim is lost, rides tend to die off and are harder to come by. The reason was that, once a fully fledged jockey, the riding fee is the exact same amount as the best rider in country.

The most enjoyable part of the whole two weeks so far had been on the mechanical horse on full-gallop mode and being shown the ultimate rider's position through a whole race from start to riding a close race finish. Then there was the riding, of course.

All horses on the establishment were between five and ten years old and all retired from racing; most by now were canny individuals ready to take on any beginner not too sure of himself. Every day up till now they'd looked after their appointed horse and rode out to the track and completed a handheld canter.*

Some of the horses took a strong pull and two or three of the group had problems holding to the canter coming alongside or passing the horse in front of them. This to the loud shouts of horror from the person assessing them.

During their time together, friendships evolved, everyone seemed to get on well and any troubles or worries were openly shared.

—

The final day of the two-week course dawned and, after a hearty cooked breakfast, the group went out to their horse, mucked out, and gave it a thorough grooming. They then had to stand to attention outside the box and wait for a senior retired jockey to inspect their work. Once done and any misses rectified, the lads and lasses were legged up. They walked around the yard until all were mounted, then made their way for this, the last ride here at the school.

Billy was third in line. They'd been instructed to trot to the end of the track, turn and come back at a half-speed gallop and to ride a finish from the two-furlong marker to the to the winning post. A member of staff already down there would set them off individually once the rider in front had travelled the first furlong.

Standing in his irons, Billy, carefully keeping three lengths behind the rider in front of him, reached the far end and circled the turning ring until told to set off.

The horse, having done the same thing many times, went straight into its gallop.

Billy checked it into the required half speed and had no difficulty at holding a steady pace. Seeing the two-furlong marker fast approaching, he gave the horse a slight squeeze with his heels and a voice command, and they immediately increased to an extended gallop. With just another hundred yards to go, he could now see the instructor was watching him closely, and, just twelve or fifteen yards from the finishing line, Billy, already bent right up the horse's neck, gave a forward flick of his right rein and voiced a command, "Come on, come on." The horse, although at full gallop, quickened again, and flashed past the post. Billy loosened his hold and sat back into the saddle. "Eeeasy, boy, eeeasy." The horse slowed into the canter into the trot, and pulled up, and with three hearty snorts was ridden off the track.

–

The group were told to report back into the gym at 9am for a final workout, wondering what it might be and why the instructor who had assessed them on the track had seemed amused. The instructor came up to Billy and asked where he'd learned that flick of the rein. "I've seen my dad use it on the telly," he said.

"Oh yes?" said the instructor. "And where was that?"

"Prix de l'Arc de Triomphe," answered Billy.

The man laughed. "Pull the other one," he said. Billy left it at that, wishing he'd not appeared a smart ass.

With thirty minutes to spare, they filed into the canteen for a mug of tea or coffee and talked of their gallop. Two or three were unhappy with their horse, being much slower than what they were used to, whilst others were elated and pleased. Billy kept his feelings to himself; however slow or fast, it hardly mattered: they weren't assessing the horse, were they? It's how one looked and how one rode it.

He thought some of the group were somewhat naïve, others a little too sure of themselves. Then his thoughts turned to himself. Was he being too sure of his own self? Why was it his own confidence was sky high? Smiling to himself, he decided he'd try not to judge others, just be the judge of his own abilities, whether well founded or not.

Once all had gathered into the gym, there was an instant hush as a famous jump jockey entered the room. "I will assume not everybody knows who I am," he said, "but I'm a jump jockey and my name is Don Rankin. You're all hoping to become jockeys and, whether or not it's over the jumps or on the flat, at some time or possibly many times you will take a fall. How you fall may prevent injury, and a fall is not only painful; it also loses one rides, and losing rides is losing income, so we're here now to teach you the best and safest way to take a fall."

Don Rankin pulled a two-foot thick foam mat into position a few feet away from and in line with a gymnastic springboard. Slipping off his jacket, he set himself about ten feet behind it and with a run and a jump sprang several feet in the air, falling onto the soft foam, landing on his right shoulder with his right arm tucked around his body.

He stood off the mat and explained, "It was probably all too quick to take in, so... You... Yes, you, come and lie down on the mat on your right side." The lad did as asked. Don bent the lad's body forward and brought the right arm across the boy's chest, pushed down the head so the chin rested on the chest, and brought the left arm close around the body. "Avoid putting your arms out in front of you; don't let them become the point of impact, otherwise you'll break your wrists. So, I'll repeat what I said again, before you try it out yourselves: bend at the waist and bring the arm across the body; avoid putting them out ahead of you. Keep head tucked in with your chin touching your chest. Main aim is to take the impact on the back of your shoulder... now, who wants to go first?"

The lad got up from the mat and was the first to try but only half succeeded; it was as difficult as it'd looked. The best of them managed it after their third try; Billy managed it on his fourth attempt.

"Who wants to give it one last go?"

"Me," said Maggie, one of the two girls who'd not wanted to try. Standing back from the springboard, she ran and jumped daintily onto the springboard and seemed to fly higher than anyone else; she did a complete somersault in the air and landed on her feet. Everyone clapped and whooped. She stepped off the mat, laughing.

"Well," said Don with a wry smile, "that's another way of doing it. I might try it myself next time I find myself being flung over the head of my horse. That concludes your work for today; now, if you all congregate in the canteen, the director will interview you individually before you leave us. Thank you and good luck in the future."

The first five had their interview; each one, as they walked back through the canteen to collect their belongings, sent the next named pupil through.

Billy was sent for, knocked on the director's door and went in. Quietly closing the door behind him, he stood in front of the director's desk.

"Ah!" said Mr Malloney. "Please, sit down... How do you think you got on?"

Billy came out with the answer straight away. "Well, sir," he said, "if I haven't got through, I would feel very sorry for the others but I think the girls were terrific."

"Billy, my man's report of you on the gallop this morning..." Malloney paused as he scanned his notes, "tells me that just before you reached the post you flicked the right rein at the horse, which surprised him as it was a very professional thing to do. Where did you pick up that little trick from?"

"Gordon Stokes, sir, when he rode our two-year-olds in the breeze-ups. I saw them quicken up after he did it on the blind side of the buyers. They couldn't see it but I was on the other side, and I did."

"He's a canny old devil, Gordon Stokes. Your Mr Henley's having a good season, since he took on your father."

"He's not my father, sir; my father lives in France."

"I'm sorry, Billy. Yes, I mean David Clayton. So, what does your father do?"

"He's French, sir; he's a jockey."

"Would I know his name, Billy?"

"Yes, sir, you would, but I don't want it known as I don't want any favours. I want to make it on my own."

"Well, Billy, that may be, but in this business even a small article in the *Racing Post* or the national papers brings one's name to the forefront and into the minds of those that may employ you... But I tell you now, you will be granted your licence, and that you came top of the group. I shall email Weatherbys and you should receive your licence within ten days. I shall also be sending a full report of your attendance here to Mr Henley."

Mr Malloney stood up, leaned over the desk and, with a firm grip, shook Billy's hand. "Well done, Billy. All of us here wish you a very successful career."

THIRTY-NINE

It was with some trepidation that Billy went back into the school building to pick up his GCSE results. It wasn't that he expected to pass anything, but he was just not programmed into accepting failure.

The assembly hall was a buzz of pupils either screaming out their delight after opening their envelope, or in groups solemnly talking over their disappointments.

Billy waited in the queue, shuffling slowly up to the desk.

"Name, please?"

"W. Brent."

The secretary sorted through the pile of those yet unclaimed, and handed him the pristine cream envelope. "Next," she said grumpily. Billy turned away without another word. Walking outside, he sat down on one of the memorial benches and opened his results.

History... Pass Grade B. Religious studies... Pass Grade C. French... Pass Grade C. English language... Pass Grade D.

Billy didn't know whether he'd done OK or not. To him grades weren't worth much but it did say he'd passed four GCSEs, and, having had less time in the fifth form than anyone else, he could hardly have expected to do any better.

Later that evening, when David had got back from Millgate, straight away he gave Billy a hug. "Edward received the Racing School's report on your assessment," he said, beaming. "Billy, you did us proud as usual; what pleased the old boy even more was it confirmed his own opinion of you, and then Grace rang me to say you'd passed four GCSEs. You never cease to amaze us, Billy. Edward wants you to start full time on the first Monday of September, as we get paid monthly. So you can enjoy a rest over the next couple of weeks and chill out."

–

Billy was now in a possession of a passport, and wondered if he dare; he also for some time now had had his own email address. With only fifteen days left before he started work, he wondered if he could fit it in.

Taking what, for him, was a giant step, he put Yve's address into his phone and typed that he'd now got his licence, was starting work on 2 September and asked whether it would be possible to meet up for a few days either here, or perhaps in France.

Billy re-read the short missive several times; his finger hovered over send, then, taking it away again, he asked himself what he had to lose. He pushed send and immediately closed his phone.

For the rest of the evening he checked and re-checked in case of an answer.

The following morning he checked again. Nothing, absolutely nothing.

Then, late in the afternoon, the phone now in his pocket bleeped. Shocked but thrilled with expectation, he ran back inside and up to his room, sat on the bed and opened his phone.

He read and re-read the email several times and could hardly believe what Yve had arranged. A car would pick him up at 7am Thursday morning, get him to Gatwick North Terminal at nine. Flight by EasyJet leaving at 11am and arriving Paris at 12.15. Yve's driver would be waiting in arrivals and bring him to Chantilly.

The flight reference was also there with a printed boarding card. Everything was pre-paid; it would cost him nothing.

Finally, Yve added that he was looking forward to Thursday and had booked everything for his return home on the following Wednesday and to please confirm by return that he was coming.

Billy could hardly wait to reply back with the answer that he was, but thought he should first ask David and Grace if they'd let him. Grace was in, and was excited for him. "You're old enough to make your own mind up now," she said. "Tell Yve you're coming; I'll square it with David. He'll be pleased for you."

Excited, Billy ran back upstairs and emailed he was coming. He thanked Yve for arranging everything, and that he looked forward to meeting up.

The next day, Grace helped Billy decide what to take. They decided he would travel in smart casual clothes and his new white sneakers, and she'd pack his best shirt, a clean change of socks and pants, and his riding gear should he be lucky enough for the chance of riding out.

Billy, who'd never flown before, had lots of questions on what and where.

Grace simply told him to look for the EasyJet desks, show them his passport, take the bag through as hand baggage, go through security, find a seat in the departure lounge close to a flight information screen, and wait until the flight says boarding and go straight to the gate number on the screen.

Billy felt unsure of himself and wrote it all down. He might have said it was way out of his comfort zone, but sense told him that, with his ambitions of becoming a world-class jockey, moving around the world would require plenty of air travel and the sooner he took it in his stride the better.

—

He was up at five, had a shower and took care of looking his smartest. He had a cooked breakfast with David. "Just be yourself," he said, "and they'll love you like we do. Be a listener rather than someone who chatters on just to fill the silence. Ask whatever you need to know by all means. Everything will be fine. Give us a call to say you've arrived safely." David gave him a hug and left for work as Billy waited, very much on edge as to whether a car would actually show.

He needn't have worried. A black Audi came up the drive five minutes before seven. The driver got out and Grace recognised him as an ex-jockey called Vince Smith; after a brief chat, Billy climbed into the passenger seat, and as they drove off Grace waved them goodbye with a tear in her eye.

It was an easy drive down to Gatwick. Vince was very interesting, keen to know about Billy's hopes and fears, and answering Billy's many questions of his life as a jump jockey. "I retired last year," he said, "but I still get rides in Jersey. I've been champion jockey there for six years in a row, and I'm still in the lead this year with only one meeting left of their season. All expenses are paid and they're always looking for lightweights so, if you want, I can give your name and contact details to two or three local trainers I ride for. The prize money's crap, but it's a lovely little course and would be great experience for you."

Vince pulled up at the drop-off point at the North Terminal, Billy collected his bag from the boot and thanked him. "I'll see you here next Wednesday," Vince said. "I'll wait for you in arrivals, have a good trip, and have a think about Jersey."

–

Everything went off smoothly, Once through security he'd sat in departures and kept his eyes glued to the departure screens. He found his way to the gate and they boarded on time. He had a window seat and enjoyed the short flight, watching the land pass below him and the short time over the sea.

Though slightly concerned that he'd not locate his French driver, he needn't have worried; a lady was holding a card with his name on it. To his surprise she spoke English with only a hint of an accent. She welcomed him to France and said her name was Matild and that she was Yve and Jeunette's secretary and housekeeper.

During the drive they chatted about their very different lives. She also told him how much Yve was looking forward to him coming. "He does speak English if he needs to," she said. "Actually he speaks it a lot better than he thinks."

An hour and ten minutes later, they pulled off the motorway into a minor leafy lined road and after a few minutes slowed to a stop in front of a huge pair of ornate gates, which opened automatically. Continuing down a narrow driveway lined either side by mature trees, Billy marvelled at the beautiful sculptured gardens and then a large lake with a fountain. The driveway took in an S bend, bringing the chateau into view in all its grandeur. Billy took in a deep breath: it looked like a palace to him. Matild noticed his surprise. "Don't worry," she said, "we don't live in there; we're in the annexe and the stable block behind."

Driving over the gravelled forecourt to the rear led them to the Tudor sandstone house with wisteria enhancing its entrance. Matild parked the car to the side of a large single-storey building, which she said was where Yve kept his collection of vintage cars.

Billy took out his travel bag and they walked to the rear entrance of the house and straight into a large beamed area housing the kitchen, huge fireplace, comfortable sitting area and a long shiny oak table with ten matching chairs set around it. Matild asked if he would like something to drink and that, as Yve had three rides today, it would be somewhere around seven before he got back and that Jeunette wouldn't return from Marseille until Saturday evening.

She made herself a coffee and Billy a glass of iced water. She told him Yve had said she should show Billy around the yard and, if Monsieur le Maistre was in his office, to say hello. "First things first," she added, "I'll show you to your room."

The room was huge, everywhere beamed ceilings, beam lintels over the doors and windows, and an enormous dark oak seven-foot-wide bed; it all looked as if it were centuries old and probably was, but conversely it still felt fresh and new. "I'll leave you to unpack and freshen up," she said, "and let's say we meet up downstairs in fifteen minutes." So nice, so welcoming, she smiled and closed the oak door behind her.

Billy unpacked his few things and put them in the huge oak press that stood high and proud against the wall. Walking into the large en suite bath and shower room, he'd never seen anything like it. Marble floors, marble sinks, marble bath and a very large and ancient-looking radiator, stone cold; in fact, although a sunny day, the bathroom as well as the bedroom room still felt somewhat chilly.

Checking the time, he went back down to the kitchen; it felt warm and cosy.

Matild had lit the large log burner that sat in the granite inglenook and was now preparing vegetables at the sink. She turned towards him as he entered. "Yes, I'm the cook as well." She laughed. "You must be hungry; can I make you up a sandwich with our lovely French bread?" Billy shook his head. "Tell you what," she said. "We might catch Yve's last ride at St Cloud; I'll put the television on."

Billy sat into one of the soft easy chairs as Matild turned on the TV and flipped through several channels to France Gallop. The horses were already cantering down to the start. "He's in black with a red cap and red sleeves... There, that's him, number five."

Matild sat down on the edge of the chair next to him, and they watched the action together. The horses reached the stalls and were loaded in; Yve was drawn in gate two. Billy watched in awe: this was his dad, doing exactly what he himself had dreamed of over the two years he'd been with Grace and David. A sense of pride nearly overwhelmed him and yet again he felt near to tears.

A pause... and the gates opened. Yve was one of the quickest out and they kept straight for 100 metres and then those drawn on the outside cut across to the rails, bunching into a tight group. Apart from a couple of stragglers, the group stayed together until the last 200 metres. The cameras now cut to close-up, and caught a full view of Yve riding his finish head on. He had his stick in his right hand and spun it three times through his fingers, changing its position in his hand, allowing with a swing of the shoulder to catch the horse on its quarters. He only hit it the once and the horse quickened, passing the winning post a nose in front of the second, beating the third horse by five lengths.

Having watched the whole race had been a complete thrill to Billy, but what had impressed him most was that professional finish in the swirling of the stick. It was something he'd have to master himself, not only with his right hand, of course, but the left as well. It wasn't showmanship; it was purely to enable the rider to reach far enough behind himself to catch the horse on its quarters and not its flanks, an English jockey club regulation to spare the horse unnecessary pain.

"That was marvellous," Billy said. "Thank you so much."

"Come on then," she said, "I'll show you the yard."

They walked out of the back door into a tree-lined garden and down a flagged stone path that led them to a small granite arch, and a half-open solid oak gate.

Walking through, Billy had his first view of the yard, as Matild closed the gate behind them. Set around a huge square of pristine lawn, there were stables on all four sides, apart from the southern end, which had a pair of closed gates as its main entrance.

Within the opposite side was the office, tack room and canteen, and the two small gates, the one they had just entered from and the other to a separate barn behind for feed, hay and straw, with a brick enclosure outside as the muck pit.

All the buildings matched the style of the chateau and most likely were two or three hundred years old, but all were very well maintained.

Looking into one of the stables, Billy judged them to be half again larger in size than he was used to. He did a quick count and judged there to be at least a hundred boxes, and almost all were full.

The yard was busy, with horses being skipped out and feeds and hay being distributed. There weren't as many girls as lads, as he might have expected, but it all looked to be operating flat out, smoothly and efficiently.

Matild led the way to the office and introduce him to the trainer's secretary, an attractive mature woman who smiled and said, "Enchanté," as she shook his hand.

The boss, Monsieur Christophe, was not in. "He's at the Deauville yearling sales," she said, "and won't be back till Sunday, and his assistant is at St Cloud with Yve."

Back to the house and Matild carried on with preparing dinner whilst Billy went up to his room and phoned home to say he'd arrived safely and he hadn't met up with Yve yet as he was away and had just rode a winner, but he'd be back home by seven.

Going back down to the warmth of the kitchen, he sat in front of the fire and watched TV, which he didn't understand: it had lots of adverts and seemed utterly boring.

FORTY

Billy kept checking the time, and it was now 6.50; he had butterflies in his stomach and his mouth felt dry. A few minutes later he heard the sound of a car crunching to a stop on gravel, the kitchen door opened and in he walked.

As Billy stood up from his chair, Yve dropped his bag on the floor, walked up to him, held each side of Billy's face in his hands and kissed his forehead.

Speaking English with a heavy accent, interspersed with French when struggling to find the English equivalent, he lifted Billy off his feet, hugging him tightly. Putting his son down, he turned to Matild and asked her to translate, holding Billy's shoulders at arm's length as she spoke.

"He says this is the best day of his life, to finally have a son, and a brother to Angelique, his daughter. He is excited that you have a love of the horse and that you are a jockey too, and that he can follow your career and perhaps help some way in guiding you through the complexities that success brings with it. He says, will you please excuse him as he needs to change his clothes and when he comes back down we will eat together and he can come down from the clouds and you can tell him all that's happened, in your life, from your time with Lucy to where you are now."

Yve kissed Billy on both cheeks, picked up his bag and went upstairs.

Matild wiped a tear away. "I think you have made him very happy," she said. "He's always wanted a son and now he has one. He'll be down in a few minutes."

Billy went back to his chair and pictured in his mind this, the first impression of his birth father. Possibly 5ft 7in tall, slim, but broad in the shoulder, and a southern swarthy complexion. His black hair – thinning, with grey showing in places – was swept back close to his scalp; his eyes were blue, a piercing blue, with jet-black eyebrows, a generous mouth and a fairly large nose.

Matild broke his train of thought. "I could tell straight away that you're his son," she said. "You look alike; he's a good-looking man, and a very nice man with it."

Billy felt pretty good, and hoped this was just the start of a full son-and-father relationship, but then a tinge of guilt entered his thoughts. He still loved David and Grace, and would never want to lose his feelings for them, but love is not divisible, is it? He'd just have love them both; it was still early days, anyway, and what was it David had told him? "Just go with the flow as everything has a way of working out its own agenda."

The three of them sat at the table and Matild served up steak and chips for Billy and steak and salad for Yve and herself. They drank a bottle of red Burgundy between them and Billy simply a glass of iced water.

During the meal, as Billy spoke of the hard times he and his mum had gone through, Yve was filled with remorse and then amazed at the coincidences that had brought Billy to Newmarket and of Billy's fortitude and determination to become a jockey. He supposed it must have been in his genes; fate worked that way sometimes.

Dinner finished, Matild cleared the table and said she would leave them to it, bid them goodnight and went up to her own quarters. Yve beckoned Billy to sit down by the fire; he poured himself a brandy, offering one to Billy, who, slightly embarrassed, refused it.

Between Billy's schoolboy French and Yve's pigeon English, they managed to understand one another. Yve said he was sorry that Jeunette wasn't there to meet him, and that she'd be home tomorrow with Angelique and the child's nanny.

He asked about Edward Henley and of the yard: how many horses did he have in training? And how was David enjoying being assistant trainer? It was a lot for Billy to answer in so much in detail, but somehow he managed. Yve, of course, knew of Henley and once before had met Her Ladyship at Longchamp, when she'd awarded him the trophy of a prestigious race he'd won and a race that she'd sponsored.

Yve then told Billy what they'd be doing over the next few days. Tomorrow morning they would ride out just the two of them together, so he could show Billy the amazing training facilities that made Chantilly the centre of French racing.

He said he had rides Friday and Saturday but had kept tomorrow free.

The evening ended when Yve explained he would be retiring at the end of next season as he'd then have been a jockey for twenty-three years; he'd had enough. It wasn't the riding; it was the travelling, which day after day seemed endless.

Even now, he said, he only took bookings for the big handicaps, listed and group races, and of course famous international events if fortunate enough to be engaged. Yve stretched and yawned, and indicated he had to sleep, told Billy to be down for breakfast at seven, and said again how the two of them having been brought together at last had affected him greatly.

Billy got up from the chair, put his arms around Yve and said it was only now he really knew who he was, and where he'd come from, and he was happier now than he'd ever been in his whole life.

—

Billy slept like a log, as we say in English. He got into his riding gear and came down to breakfast. Warm croissants, jam, fruit and coffee. Matild was already seated and Yve joined them minutes later. He asked how Billy had slept, and, not knowing the French for log, Billy simplified it by a simple, "Tres bien, merci."

Yve wanted to know more about David and Grace and, with help from Matild, Billy said how wonderful they'd been to him, and that he loved them and would always, and, although legally he was still in care, he would be free of social services on his seventeenth birthday. Adding that they seem to have forgotten about him as no one had heard a word from them since they'd given him their permission to leave school, and it would make no difference now anyway as he never wanted to distance himself from his foster parents.

Yve looked concerned and started speaking rapidly to Matild, who continued to translate. She asked whether Billy had ever wondered about Yve's name, "de Montagnes", which translated is "of the mountains". Billy shook his head. Matild continued that Yve had been left wrapped in a blanket in a religious retreat in the Pyrenees halfway up a mountain. He was found by a monk and taken down to the village. He never knew his mother or father or where he came from, so they gave him the name de Montagnes.

She went on to say, "He's completely amazed at the coincidences between the two of you. Not only the involvement with the horse and racing but that both of you were taken into care." With a look of concern and a shake of the head, Yve put his arm around Billy and led him outside.

–

Picking up saddles and bridles from the tack room, he took Billy to the horse he thought suitable, and moved three boxes down to tack up his own. He'd chosen a time between the first and second lots when the staff were having a short break, so the canters, gallops and heath would be less crowded.

Leading his horse out of the box he waited for Billy, who was having a job reaching up to get the bridle over the animal's ears. Finally he managed it; Yve, who'd been watching, tried to hide his amusement but Billy noticed and they both had a good laugh.

Jumping onto their mounts from a granite hop-up,* they rode out of the gates onto a grass walkway that led them into the forest; lush green trees lined each side.

A strange quietness and feeling of calm filled the air, and, with the smell of pine oak and cedar all mixed together, gave a sense of peace, calm and tranquillity.

The narrow walkway opened out; two white posts heralded the start of an all-weather fibre sand track, but, unlike its ten-foot British counterpart, it was over thirty-five feet across.

Yve broke into a trot, and Billy, now upsides, still on a long rein, did too. He was watching Yve closely and shortened up as they broke into a canter.

The horse took a strong but steady hold with no fighting of the bit or being difficult.

The two of them held the canter for perhaps four or five furlongs, and pulled up back into the trot, then gently eased into the walk. Two hundred yards further on they came out of the wood into the sunlight.

For a second the brightness dazzled him and then the wow factor kicked in as he witnessed the sixty-five hectares of pristine green turf, the multiple white-posted gallops, some flat, some undulating and more than one post and railed oblong training track, which Billy guessed to be perhaps a mile round. It was all so beautifully maintained, so different.

They continued at the walk, and Yve managed to explain they would do a half-speed gallop and when he shouted, "Allez, allez," to quicken and to ride a finish from the 900-metre marker to the 1,000 and said he'd be upsides all the way as his horse had much more to give than Billy's.

Yve wanted to watch closely on how the lad performed and if he'd the ability to transfer riding a finish on the mechanical horse to the real thing. It would also be a chance to improve the lad's technique, not forgetting the boy was still only sixteen.

Walking onto the gallop, Billy made sure he had a loose rein, and with a plunge forward the horses immediately broke into the gallop. Within three strides he'd gathered up the reins and held the horse's head close to its chest, keeping it at the controlled pace and tight alongside Yve.

Billy was riding an older horse and it knew exactly what was expected, and that of its rider: light, strong and confident, but having sympathetic hands.

This horse had often been jagged in the mouth and pulled up short. It showed respect in its behaviour to someone who played him in the mouth gently and without hurt or pain.

Yve made a sign for Billy to bend forward more and lower over the horse's neck and nodding as Billy adjusted. Holding the horse together at this slower pace felt as if it was pulling his arms out of his sockets; they ached, and all his muscles throughout his body responded to the effort. "Allez, allez vite!" shouted Yve. The 900-metre marker flashed past.

Billy let the reins slip through his fingers, still keeping the horse on the bit.

Immediately it stretched its neck and lengthened its stride. Billy pumped his hands and arms alongside each side of its neck in time with each stride of the forelegs. He could see the 1,000-metre marker ahead, and, flicking his left rein toward the horse's face, it quickened again and they flashed past it.

Through riding his finish, Yve had kept upside, still holding his mount together without any other movement or aid. Billy had edged ahead of him by a few metres and managed to pull up well before Yve, whose horse had been very keen to carry on.

Billy trotted up to join him and they walked off the gallop. Yve had spotted that flick of the rein and as they weren't carrying sticks it'd impressed him all the more. Generally, lads were not allowed to carry whips when exercising. It was not an official rule in France but an issue most trainers adopted in order to prevent misuse.

Walking to the all-weather track again, they gently hack cantered back to where they'd started from, and, after a leisurely walk along the path, they rode back into the yard.

—

Billy accompanied Yve for the rest of the day. They had a light lunch at a bar and restaurant in a small hamlet of stone cottages just outside the forest, then drove to a stud owned by a Monsieur Fredrique Boutins, a close friend of Yve.

Fredrique, who spoke good English, insisted on showing them his stallion, who was very much in favour as having sired three group winners this season and was also keen to show Billy the foals, now nearing the day they'd be separated from their mothers.

Next, they walked through a modern barn, with twenty stalls down either side but, apart from a few yearlings, most were empty. Fredrique explained these were thought too immature to sell at the Deauville sale, now in progress, but would be held back until the later sale in December.

Yve, of course, had seen it all before, but was very patient, correctly believing it was all of great interest to Billy. Having seen over this magnificent property, the proud owner took them into the house and offered them a glass or two of champagne.

Billy could see straight away that this was something of a quite normal occurrence for Yve and their host, but certainly not for himself, and, when offered the glass of sparkling bubbly, he didn't feel he should refuse. Taking a sip, he couldn't decide whether he liked it or not, but thought perhaps it was something he needed to get used to.

He'd heard lads back home saying it was the least fattening drink of all, and that most jockeys who could afford it preferred it to any other when watching their weight. Billy took another sip, a little more this time, and started thinking that perhaps it was quite nice.

The two men were chatting away in their own language as Billy took in his surroundings, admiring the grand room they sat in and the fine oil paintings that adorned the walls. He felt a little light-headed and really happy, and quickly realised the champagne had affected him.

Putting down the near-empty glass on the table next to him, he tried to concentrate on what was being said, pretending to show an interest even though he hardly understood a word of it.

Fifteen minutes later, Yve stood up and thanked Fredrique for the drink and Billy thanked him too. They were seen to the door and were waved goodbye from a lovely man who returned to his sumptuous rooms to finish the bottle.

On the way home, Yve asked Billy if Lucy had been told they had found each other and that he was the father. Billy told him no: the only ones who knew were David and Grace. "But surely she would have guessed," he said, half in French and part in English. "It's not that difficult to work out."

"You'd think so," said Billy, "but perhaps she can't remember the dates as it was sometime before she fell off the stage and rushed into hospital; her memory's not too good even now. Perhaps she doesn't remember you."

"Perhaps so," Yve mumbled. "Anyway, I think we should tell her, don't you?"

By the time they arrived back at the house it was near 5pm. Billy went up to his room and lay down on the bed, and Yve went to his office to make a call to his agent to confirm his rides over the weekend.

–

Billy had fallen asleep, and woke to a loud noise. Increasing, it reached a pitch where it continued for at least ten minutes; it then slowly faded and finally stopped.

Swinging his legs off the bed, he went into the bathroom, washed his face in cold water, combed his hair, and, having shaken off his drowsiness, he went back downstairs.

Done up to the nines, Matild had set the table, and told Yve she'd made a coq au vin for their dinner and it was there ready in the oven, and that she was now on her way out. Bidding them goodnight, she left through the back door.

Yve had been sitting in his chair by the fire, reading the French equivalent of the *Racing Post*. As Billy walked in, he folded the paper and stood up. Billy asked what the noise was. Yve laughed and said it was the wife returning from Marseilles.

Minutes later, a young woman walked in, carrying Angelique. The woman put the child down and the little girl dashed across the room and jumped up into her father's arms. Billy felt a warm glow in seeing this spontaneous love between them, which made him realise even more just how much he'd missed out on as a child himself.

Billy's thoughts were suddenly forgotten as someone else had just walked in, followed by a smart man in uniform carrying a host of bags and cases. The woman was the most beautiful-looking female Billy had ever seen. So elegantly turned out, her hair fine and shoulder length, dazzling blue eyes, she simply took his breath away.

Yve put Angelique down and embraced his wife and she kissed him on the lips.

"This is my wife, Jeunette, and my daughter, your sister, Angelique." Billy was about to shake hands, but she put her arms around him and this beautiful woman hugged him and kissed him on both cheeks. She said how excited she was to meet him, returned the child to the nanny, and said she'd go up and change and be back down in a few minutes.

The man in uniform said hi to Yve, put the bags down on the floor and said he'd back at 9am tomorrow. He then left, closing the door behind him.

"You looked surprised," Yve laughed. "He's the pilot. Thanks to Jeunette's film contract, she can come home from wherever they're filming, and I get to use it too. We're off to Deauville tomorrow; we'll go and find Christophe at the sales first, and I've three rides in the afternoon. It's too long a drive so we'll take the helicopter."

Billy began to realise that Yve's English was far better than he let on, and although he often struggled to find a word, he actually managed quite well and could be understood.

That they would be travelling by helicopter would be an experience, but seeing and being up close to what it meant to be a famous French jockey was something he could only have dreamed of, and now it would all be happening tomorrow. Billy felt blessed: everything was happening his way, paving the way to what? Could he ever match all of this? It was a lot to ask, perhaps almost too much to hope for.

FORTY-ONE

The helicopter was sitting on a helipad within the chateau's extensive grounds. It was shiny black with a small yellow emblem depicting a coat of arms and the letters F F Films Corp.

Billy was excited as he climbed aboard and sat himself into the red leather seat. Yve, with just a small bag, climbed in beside him, placing his bag on one of the two empty seats behind them. The pilot was already aboard and, after a brief chat, he fiddled with the controls, the rotor blades started to turn slowly, then, with a roar and a burst of sound, the engine fired up. Henri, the pilot, turned in his seat, gave a thumbs-up, returned to the controls and they rose up from the ground to the regulation height of 1,000 metres.

Billy watched the landscape below him, countless small fields and stone cottages, hamlets and villages. It was fascinating to see the traffic below them, reminding him of the joy he'd had playing with his dinky cars as a child.

As they flew north-west, time had little matter and before he expected he could see the green of the racetrack set out within the white post and rails. Henri brought them down and skimmed over the grandstands to land in the centre of the course. So easy, so quick, and here they were at Deauville–La Touques racetrack, with the sales ring close by.

Having had to wear ear protectors during the flight, he'd had no conversation with Yve and, although the views had kept his attention for part of this short flight, his thoughts had returned to how kind and lovely Jeunette had been towards him over dinner last night. She spoke almost perfect English, save for a slight accent, and was so interested in learning about his short life. Translating the most important bits to Yve, she'd been able to fill him in with detail, so that now he had the full story.

She even indicated that she hoped to meet Lucy sometime soon, and how lovely was that?

Billy could visualise how thrilled his mum would be to be befriended by a famous film star. Even though French, she had been in several Hollywood movies, including the one presently being filmed in the south of France. It all made him realise he must see his mum as soon as he could, to explain all that had happened and that probably he should have done so long before now. Anyway, it was too late to be worrying about things from here. He'd sort it once he got home.

Unfastening his rather complicated seatbelts, he followed Yve out onto the grass, ducking unnecessarily under the still-rotating blades. Henri stayed behind and said he'd be ready to take them back half an hour after Yve's last ride at 15.40.

A fifteen-minute walk took them to the Deauville sales ring, offices and paddocks. The three-day sale of yearlings was within its last three hours, with most of the top lots already having been snapped up. Yearlings were being led around the parade ring before being taken inside to be auctioned off. All of it very similar to that of Tattersalls.

Deauville was very popular with British trainers, and Billy caught sight of some he knew of; Yve pointed out others.

There was no sign of Monsieur Christophe, but Yve suspected he might be elsewhere and they found him in the bar sat at a table with a large whisky in his hand, deep in conversation with three others.

Yve joined them, introduced Billy as his son, asked them if he could get them all another drink and walked over to the bar. He reached in his pocket and took out a wad of money. He peeled off a fifty-euro note. He handed it to Billy. "I'll stay here for a while," he said. "Why don't you go inside the sale ring and watch some of the yearlings go through and get yourself something to eat from the kiosk outside? My first ride is the 13.40, so meet me back here and we'll walk back to the track at 12.15."

This suited Billy; he wanted very much to do exactly that, and made his way into the sales ring. Sitting down in a row halfway up the tiered seating, he wondered where the money was coming from, as there didn't seem to be enough people inside for yearlings to still be fetching thousands of euros. He stayed until he started to lose interest, then, leaving the building, he joined a queue and got himself a burger.

–

Yve and Billy walked back to the racecourse, which didn't seem to Billy to have anywhere near as many of the public as in at a similar track in the UK. The 15.40 was the feature race La Grande Prix de St George, a top-grade event with a first-place prize of 250,000 euros. There were two English trainers with horses entered, an Irish challenger, a German, and twelve French. One could have expected a huge crowd but there wasn't one.

Yve asked if Billy would like to come into the jockey changing rooms with him, which of course he did. The room was half full, some sitting around on a bench that surrounded the room, some changing into their breeches, boots and colours.

The first race of the day was a handicap so valets* were busy weighing their man before slipping lead into the weight cloth* to achieve the assigned weight of both it and the jockey. Various silk colours were hung in pegs above the bench, the whole blending together in a colourful display, very organised, efficient and professional.

Yve introduced Billy to his valet, Jean, proudly telling all in earshot that this was his son, who'd just been awarded his licence.

Several now started to file out into the weighing room to stand onto the scales, carrying their weight cloth, saddle, girth and surcingle,* for the clerk of the scales to check that their combined weight corresponded to the weight allotted to their horse.

As they filed out for the 12.40, others filed in for Yve's first ride of the day.

All seemed keen to engage with Yve and shake Billy's hand, wishing him "bon chance" for the future, but now it was time for Yve to get changed and ready for his first ride.

Fifteen minutes later, jockeys from the first race, having weighed in, were now returning, one or two beaming with delight, most of them looking rather glum. Yve suggested Billy go and look out for Christophe and join him on the owners' and trainers' stand to watch. Yve was riding for someone other than Christophe in his first two rides but was on the yard's horse for the big one.

–

Billy couldn't understand any of the French commentary, but looked out for Yve's colours on the big screen. Riding a finish from midfield, he made ground to be beaten by a short head. In his second race, Billy saw Yve get boxed in on the rails and unable to get a run until things opened in the remaining few metres; he finished fifth. Slightly disappointed, Billy soon put those feelings aside, and now pinned all his hopes on the big one run over 2,000 metres; his excitement grew by the minute.

Walking to the parade ring, he reserved his place at the rails and waited. An extremely pretty girl led in a particularly fine-looking mature horse; it was number 6, Yve's mount. Billy didn't know whether to watch the girl or study the horse until his attention caught sight of Yve walking in with the other jockeys. He was wearing dark blue colours with yellow dots, and a yellow cap. He joined Christophe and the owners, a very old man and a younger woman in the centre, and whilst they were in a deep conversation the bell rang for jockeys to mount. Yve was legged up into the saddle and led around just the once. As he passed, he caught sight of Billy and, such was his concentration, he simply gave him a nod and a slight smile.

Weaving his way through those standing behind him, Billy ran back to the stand to catch sight of them cantering down to the start, and, having watched both the previous races from where he'd been told, he'd not seen Monsieur Christophe.

There were plenty of spaces left so he could hardly have missed him, but he needn't have worried as there he was now, climbing up the steps. Billy waved and the trainer, slightly out of breath, came and sat beside him.

Tension and anticipation rose as the horses were guided into the stalls, but one animal was proving extremely difficult to load, and causing the handlers problems, but after several attempts they managed to get it in.

A brief pause and the starter dropped his flag, the gates sprung open, and they were off. Christophe watched through his binoculars; Billy watched on the big screen opposite on the other side of the track.

Christophe had only briefly acknowledged Billy, but now both were totally committed to the outcome over the next four or five minutes.

As they plunged out of the stalls, Yve kept in a straight line and was able to hold his position six from the outside rail. All but one of others had crossed over and formed a group behind one lone runner, which stormed into the lead and was already eight lengths ahead of the pack. It, and two other horses, were now ahead of Yve, yet not one of them had made a move to rein in the leading horse, and the gap had now increased to fifteen lengths. Two other horses had now passed Yve, and he made no attempt to fight them off. Christophe was mumbling to himself.

Billy, although concerned, could see that Yve sat still; the horse was tight on the bit and still full of running. With 500 metres to go, they swung into the straight; Yve was now lying seventh until a gap opened up. This was his chance and Yve gave his horse an inch of rein and squeezed through, passing two, but still with five horses ahead of him.

With a clear track now in front of him, with that wonderful twirl of the stick* in his left hand Yve rode his finish and passed the four horses immediately ahead, leaving just the horse that had made all the running from the start ahead of them.

Two hundred metres from the post, its lead had now reduced to six lengths.

Monsieur Christophe, much to Billy's surprise, was jumping up and down, urging the horse on; it looked an impossible task but the lead horse was tiring. Its jockey used the whip, the horse seemed to recover and renewed its effort, but Yve was closing fast. Fifty metres remained, and for a few strides they were locked together but as they crossed the line Yve won by a neck.

Christophe turned to Billy, picked him up and spun him around. Putting him down, he was about to rush back to the parade ring; Billy sat where he was.

Stopping halfway down, Christophe turned and beckoned Billy to follow him.

The first four horses were ridden in: the first three finishers into their allotted place; the fourth as a reserve in case of an objection. Yve jumped off and removed the saddle. He had a quick word with Christophe, then waited for the owner and his companion to come down in the lift from their private box. Christophe introduced Billy as Yve's son, and photos were taken in front of their horse, insisting that Billy be included.

Yve left the paddock to weigh in, and a few minutes later returned for the presentation. Billy didn't know quite what he should do or where he should go, but his mind was made up for him when the old man insisted that he join them onto the platform to receive their gold trophy, and, a little self-consciously, Billy stood alongside Yve, who also received a small replica.

Presentations concluded, and making their way through the crowd, Yve was waylaid by the press. They first asked where the horse might run next and where, and then if the rumours were true that he was retiring at the end of the season. Yve said it was incorrect and that he'd decided on having one more season next year. Typical of the tabloid press, they then asked who Billy was, their photographer taking copious shots as he spoke. What could Yve possibly say but to tell them he was his son, and then the questions came thick and fast, Yve saying he wasn't answering any questions on his private life, and pushing himself and Billy out of their way.

There was a scramble to detach themselves as they were followed all the way back to the weighing room, the reporter asking who Billy's mother was and other personal questions relating to "your film-star wife" and whether she knew about the boy.

Billy, insulted, turned towards the man. Yve pulled him away just as the photographer took another shot. They made it to the building, leaving the press believing they were onto something big here, worth further investigation.

Telling Billy to wait for him to shower and change, Yve left him as jockeys came in to weigh out for the next race. Now finished for the day, he was back out within fifteen minutes and made a call to Christophe that they were ready to leave.

Checking that the press had dispersed, the two of them dashed across the turf to the helicopter. Henri was already in the cockpit, and had been watching the action on his iPhone. He congratulated Yve and was about to start up but told to hang on for the boss. They had a wait half an hour before Christophe arrived, and without apologies climbed into the seat next to Yve, with Billy sat behind and, without further incident, Henri took them home.

FORTY-TWO

They landed at 18.15. Christophe stumbled out and with a few grunts of good nights walked towards the big house, where he and his wife lived in the South Wing.

The main part of the chateau and its gardens, much to his chagrin, were open to the public during the summer months, partly funding its huge upkeep. Yve and Billy walked a hundred metres the opposite way, through the gate and into the cottage.

Matild's day off, and with Jeunette disinclined to cook, they had planned to go out for dinner. She was already smartly dressed, made up and ready to go, but Yve opened a bottle of champagne, sat down in front of the fire, and asked the two of them to sit with him for a few minutes that he might have time to relax and settle his thoughts; he said he needed to say something to Billy and asked whether she would translate for him.

As he spoke to her in French, Jeunette took Billy's hand in hers, and, with a concerned frown, said, "Yve was upset that the press were asking about you, Billy, and they're likely to make a big thing of it. He says you have to let your mother know where you are now, and that you've found your birth father. If this gets to the tabloid press, and Yve thinks it will, they'll be knocking on your mother's door for her part of the story. He says you should think about it carefully overnight and call her first thing tomorrow."

Jeunette squeezed his hand and let go; Billy reached for his glass and took a brave sip of champagne. "I can't tell her over the phone," he said. "I know I should have told her ages ago. I'll call her tomorrow and tell her I'll come to see her when I get back on Wednesday. Would you mind if I asked your driver to divert there before taking me home?"

Jeunette put the suggestion to Yve. "He said it's a risk that they might try and contact her before then, but it's up to you; he agrees it's a bit much trying to explain it over the phone. He's quite happy for Vince to take you there but you better let him know. Yve will give you his number."

So, having talked the matter through, they got up and drove to the same little restaurant they'd had lunch at yesterday. Of course, the "a la carte" was in French, so Billy played safe and ordered the same as Yve, and, not knowing what to expect, rather enjoyed the lobster bisque to start, and pan-fried scallops to follow.

—

Unless France's premier tracks had a feature race on their card, Yve refused to take bookings on a Sunday, so the whole family spent a relaxing day at home with Billy having a fun time getting to know his little half-sister. He'd called Lucy, of course, and she asked whether anything was wrong; she said she would be so excited to see him and at last be able to show him her lovely house, and see how well George was doing. He and his brother's plumbing business was going from strength to strength. Billy bit his tongue and made it seem he was just coming on a surprise visit.

Christophe had asked that Billy ride out for him on this Monday morning, and at 7.10am, as they came out of the forest, four three-year-olds pulled out of the string of twenty and headed for one of the testing gallops.

Yve and Christophe had previously taken the car the long way round and stood twenty metres from the edge opposite the 1,500 marker. Catching sight of the horses through their binoculars as they emerged from the trees and into the sun, they watched the four of them trot over to the white-railed entrance to the gallop. Two horses, now upsides, were quickly into their stride, followed by the other two, maintaining a twenty-metre gap between the two in front.

The trainer wanted to test whether or not one particular horse was ready to be entered into a race next Friday, as he thought it could win. If it was ready, it would show it here. The horse on the far side had Billy atop, and the horse upsides of him; the one of specific interest would pass closest to the two men watching.

The riders had been told to ride a finish from the 1,400 marker; neither was, of course, carrying whips. A few metres before they reached the marker, Billy had got busy a second before the other, easing three-quarters of a length ahead. Both riders now urged their mounts to extreme effort over the final 100 metres. Billy rode his finish using everything Yve had explained to him on Friday.

Getting his body low up the horse's neck, and pushing and extending hands, arm and reins in time with the horse's stride, he got the horse to extend its neck and lengthen its stride.

The other horse had come back to him and as they passed the 1,500 was a nose in front. Before the blink of an eye the other two flashed past as if nailed together.

Christophe turned and said how pleased he was at the outcome. With Billy's combined weight likely to be in imperial terms around 8st 7, he'd be over a stone lighter than the other work rider, and Billy's horse was no slouch, having already won twice this season. The trainer now assured that he knew his horse would have a real chance of a maiden win on Friday, and Yve was not amiss at having a bet on it too.

Walking back to their car Christophe said he was impressed with the lad's ability, and that if he'd been fluent in French he would've offered him a place here and now. He also added that he thought the boy had a natural talent and that if he had the dedication to overcome the many setbacks he was sure to have, he could surely make it to the top.

—

The helicopter woke Billy at 5am the next morning to return Jeunette to Marseilles, and they'd already taken off before Billy got downstairs. It was his last day here and, although he would feel sad to leave, he was looking forward to starting work in just a few days' time.

Billy rode out another two other lots, and went into the office and thanked Monsieur Christophe for using him and said how much he'd enjoyed Chantilly.

The trainer stood up and they shook hands; he said he'd keep in touch with Billy's progress and hoped he'd be able to ride out his apprenticeship and go on to greater things. He added that, whenever Billy decided to return, to let him know in good time and he'd try find a suitable race for him.

Billy was fast gaining first-class contacts, sure to become useful sometime in the future, and now, on his next visit, he might look forward to riding a race for a famous French trainer on a premier racetrack.

Later in the day, Yve had two rides for a different trainer at Longchamp Racecourse, in the Bois de Boulogne area of Paris. Yve's driver took them the 50km in the Mercedes in just over the hour. Billy kept himself to himself and stayed out of the parade ring. With Yve only managing a third place in the 15.45 and coming from nowhere to gain a second place in the 17.00, they were quickly away and got back to the cottage by 19.45.

Matild had prepared the two of them and herself a hot meal followed by cheese, enjoyed with the wonderful taste of a fresh French baguette. As she was clearing up, Billy asked Yve to show him how to twirl the stick when riding a finish. Yve got up from the table and rummaged in his bag, still on the floor where he'd left it. He took out the stick he'd used and a brand-new one that he gave to Billy. Billy stood up and held the stick in his right hand as he would when riding.

To reach the hindquarters, the whip needs to be held differently, which is not an easy thing to do at a speed of 30k. Yve showed him how by spinning it three times through his fingers. They laughed and laughed as Billy tried, dropping the stick each time to the floor.

"Now you know how it's done," Yve managed in his broken pigeon English. "If you keep trying, it'll suddenly come to you. But don't attempt it when racing until you're a hundred per cent certain you won't drop it. I wouldn't worry too much; there won't be many of the younger jocks who can do it... Please... keep the stick." Yve returned his own whip to the bag, rummaged into it again and brought out a small red leather box, which he handed to Billy. "They gave me this at the presentation on Saturday," he said. "I'd like you to have it as a memento." Billy opened the lid and took out a gold Cartier watch.

Putting his arms around his dad, father and son had a long and meaningful hug, bringing Billy close to tears.

–

Up early the next morning, the same driver as the previous day turned up at 6am sharp and it was time to leave. Yve took Billy's hands in his and told him how proud he was to have him as a son, and to have a son who was a jockey made it all the more special. "Thank you so much for letting me come here," replied Billy, "and thank you for being my dad. I feel so different. I've got nothing to brood about in my head anymore." Yve couldn't quite understand what he meant but Matild chimed in and explained.

The driver stood at the door, waiting, Matild gave Billy a huge hug and Yve drew him close and kissed his head. Billy gave a deep sigh, and looked down to the floor as he tried to hide two uncontrollable sobs. Then, turning back to Yve, he managed a weak smile and walked out of the door.

FORTY-THREE

The plane landed on time, and Vince was waiting for him in arrivals. With a friendly handshake, they made their way to the car and sped off towards London.

No problems with traffic, they reached Muswell Hill in an hour and turned into Roseberry Road. Checking the house numbers as they drove slowly along the row of nice-looking Victorian terraced houses, they turned into the single parking space to the front of the house.

To the side of where they'd parked was a small front garden, a tiny patch of mature lawn surrounded by a border of roses neatly trimmed and cultured.

The front door opened and Lucy rushed towards Billy and threw her arms around him. Kissing her on the cheek, he introduced Vince, and explained they could only spare an hour as Vince had another delivery to do.

Lucy ushered them into the front sitting room, and went to the kitchen in the back, and brought them tea and biscuits.

Vince quickly realised that he shouldn't have come in as he was well versed in what Billy was about to tell her. Apologising, saying he had some calls to make, he returned to the car.

"Mum," Billy said, "I have some news." And, with that, he proceeded to tell her the full story. Lucy just sat there, not interrupting him once. As he finished, she lay back into her chair and said, "So he did try to find me? Weren't we stupid, not knowing each other's surnames? And you've just come back from seeing him. Was he nice to you, Billy? Oh, I do hope so. Married to that Jeunette Jeneaux actress, eh? I've seen her in a DVD we have. Don't think I could have matched that, but we were so young, Billy, and he was so lovely to me. I'm so pleased he's happy and so successful, and really pleased for you, love. Did Jeunette really send her regards to me? How nice."

She then went on about George and the holiday they'd had in July and how they'd driven all the way up to Holt in Norfolk to see his sister. Billy tried to show interest, checked the time and got up saying he had to go. First, though, she insisted he had to see over the house and how the kitchen doors opened out to the patio and the back garden.

Although somewhat naïve, it made Billy feel hugely relieved how she'd taken it all in and that she in herself was now very settled and content.

They said their goodbyes, kissed and hugged, promising to see each other soon.

"I'll ring you next Tuesday," was his parting shot, "and let you how I get on."

"Why's that?" she called from the door.

"Because it's my first day at work as apprentice jockey to Mr Edward Henley at Millgate Stables… See ya."

—

On the way back, Vince went on again about Jersey. He was off back there on Monday, all expenses paid, for the Jersey Race Club's Bank Holiday Meeting, the last meeting of their season at Les Landes Racecourse. "Prize money's rubbish," he said, "but it's a great day out and I've got four rides and I just need one winner to get my seventh trophy. You'd get plenty of rides as a lightweight. I'll give your number to my trainers so they know how to make contact. It's a bit rough and tumble out there but you'll get two or three rides in the day and it's a nice little earner."

"I'd have to get my boss's permission, though," Billy added. "Anyway, I thought you said you'd retired."

"I have, three years ago, but I have a Jersey licence to ride and most of the jocks who go from here are either retired jockeys, amateurs, or simply work riders. Good fun, though."

–

Vince dropped Billy off at Home Farm at 4.30 and drove away with a promise not to breathe a word to anyone about who'd paid him for the job, where Billy had been or who he'd met, especially if contacted by the press.

Grace was so pleased to see Billy, and wanted to know everything on how he'd got on with Yve and fascinated to hear about Jeunette and his new sister, Angelique.

Billy was quite brief in answering as he knew he'd have to tell it all over again when David got home. They still had no idea that the French press had found out about them and most likely sooner or later would be wanting the full story.

It wasn't until late Friday morning, when David got home and opened his *Racing Post* to find a full-page article with the headline "YVE DE MONTAGNES'S SECRET SON", with a large picture of Yve pulling an astonished-looking Billy to him, amongst a crowd of racegoers, that the phones started ringing. David and Grace simply turned off their smartphones and left the house phone off the hook.

Between one and two o'clock, they had the press and three vans in the drive with reporters and photographers shouting offers of silly money for an exclusive.

Within a further ten minutes, in drove a large TV van with an ITV reporter asking for an interview.

From the front door, David tried to calm things down and shouted over the din, saying he would go back inside and discuss with his wife and Billy what they should do and how to go about it. Shutting the door, the clamour abated and the three of them sat at the table to talk it through.

"Do we give one of them an exclusive?" David asked. "Or just go out and answer their questions? What's our best chance of getting a positive response to all this? Probably if a free for all, each of them might well add fictional spice to generate mass public interest."

Grace suggested she didn't want it known they were being paid for an exclusive, and thought they should agree to an interview with ITV, and let the press print their story from facts taken from that, thereby sorting this mess out in one go.

"As I see it," David said, "all of us, including Lucy, have nothing to hide. It's a heart-warming story and I'm going out there and tell them exactly how it is."

David opened the door, and there was a hush of expectancy. "We've decided I should tell all of you how things have worked out, and the heart-warming coincidences that have got us here. Before I do, however, I want you to know that, for the two and a half years that we've been foster parents to Billy, he has at all times been the most single-minded, hard-working and polite child that we could ever have wished for. We love him dearly and, as he is about to start his career as apprentice jockey to Edward Henley, I know that you all, as we do, wish him huge success. It has been his own personal ambition of becoming a jockey long before ever finding his father, Yve de Montagnes." There was a clamour of questions and flashing of cameras. The ITV crew were filming everything. "Please allow me to finish what I have to say, and then I'll answer your questions. After that we would be quite happy to grant an interview with you TV people in the house. So please, I beg of you, judge for yourselves; this should be nothing but a heart-moving story of one little boy's grit and determination to seek a better life for himself and all those around him. Thank you. So, this is how it all began…"

—

It was sometime after five before the last hangers-on had driven away. David called his boss and warned him that he would probably be approached, and told Billy to ring Lucy. "Tell her the press might be turning up within the hour, and to be sure she tells them exactly why you were taken into care, and to be brief about her relationship with Yve. Simply tell them they lost touch with one another before she knew she was pregnant. Tell her to just stick to the facts so that our version of events matches her own."

Of course, the whole thing didn't end there. On Saturday morning there was a quarter page-article in the daily paper and on Sunday there was a photo of Yve and Billy splashed over the front pages, with page numbers leading to a full page of the complete story with four photographs. One of Lucy holding Billy in her arms as a nine-month-old baby and one taken just before he left her at thirteen. The other two were of Billy and Yve at Deauville. Details followed of Yve's big race victories and a picture of Billy riding that finish on the gallops at Chantilly.

"Well, Billy," said David, as he carefully folded the Sunday paper. "You're famous, before becoming famous. I suppose it could be a lot worse; they've treated it as good-hearted news, and I suppose it might even be good publicity for you. Mind you, everyone will be looking to see how you get on in your first ride; I think I'll have to discuss this with Edward."

Sunday evening news on ITV and BBC included the interview and shots around Home Farm of Billy dressed in full racing gear. When asked what his ambitions were, he'd answered simply to be half as brilliant as his father and later, if ever he became a trainer, then half as good as his boss, Mr Edward Henley.

So, hoping all the fuss would now blow over this Monday morning, Billy helped Celine by driving the tractor to cut the grass over two of the empty paddocks and later rode out through the lanes with her and Cindy, and enjoying a hack canter across a couple of fields.

David had gone to work early and, before first lot, sat down with Edward to talk things over. "When I heard about all this," Edward said, "I was none too happy about it on Saturday evening. Now I'm not so sure; yesterday I had four people phone up and have already got three new owners and sold them three of the remaining two-year-olds. The other enquiry is coming to see the horses out third lot. This, of course, puts a lot of pressure on your lad; the press will be all over him."

"That worries me somewhat," David answered. "Normally we'd give an apprentice five or six rides before anything that had a chance, but now, with all this fuss, I think we should look for a suitable race he could win."

"I'm inclined to agree with that, David; it's my reputation on show, too, but it was very nice the lad showed me the respect in mentioning me in his interview. I was rather touched. So let's do it. He starts tomorrow, doesn't he? I'm thinking that as we took Hot Potch out that race on Wednesday when the going was soft to heavy, and we know he hates that, he's desperate for a run. I'll look through the calendar for a suitable race next week. We know the horse is fit enough to win, but do you think Billy can handle that sort of pressure?"

"Actually, I do, but I don't think we should tell him we're expecting a win; let him think it's a normal entry and an easy ride. Whatever we tell him, he'll give it his best. I can guarantee it."

—

Tuesday morning, September the first 2011, and Billy was excited and could barely wait to get to work. As David had driven there separately, Billy took his moped, and arrived fifteen minutes early at 6.45.

First lot, David had booked a time for use of the practice stalls situated racecourse side. It would be opportune for Billy to ride one of his unraced youngsters through the stalls: first time for them both.

As Billy pulled into the yard and parked his moped, David pointed him over to a box with its two-year-old filly by the name of Inspired. Billy got his tack and grooming kit out of the store and set about mucking out, brushing the horse over and picking out its feet. He tacked up, then stood by the stable door and waited.

Mount up was called and the string started to line up around the square. Billy noticed Angela sitting tall in the saddle on Black Sunday.

The filly looked truly magnificent, her black skin shining in the morning sun, her one white sock and the white star on her forehead washed clean and as white as snow. Billy was none too pleased he hadn't been assigned to the filly himself but thought it might well be they didn't want to jog Angela off, as it could obviously be seen as favouritism.

David gave them the instructions that all were to do a half-speed gallop along the all-weather* track racecourse side, and the six two-year-olds were then to break away and walk behind the stands to the practice stalls. He would be there waiting for them. The rest were to come back at the same pace down the wood chip and make their own way home.

The string pulled out of the yard, led by the colts with fillies behind. To Billy, Inspired seemed very immature, all legs and unbalanced; he thought the horse was unlikely to get a run until next season, but thought he should keep his opinions to himself.

Coming up the track, it was so much on its forehand that the power that should come from behind was virtually non-existent. Pulling up as they neared the end of the track, the horse, totally unbalanced, stumbled, but luckily kept on its feet by Billy pulling its head up and sitting back into the saddle. Breathing a sigh of relief, he knew full well that if he'd fallen off on his first day of work he would have been the laughing stock of the month.

Plenty of time to relax again as they walked over to the stalls. David was already there, waiting, the stalls open, front and back.

None of these youngsters had been put through before and this was to be their education of what to expect when their time came to run. They circled around David, awaiting instructions. "I want you to simply walk your horse straight through the open stalls in pairs, leaving one empty stall between you. Come on, now, sort yourselves out."

The first two walked through quite happily; one of the next pair was a little on edge and rushed through. Next, Scot, paired alongside Angela on the filly, walked up together; he rode straight through but the filly refused, the whites of her eyes showing her wilfulness and sheer reluctance to even approach the stall.

Angela took a turn and tried again, this time being far more aggressive, digging in with her heels and urging the horse on. The filly reared up, came down and backed away at speed, then, spinning around, tried to take off. Somehow Angela managed to regain control and walked back to the group.

David complimented her for sitting tight, and told Billy to get down and see if he could lead them through. Sliding off Inspired, he handed David the reins, took hold of the filly, and ran his hands from her brow and over the eyes and blew his breath into her nostrils. Then, leading her up to the stall, walked her straight through.

This procedure was repeated by everyone, but the filly again refused Angela's insistence until she was walked through by Billy afoot.

The horses were now ridden back into the stall, but this time the front gate was shut and the rear doors closed behind them. They were now shut in. David told them not to jab the horse's mouth, to grab hold of its mane and on the count of three he would pull the lever and the stall would spring open.

"Gee the horse up," he said, "and from the standing start get it straight into a gallop for a hundred metres or so and then walk back."

He pulled the lever down hard, and with a loud clatter of steel against steel the gates sprang open, and, half in fright and blind panic, the horses shot out at full gallop and left to run over fifty yards, before being restrained to a canter, trot, and finally the walk back to the others.

Billy got legged up on Inspired and with a little encouragement the horse went straight in, and galloped out as if the two of them had already been here and done this many times over.

Now for the last two: Black Sunday, still with a slightly nervous Angela aboard, and the head lad, Duncan, on a classy-looking filly called Ballet Royale. Duncan rode into the stall and the rear gates closed; Black Sunday spun around and tried to take off but Angela managed to regain control and walked it back again.

She suggested Billy might try if they swapped horses. David was pleased as this was what he would have preferred but had been loath to upset Angela, perhaps making her feel upstaged. So, without further ado the two riders exchanged horses and David legged them up. Duncan, with growing concern, was waiting, still locked in his stall, his horse stamping the ground, impatient, fretting.

Billy rode the filly away from the other horses and trotted her three times round in a large circle and then brought her back. David, catching hold of the bridle, ran with her towards the gate, encouraging her with each step with a loud, "Come, come, come, come, COME ON, THEN!" Billy rode straight into the stall; she, confused, did not quite realise where she was as the rear doors slammed shut behind her. David ducked under the front gate and, as fast as he could run, went to his left and, shouting, "one, two, three," pulled down the lever. The gate flew open and Black Sunday came out two lengths ahead of the other horse, giving Billy plenty to think about when trying to pull her up, taking at least another seventy-five yards further on than Duncan, who waited so the two of them could walk back together.

"Well done, all of you," said David. "Let's leave on a good note, so off you go, cool them off, easy walk home, and you, Billy, hang on a bit. I can just see the other horse coming. I want to put you through a couple of times more on a horse that really knows its business."

Four minutes later, one of the older lads came up to them and slid off his horse to take the filly home, whilst Billy was given a leg up onto the three-year-old.

Billy could immediately feel the difference; this was a ready-made racehorse.

"What's its name?" Billy asked.

"Top Notch. You galloped him ten days ago, remember? He's due to run next week as long as the ground doesn't turn heavy again. We'll just put him in the once; remember to grab a hold of the mane as he comes out, and gallop on until you can pull him up. He knows how far he goes here, so shouldn't give you too much of a fight. Pull him up as gently as you're able, and then come back to the yard."

Billy nodded, his face fixed in concentration as he walked the horse straight into the stall. David shut them in, raced to the side, called out his one, two, three, and the gate clanked open.

It was all Billy could do to hang on against the force of being taken from a standing start to somewhere close to 28mph. Within three strides he managed to come out of the saddle into his crouched racing position helped by the horse's strong hold of the bit. Within a few seconds, Top Notch slowed, Billy eased his hold a little and they slowed through the paces to a walk.

Billy's thoughts were mixed. Why had David brought him the horse to do this stall test? Did it mean they might be thinking that this horse could be the one? Billy hoped so; it was probably the best horse he'd ever sat on.

–

When he'd got back and seen the horse safely into its stable, he walked across the yard to the tack room. He hung up the bridle and put the pad and saddle on the rack. As he walked back with a slab of hay for Top Notch, the secretary called across to ask him to come into the office as the boss wanted a quick word.

Dropping the hay into the corner of Top Notch's box, he hurried over.

The boss, Edward Henley, sat at his desk. "Ah, Billy! You've hit the headlines, they tell me. Well, the press have been onto me to let them know when you're entered for your first race. I would've preferred it if they'd wanted to interview us on having won the group 1 at Newmarket last week, but never mind that; we have a newsworthy sixteen-year-old lad instead. So, all eyes on you, eh? And Millgate's reputation resting on your head. No pressure, then."

Edward Henley smiled at Billy, who was now looking aghast and greatly worried. "Don't be upset, lad," he continued. "That's just the old man in me being cynical. Actually, we're all very pleased for you, and do you know we have five new owners all because of the nice thing you said of me. Your father, Yve, also rang me last night offering us his services if ever we were short of a big race jockey, and how nice was that? Anyway, I wanted to be the first to tell you that we have entered Top Notch next Saturday at Sandown in a class 2 handicap at 3.05 and hopefully you'll be riding it. It's over one mile, one furlong, and most likely your handicap rating will be 9st 4lb less your 7lb allowance, making it 8st 11." Billy's whole demeanour changed. "Now," Edward continued, "let's get you weighed."

Standing up, the secretary walked over as Billy stood onto the ancient scales. She slid the brass weight back and forth until the scale balanced equally.

"Eight stone two pounds," she called back.

"That's fine, then," said Edward. "With a 3lb saddle you'll need to carry about 3lb of lead. Gordon's valet will sort that for you, so don't worry about it. But you do realise, don't you, that under normal circumstances you'd be running on the all-weather tracks through the winter months with little hope of a win. So don't let this go to your head; it's a one-off, just to get the press off our backs... OK?"

Billy took it all in, and then asked whether the owners of Top Notch were happy with someone with no previous experience riding their horse.

"Top Notch is owned by Lady Worlinton, and she insisted you be given this chance, so that's all for the moment."

Billy thanked him and the secretary and scurried to the canteen for a quick mug of tea, before tacking up for second lot.

FORTY-FOUR

The lads and lasses were eager to find out how Billy had got on in Chantilly.

What it was like compared to Newmarket? How had he got on with Yve? And the girls all wanted details about Jeunette. None of them seemed upset or jealous of all the fuss in the press, all except Gordon Stokes, that is, his nose put out of joint having now lost the ride on Top Notch, who'd already won for him twice. Jason Scott, previously the yard's apprentice and now second jockey to Gordon, couldn't have been more pleased for him. Jason had been having a relatively good season up till now, having ridden fifteen winners, mostly on the all-weather.

–

Later that evening when just finishing supper, the house phone went and David answered. Grace couldn't quite pick up what was being said, but gathered that he was talking to June from social services. She looked at Billy and grimaced; anything from social services was invariably bad news.

"Well," said David, as he sat back at the table, "you might have guessed that was June. Finsbury have been onto her about Billy having located his father, someone of financial means. Yve's lawyers had made contact with them asking for Billy to be released from their care and that he would vouch for the boy's keep, care and control, and that he, through his lawyer, would compensate us, the foster parents, financially if the boy intends to stay with us and as long as we're happy to have him."

"Well, that's a bit of a shock," Grace said. "I think it's very kind of him. I'm happy for Billy to be out of their control, but that Yve has control I'm not so sure. Can we trust him to leave Billy with us? Not that you need controlling, Billy; it's just the legality of it that worries me somewhat. Perhaps he should have talked to us first."

"He doesn't speak English well enough," Billy chipped in. "I can't believe he would want to control me."

"It's just a legal term, Billy," said David. "I'm sure we all agree, after all, it's only eighteen months before you're eighteen and have the right to decide whatever you wish to do with your life. So I'd say... Who the heck cares about that now?"

The phone was ringing. David got up wearily. Grace and Billy took scant notice, tucking into their apple tart and custard.

After a few minutes David returned to the table. "That was Matild, translating for Yve, thanking us for looking after Billy and that he understands how well he's been brought up and how much Billy cares for us. He offered to either forward us a one-off payment to replace the fee we receive from social services or a monthly allowance. He wants to assure us that he wouldn't wish to disturb anything that Billy is happy with, and fully agrees that he should stay with us, as long as we are happy with the arrangement. I said, of course, that we were."

"How nice of him," said Grace. Billy, all ears, sat silent. "What did you say about the money?"

"I told her to thank him, and that we wouldn't want any payment from him as Billy had already started work and would want to pay for his own keep. I also asked her to say how pleased we'd all be if Billy was removed from the control of social services, and that it was very kind of him to have thought this through. She asked if she could hand the phone over to Yve as he wanted to thank us personally, so we exchanged a few words. He said he was looking forward to meeting us, and would be sending Billy an email to wish him luck. He'd seen the Doncaster entry for your first ride, Billy, and would be watching the race on his phone between his own three rides at Longchamp on Saturday… Now, Billy, about your rent. Your first pay day is October the first, so I suggest you pay Grace that week and on the first day of each month. We'll also stop your monthly allowance, but whenever I ask you to do anything for us here I'll now pay you by the hour."

"That's a bit harsh," said Grace.

"Not really. If he was living in the lad's quarters at Millgate, or at any other yard, he'd be paying for board and lodgings. He can't expect to be different to any other apprentice, and I'm sure he understands."

Billy answered as Grace was about to disagree. "It's OK: you've both done far too much for me already. I want to be independent; it'll make me work all the harder, and I'm sure I can manage very well. I'd better go upstairs now and call my mum."

Thanking Grace for the meal, he went to his room, sat on the bed and, taking the whip Yve had given him, practised twirling it through his fingers for the umpteenth time, only dropping it a few times now but mostly in his left hand, from where it again fell to the floor. Leaving it there for the moment, he reached for his phone and called his mum.

She sounded bright and cheery; the press turning up and wanting to interview her had thrilled her. George had kept well out of it and was none too pleased about her going on about Yve, but she'd got through it, hadn't said anything she shouldn't have, and was treated sympathetically.

She asked him about Saturday, wished him luck and hoped it would be on ITV4. She looked forward to seeing him soon, and only then did he tell her that Yve was taking him out of social services' control. "Thank the Lord for that," she said. "I can at last hold my head up high after all these years of feeling so ashamed. I'm very pleased for us both, love."

Her reaction to this surprised him, and there wasn't much more to say, was there?

—

The routine of normal stable work and riding out all became the norm. His workmates, however, had noticed a change in the new boy's personality. He was now engaging in their chat, opening up about his previous life, and answering all their questions. Questions about Yve, Jeunette and Chantilly. What did he think of the Deauville sales and French racing as a whole? It all came out instead of a few mumbled words. Previously seen to be so deep within himself, he now seemed a different person and most of them now sought to interact with him.

Billy, of course, noticed the difference in himself too, and, as long as he could sometimes find his own space somewhere, he felt for the first time comfortable and happy in being part of the team.

That may have been how it now was, but Billy was counting down the days before the very start of what he hoped would be a long and distinguished career.

–

Saturday morning dawned to a slight breeze and sunshine. He packed his still unused saddle into his travel bag along with his breeches, white polo-necked shirt, and brand-new shiny lightweight boots, zipped up the bag up and slid the whip Yve had given him on top. This morning he went in with David, with Grace seeing them off at the door shouting out her best wishes.

Once they'd arrived at Millgate, David told Billy to go into the office as the boss wanted to have a pre-race briefing.

"Ah, Billy," said Edward, looking up from his *Racing Post*. "So this is a big day for you. If I don't see you before, I tell you now that one of the worst things an apprentice can do early on is too much use of the whip. Legally, one is allowed five cracks, but five is also too much, as, in my book, if a horse doesn't respond after two there's little use in any further chastisement. You're drawn stall four, so get an early position so you don't get swamped by those outside you coming across. Then, after that first rush, try and settle the horse and wait your chance, and if a jockey screams at you to let him through on your inside don't let him. Have you anything you'd like to ask? No, well, good luck to you... Oh, and one more thing. Would you like to go with Gordon, as he has Finagan for us in the two-year-old listed race before you and then the filly you sold us, Black Sunday the two-year-old in the one-mile maiden at 4.05? Why Her Ladyship called her that only Heaven knows, but I digress. If you'd rather, you can go in the horse box with Duncan; they leave here at ten. Just time for you to ride out first lot. I'll tell them to wait for you... Off you go, then."

That his filly was running today shook Billy out of the constant thoughts of his own race. He couldn't understand why David hadn't let him know.

Speaking to Angela on their way to the heath, she told him she'd guessed the filly was close to having her first run, but hadn't known she'd been declared until they told her she'd be taking the filly to Doncaster late yesterday, and she was as surprised as he was. "But I'm glad in one way," she added, "because I'll be able to watch your race first."

Well, thought Billy, *both of us being put into the deep end on the same day.* But, be that as it may, he couldn't stop worrying whether the filly would behave herself down at the stalls, and whether she would allow the handlers to load her.

They rode down Hamilton Road and just did a bit of light work with a couple of circuits around the Hamilton Hill canter, and, with not having to do second lot, they had plenty of time for a leisurely break. Then, collecting all the necessary tack and gear, they loaded the two horses into the horse box at 10.12, pulling out of the yard minutes later, Duncan in the driving seat, with Angela and Billy alongside him.

FORTY-FIVE

The drive to the racecourse took them just over three and a quarter hours, arriving at 1.30. They unloaded the two horses and Angela and Billy walked them to the stable block, where, after showing the guards their security cards, they led the horses to their consigned boxes. Duncan followed, carrying the tack, grooming kit, pads, blankets and Billy's kit. Gordon Stokes would have his own gear, including the colours of Lady Worlinton and those of Finagan's owners.

With the horses safely installed, the three of them found the lads' and lasses' canteen. Duncan and Angela had lunch of the day, a choice between cottage pie and lasagne. Billy, slightly worried about the weigh-in, simply had a mug of tea.

Time seemed to drag; Billy just wanted to get on with it, and sitting watching the other two tucking into a hot meal didn't help. Picking up his bag, he excused himself and went off to find Gordon to get the colours, proper racing silks* in Lady Worlinton's colours that he'd be wearing for the very first time.

Billy walked through into the building, passed the clerk of the scales, took a deep breath and straight into the men's changing rooms. The smell, a mixture of sweat and body lotion, filled the room. It was a hub of industry, some jocks being weighed by their valets, slipping in extra lead into weight cloths, sometimes taking it out. Jockeys changing into their breeches and having trouble sliding their legs into their racing boots. Some carrying their saddles, girths and surcingles out to be weighed out, and the clerk checking that their combined weight coincided with that of their allotted handicap.

Standing there not really knowing what he should do next, he caught sight of Gordon talking to a middle-aged man of medium build, holding Her Ladyship's colours. Billy noticed that Gordon, already kitted out in Finagan's colours, was ready to be weighed out for the 2.30.

Billy walked across to them. "Billy, this is Mark," Gordon said by way of introduction. "He's been my valet for the last eleven years, and he's going to look after you. If you're happy with him, and you'd better be, you'll sign an agreement with him and it'll be registered at Weatherbys. You don't have to, mind, but I would advise it. Just hand over all your gear and he will sort out everything you need. By the way, Mark, this is Yve de Montagne's son, so take good care of him, eh?"

Gordon hurried away; Mark smiled at his new client. "Don't worry about a thing; you'll soon get the hang of all this, and it's my job that you do. Blimey, I love that saddle; it's American, isn't it? Lucky boy, aren't you? I've always admired your dad; to me he's the most stylish rider when riding a finish. If you copy him, lad, you'll go places. Anyway, let me help you on with those boots."

Dressed and booted, Mark led Billy, carrying his saddle and girths onto the scales, which displayed the combined weight as 8st 9lb. Mark took the weight cloth and slipped a one-and-a-half-pound weight into the pockets each side. The scales now showed the weight as 8st 12. "Now you can take this outside and weigh out and, once that's done, hand the lot over to one of your lads so they can saddle up, and then we just wait in here for the call to the parade ring. OK? Anything you'd like to ask me?" Billy shook his head.

The clerk of the scales weighed him out in the adjoining room, and there was Duncan already waiting. Billy handed him the saddle, girths and surcingle, and returned to the changing room and watched the action on the large-screen TV.

The horses were just cantering down to the start, and for a few seconds picked up Gordon. Finagan was throwing its head about, looking very keen, but Gordon kept him at a steady pace and then the camera lost them amidst the other fourteen milling around before being loaded.

It all looked so simple, really: the gates sprung open, Finagan led for the first furlong, then made all from the front; it was never headed, winning by four lengths.

Billy thought it a good start to the day and wondered whether it might lessen the expectations they had of himself. Possibly not. Sitting waiting to be called, butterflies in the stomach, he thought over the talks he'd had with David last night.

They'd gone over the race in detail, watched Top Notch's two previous wins on DVD and analysed its strategy in detail. David had been very upset not to be coming to the meeting, but had to remain in charge of the yard as Edward was being picked up by Her Ladyship and driven up to Doncaster in the Rolls by her chauffeur.

Billy, slightly upset, had asked why no one had told him the filly was also entered to run. David explained they had specifically not told him so he wouldn't start worrying about her race and not concentrating wholly on his own.

Billy's thoughts were interrupted by the call, loud and clear, of "jockeys out".

Jockeys out caused an immediate commotion as jockeys jumped to their feet and started to file out of the door, Billy joining them two from last.

With his whip tucked under his arm, head held high, he walked into the paddock and caught sight of Angela leading Top Notch around the ring, and the boss and Her Ladyship standing on the far side. He walked up, touched his cap in deference, and gave a polite "good afternoon". Lady Worlinton smiled warmly and said how pleased she was that his first ride was for her and that both she and Mr Henley had great hopes for his future, no matter what the result was today. The boss simply said that they'd talked through the race this morning and just do your best and bring the horse back safe and sound and that was all they should ask. The bell rang for jockeys to mount. Angela legged Billy up and led him around to the exit, wished him luck, and watched him canter away.

Once Billy was seated into the horse, his nervousness left him. With Top Notch taking a firm hold, he maintained a steady pace down to the start.

Within a few minutes the sixteen runners were walking around in front of the stalls, odd numbers going behind to be loaded first, then the evens. Billy, drawn stall four, waited. His colours, dark green, pink sleeves, pink croix de Lorraine and pink cap, were picked up by ITV4 cameras, the commentator noting that this was the lad all the fuss was about, the long-lost son of the international jockey Yve de Montagnes.

Back in the yard, David watching in the lads' canteen, Grace watching at Home Farm and Yve on his phone picking up the scene from Racing UK, each not knowing quite what the expectations were, and all fixated on the screen.

Top Notch entered the stall with no help from the handlers; the gate shut behind him. The last two loaded, a shout: "ALL IN." Billy shook his reins, felt the horse tighten up, the gate sprung open, a loud clatter, a surge of power, and within the first four strides Billy was up out of the saddle, bent low over the horse's neck at an all-out gallop. Other horses were now cutting across from the outside to come over to the inside. Now, Billy was hemmed in with four in front of him, and three others alongside him. Sitting tight, he was now able to ease Top Notch into a settled pace two from the rails. The following group stayed within three or four lengths behind the leaders and no one yet had made their move, and, apart from those who were strung out behind, now trying without much success to make up ground, Billy felt Top Notch had plenty more to give. The last corner was coming in close; Billy waited his chance and as the three on his offside swung out wide, he gave Top Notch an extra inch of rein and the horse sailed through, but now they found themselves leading the chasing group with a good two and a half furlongs to the post. Top Notch was still on the bridle, taking a strong hold. Billy bided his time.

One of the four of the chasing group came abreast for a few strides, then faded and dropped away, giving Billy at this point the feeling he had a chance.

Now in third place, sitting still and balanced, two of the horses he'd just passed came up aside of him. Billy let them inch ahead, but the jockeys were working hard trying to keep their mounts on the bit ready for the run in and trying to put a distance between them.

A furlong to go and Billy started his push to the post. Hands pumping, and pushing the horse's neck in time with its off fore, he gave it one crack of the whip and sailed past into the lead and crossed the line two lengths ahead of the second and four lengths from the third.

Easing Top Notch down, he came back to a walk, and was approached by Maureen Phillips from ITV, and now, still out of breath from his efforts, he answered her questions, summary and compliments as best he could.

David, Grace, Yve, Angela and Duncan, and even Henley and Her Ladyship, had all been calling the horse home, jumping up and down, urging their boy on with shouts of encouragement and hugs of joy. A thrill that one can't otherwise imagine if one hasn't watched your horse nearing the finish with the chance of a win, and it was no different for all those associated with the horse and Billy. It matters not, over these few minutes, from where one comes from or who you are: racing can be a great leveller and often is.

FORTY-SIX

Angela and Duncan ran out to meet him, beaming with joy and patting both the horse and Billy in equal measure. One either side, they led them into the parade ring and into the number one spot. Billy slid off the horse, undid the surcingle and girth, and removed the saddle. Holding it over his arm, he was greeted by a beaming Lady Worlinton, who, much to Billy's surprise, kissed him on the cheek, and Edward, who stood back a little, looking rather proud, and with good reason. He'd just trained Finagan to win a listed race worth thirty-two thousand pounds, and now another a grade 2 handicap worth thirty-five thousand pounds.

The horse Billy had narrowly beaten stood next to them and, as its jockey walked past, he stopped and put his free hand on Billy's shoulder. "No apprentice having his first ride," he said, "should be as good as what you showed me just now. Keep away from the happy pills and the drink and you'll have a great future."

With a nod to Edward, he hurried off towards the weighing room.

"Was that who I thought it was?" Billy asked.

"Yes," whispered Angela. "Frank Osbourne. He's a star, best there is."

Photographs were taken of owner, trainer and jockey in front of their winner and, as Billy hurried out to weigh in, he was stopped by the press. More photos taken, and a short interview with ITV's lead man, David Blakeny. Billy cut it short, knowing the official result couldn't be declared until riders had weighed in and their weight matched the same as when they weighed out. He hurried on, and after the clerk of the scales gave him the nod he rushed into the jockeys' room and changed back into his day clothes.

Hardly thinking of what he'd just achieved, he needed to get back out there to watch the filly in the parade ring to see if she was behaving herself. As he packed his riding gear into his bag, Mark came up to congratulate him and said there was no need to employ a valet yet, not until he was getting two or three bookings a day, and he'd make no charge for today and hoped that sometime, in the not-too-distant future, Billy would remember him when needed.

Jockeys were called out for the next race and, as Gordon Stokes joined others in the rush for the door, Billy wished him good luck. All he got back was a grim nod of recognition and not a word else. Billy surmised Stokes was not looking forward to riding the filly Black Sunday, but hoped she would produce what she was capable of and was sure she would, as long as she behaved herself.

Looking over the rails as the filly passed by, he could see the whites of her eyes, throwing her head about and giving Angela a hard time hanging on to her.

Duncan entered the ring to help and took hold of the bridle on the offside, and they seemed to have more control, but the filly had other ideas: ears back and swishing tail showed she wasn't in the best of moods, and that, most probably, was a serious understatement.

The bell rang for jockeys to mount up. The filly wouldn't stand, so Angela ran beside her and Duncan legged Stokes up on the move, then led him out of the ring.

Billy breathed a sigh of relief, and ran across to get a good view of the big screen.

As they cantered down to the start, Stokes managed to hold her into a controlled half-speed gallop, and pulled up in front of the stalls without incident.

So far so good, thought Billy, *but now the big if: will they get her into the stalls?* He watched in bated breath as Stokes walked her behind and joined others waiting their turn; several were already loaded.

Two handlers came up to the filly and led her towards her stall; all looked to be going well but, ten feet away, she planted herself and refused to move. Two other handlers came up either side of her quarters, each holding the handle of a leather strap, which they stretched behind her, pulling her forward with all their strength.

The filly was forced to move but after only two stuttered steps she spun ninety degrees, knocking one of the handlers to the ground. Gordon Stokes sat tight and forcibly turned her head back to face the stalls. She immediately ran backwards and Stokes, losing patience, gave her a crack. The filly reared up; she didn't fall backwards, luckily, but took two plunges forward, nearly having Stokes off. Managing to pull himself back into the saddle, for the moment he'd lost control as he galloped away. Using all his guile he managed to turn her and trot her back.

All the horses were now loaded, and the starter was becoming impatient and called out that he'd give her one more chance.

The handlers put a blindfold over her ears, eyes and face. They walked her away, turned her around three times, and led her to her stall. Halfway in, they pushed and shoved but she backed out again at speed, then gave a double-barrel kick, her hooves narrowly missing the handler's head. "That's enough," shouted the starter.

"All in," shouted a lad. The flag dropped, fourteen stalls opened to their usual loud clang and all thirteen horses were on their way to the post.

Black Sunday, the horse Billy adored so much, was left behind. Stokes, red in the face, walked her back to the stands as if on a different horse. She was cool, calm and composed, ears pricked forward. All the signs of a horse that knew full well she'd scored a victory of her own making.

With no sign of Edward or Her Ladyship, Duncan decided to leave early. Stokes had one more ride, but it wasn't for one of theirs, so, collecting all the gear together, they loaded the filly next to Top Notch and set off on the four-hour drive home.

—

David saw the horse box drive into the yard and waited for the two horses to be fed and bedded down, before taking himself and Billy home. On the way they discussed his ride and how pleased they all were that he'd done the yard proud, but the filly had been the disappointment. He said Edward had phoned, impressed with Billy's ride, but the filly was another matter and he wanted to talk it over first thing tomorrow and decide what should done with her.

Once home, Grace, running up to the car, hugged Billy as he got out, so thrilled, so pleased. She'd taped his ride, and could hardly wait to show him the rerun, and, as soon as he came back down after taking a shower, the three of them sat down to watch it.

Billy was transfixed; he almost felt he was riding the race at this very moment, and, when the cameras panned into a close-up of the finish, he was astounded to see himself twirl his stick in the right hand and give Top Notch just the one crack behind. He had no memory of changing the whip's position in his hand, and certainly not chancing the professional twirl. "I had no idea you could do that," David said, with a huge grin from ear to ear.

"Nor did I," answered Billy, laughing.

–

"I was pleased with the boy," Edward said, "but that temperamental filly. I had such high hopes of that one; she made a fool of us, David, and for Stokes; no way will he want to ride her again. I think we have two alternatives. One is that we turn her away until next season and see if she matures, or, and I'm going against all normality, that I enter her now for Newmarket next Saturday, and see if your lad can give her another a chance. I don't really understand it, but she appears to accept him somehow."

David left a few seconds of silent contemplation. "The boy has a special relationship with this horse, boss; he's spent time with her nearly every day since she was a foal. I wasn't going to suggest it as I don't want to be seen favouring the lad, but if he could get her accepting the practice stalls on the heath and we enter her here in

Newmarket, the stalls are no more than a few hundred yards apart; maybe it wouldn't seem any difference to the filly, and we can simply walk her over, no horse box, no fuss. It may just do the trick, and definitely worth a try."

"Let's give it a go, then," Edward said with a sigh. "We have nothing to lose and everything to gain. I'll let Her Ladyship know and I'm pretty sure she'll be happy with whatever we decide. Luckily, there's a seven-furlong listed race for two-year-olds that should suit the filly, and, if she behaves herself, being a quality race, it could really tell us what we've got there. From tomorrow, then, put her through every day until Friday. If she doesn't perform, we'll turn her away."

David had an idea and asked the time of the race and was told it was the first race on the card at 1.50. "How about we take her to the practice stalls each day for 1.50?" he suggested. "Then, on the day, we walk her over the heath to the course and she might think it just a normal day's outing? The only thing that does concern me a bit is that putting her straight into a listed race and giving the ride to a novice will make it look as though we prefer Billy over Gordon, and I don't think Gordon will accept it."

"I don't give a damn about that," answered Edward. "He's about to retire in a few weeks anyway, and I do find he's becoming more difficult by the day. I think your idea may or may not help but it's worth a try; let's just hope we get a result."

When David got home, he told Billy the filly was to be entered to run at home on Saturday at 1.50, and of his idea, and that Billy cut short his break after third lot each day from tomorrow. He made no mention that Billy would be given the ride.

FORTY-SEVEN

Sticking to the plan, the filly and the yard's old lead horse were ridden down to the practice stalls, arriving a few minutes before 1.50. David was already there waiting for them.

Walking in a large circle as David opened up both sides, they made a turn.

The old yard man Horace, who'd jumped at the chance of a few extra quid, rode the lead horse, Gainsborough Lad, towards the open gates, and, with Billy following, both walked calmly in single file straight through to the other side. David asked them to circle and to go through once more. This done, he asked they now walk upsides through the two adjoining stalls. This was again done twice, also without incident.

Confidence was growing. David pondered calling it a day on a good note or testing the filly further and risking an upset. Deciding against risk, he patted the two horses and made much of them and sent them on the way home.

On Tuesday they repeated the process, after which David closed the gates behind them with the front still open and made them stand there for the count of ten and then walk out.

On Wednesday he had them walking into the stalls side by side with the front gates closed, and to stand there for the count of ten. Then, very quietly, he closed them in, and said he would spring the gates open on the count of three, let them find their own way out, whether at a walk or a gallop, but not to encourage them in any way. "One… two… three." Clatter, bang. The gates opened, the old horse came out fast; the filly dwelt on her hocks for a second, then plunged into a flat-out gallop, passing the older horse, who was already pulling up.

Billy didn't want to disappoint the filly so let her run until they reached the two-furlong marker. Gently playing with her mouth and using his vocal "woo hoo" three times, he now had her, and she slowed into a canter, a fast trot, and then her walk.

Billy turned and trotted back to David. "Well done, you two; we'll leave it at that and do the same tomorrow and, if that goes as it did today, I think we may have cracked it."

–

David was in an extremely good mood when he came home and gave Grace the hopeful news that the filly behaved as she did. His phone rang. Answering, he was surprised to hear Yve, who, in his heavy accent, apologised for not ringing earlier to congratulate them over Billy's win but he'd already been away for three days now, getting ready for the US Breeders Cup in four days' time, sorting out his ride for the Qatar Prix de l'Arc de Triomphe in the three weeks, and with trying to limit his normal engagements his phone hadn't stopped ringing.

He just wanted to ask if David was sure he didn't want to be recompensed for Billy's keep and expenses, and were they still happy with the arrangement. He also thanked David for giving his boy the ride and whoever had taught the lad to ride a race as well as he did. He said how very proud he was, and asked whether David could put Billy on.

Grace, realising who it was, had already called him down. David wished Yve good luck with his coming rides and passed Billy the phone. There was some fun talk over the twirling of sticks and the news of the filly's antics and what they'd been doing about it, and they hoped to meet up again soon.

Billy put down the phone and went quiet for a few minutes. Grace wondered what was troubling him and asked if he was all right. "I'm OK, thanks," he said. "Just wish I could see him more often, but I do understand how busy he is, and when I start getting rides as well there won't be much chance anyway."

—

Thursday's trip to the stalls went as well as they'd hoped and all was now set for Saturday's trial. The yard had runners in all three meetings: Newmarket, Newbury and Lingfield. Billy knew Gordon was at Newbury and Scott on the all-weather track at Lingfield, and wondered who'd be riding the filly, and could hardly wait to get hold of the *Racing Post* Friday morning.

Finding a copy in the canteen, he thumbed through it and there it was the entry for tomorrow's race: Newmarket. 1.05 Dubai Nursery (2) (2-Y-0) £18,000 added (£11,960) 7f (9) and the eighth of the nine runners: Black Sunday 9st jockey Billy Brent.

Billy re-read the entry three times; he could hardly believe it, but on reflection realised that the filly had more chance of accepting the stalls with him on board than anyone else at this particular time. If she behaved and ran well, it would almost certainly be a stepping stone to her future career, or on the other hand, if she didn't oblige, possibly sold away to who knows who or where she would go if sold in Tattersalls November sale.

He had difficulty sleeping that night, but got up in the morning feeling pretty good. David, after talking him through the race last night, had told him there was no need to go into work until eleven but to pack his kit and he'd take it in for him. Billy had checked out that his breeches and polo neck had been laundered, nicely ironed and folded, cleaned up his boots and saddle and packed them with great care into his travel bag, and left it by the front door.

When he went down for breakfast, it was gone. Grace was already outside with her chickens and vegetable patch, and Celine and Cindy were busy mucking out.

The sales were only a few weeks away and there was still the mare and her foal to sell, and the yearling David bought as a foal last year.

David had now finally decided to commit himself fully to his job and was giving up on the risky annual pinhooking* so, once this lot were sold, then that was to be the end to it.

This was not much of a concern to the girls as they were already doing rather well in continuing with David's previous involvement of retraining and selling away retired racers.

–

Already looking very smart in his best jacket, blue shirt and tie, slacks and polished brown shoes, Billy was at a loss what to do. It was still only eight, with over two and a half hours to kill. He chatted to the girls but they had work to do, so he found Grace on her hands and knees, weeding her vegetable patch. She looked up at him. "My, you look very swish," she said. "I thought you were riding over."

"I am, but I'd feel a bit of a nit if I turned up in the yard looking as if I were ready to race; it'd look as if I was showing off to everyone that I had the ride. I've already rubbed a few noses out of joint. Perhaps you're right, though; I wasn't thinking straight. I'll go and take this lot off now, and ride over in my normal working clothes. David can bring over my racing gear."

"No, dear," she said. "When he got to work, Henley told him he had to go to Newbury as Her Ladyship had changed her mind and decided to watch the filly instead of her runner there. He was very upset at not being there for you, but wishes you all the luck, and he'd be watching the race on his phone."

Billy, thinking it pointless hanging around here any longer, ran back to his bedroom and changed into his old jodhpurs, T-shirt and zip-up jacket. Feeling far more comfortable, he hurried back out, hopped onto his moped and sped off to Millgate.

As he arrived, Angela was just finishing off grooming and turning out the filly to look her best. The one white sock and the small white blaze on the forehead were washed white and bright, hooves were oiled, and mane and tail shampooed and brushed into place; the coat was shining. The whole was finished off with two brushed watermarks down each side of her quarters, adhering to Her Ladyship's hate of diamonds and other patterns that are created on the quarters through a plastic stencil by brushing against the natural hair line and leaving the pattern. Her Ladyship and Henley were staunch traditionalists, and the brushed watermarks was just something that was done.

Angela was keen to accompany Billy across the heath on the same old horse, keeping things as close as possible to the training sessions. So, after a mug of tea and a burger in the canteen, they were legged up, and set off.

The travelling head lad, who had already left with David for Newbury, had again nominated Duncan to the Newmarket race and, as the two horses arrived at the course, he'd already driven there and was waiting with Billy's kit and old Horace, who was only too pleased to walk the old horse back home. Billy and Angela jumped off and with a bit of a struggle legged the old chap up into the saddle. She then took hold of the filly's bridle and walked the horse through security and into its reserved stable.

Billy, his kitbag in hand, walked his way to the course official's building, ran up the steps, gave a nod to the clerk of the scales and settled himself down in the male jocks' changing rooms. Gordon's valet was in Newbury, so Billy wondered whether he should look after himself, but, as he stepped onto the scales, one of the valets came over and helped him adjust his combined weight to the riding weight of 9st. Holding his saddle, weight cloth and girths, the scales read 8st 10lb, one pound more than the week before. The valet slipped 2lb of lead weight into each side of the weight cloth and now the scales tipped to 9st. No claiming 7lb today: this was a listed race, a class 2, and a race where apprentices had no weight advantage over experienced jockeys and therefore were seldom used, if ever.

Jockeys were called out for this the first race of the day, and made their way into the parade ring. First sight of his filly: things looked promising. No wild-eyed look this time, and, as she was led past, Angela gave Billy a wink and a nod.

Walking into the centre, Billy touched his cap to the boss and Her Ladyship. Duncan stood a few feet away, closely watching Angela in case she needed help.

"Let's pray the filly doesn't play up again," said Henley. "Try and keep in touch with the leading group, and then see what she can give us from two furlongs out. Good luck, anyway; we know how much you've put into this. Let's hope our novel idea has done the trick." Billy smiled up at them as the bell rang to mount up.

Angela kept the filly at the walk as Duncan legged Billy up on the move. The paddock started to disperse: trainers, owners and officials to the stands; horses to the start.

Going down, the filly took a very keen hold, and as she broke out of the canter into a half-speed gallop it was all Billy could do to hold her there, but she allowed herself to be pulled up in front of the stalls.

He drew stall six out of the nine. Odd numbers were put in first, so he joined the others and waited to be called. Minutes later, even numbers walked behind and started loading, but the handlers had already been informed that, as the filly had refused to be loaded a week ago, she would be the last to be put in, and, if she gave them any trouble, she'd not be given a second chance.

All in apart from Black Sunday, the handlers came up to lead or push her towards stall six, but Billy told them to stand aside until he had had one try at walking her in himself without their help. Walking her in a wide circle, he turned her to the open stall and she walked straight in; the gate was slammed behind her... "All in," was called, the flag dropped and they were off.

Back on the stands, Edward, watching through his binoculars, breathed a sigh of relief; Her Ladyship squeezed his arm.

The difference of nine runners rather than fourteen was immediately apparent.

No flat-out scramble to cross over to the rails, no one to block him in, but no place to cover her up for a last-minute effort. Billy was shocked to find himself four lengths ahead and making the running. He'd a split-second decision to make: either rein her back into the pack behind or make all. Slowing her down might well disappoint the filly and make her lose interest. He decided to let her run her race and ignore the boss's instructions.

The straight seven furlongs of the Newmarket course is often quite daunting to a young horse, and it was a worry that she mightn't stay the distance. When they got to the rise,* three other horses came abreast of him with just half a furlong to the post.

Now, and only now, Billy rode his finish, never touching her with the stick, just using his voice, urging, urging, urging her on in time with each stride, pushing the bridged reins up her neck, hoping she'd stretch and increase the length of the stride. As they crossed the line, the filly was in full stretch, with neck, head and nose thrust forward.

Billy thought he'd lost it by a nose. Pulling up, he patted her neck, telling her she'd run a great race and he was proud of her and as they walked back towards the paddock an announcement over the loudspeakers stated the result would follow, the decision by photograph. Billy's heart jumped: perhaps he'd got it wrong; there was still a chance.

He and the other two in contention circled in front of the stands, awaiting the result before returning to the winner's enclosure.

The loudspeaker crackled. "And the winner is number 8, Black Sunday."

The rider of the second rode up alongside to shake Billy's hand. Billy, trying to hide tears of emotion that welled up inside him, smiled back in acknowledgement of the sportsmanship that exists between jockeys in this highly competitive sport.

Stroking the filly on the neck, pulling her ears, now feeling ecstatic, he turned the horse and started to walk back to the paddock. TV cameras were filming him and a long pole with a microphone was thrust up to him by ITV's Maureen Phillips, asking what it felt like to be winning a listed race in only his second ride and at the age of only sixteen. He waited a moment before answering. "I might only be sixteen," he said, "but my uncle bought this filly as a foal, and for the last two years she's been my best friend... I also want to thank my dad, Yve de Montagnes, and my aunt and uncle, who've always supported me, and say how much I appreciate Mr Edward Henley and Lady Worlinton having given me this chance. I shall try my best never to disappoint them."

"Well, you certainly didn't disappoint anyone today. Well done, Billy, you're a star."

As Angela and Duncan, each side of the filly, led them into the winner's enclosure, Edward and Her Ladyship showed their obvious delight, patting the filly and shaking Billy's hand and affectionately gripping his arm. Billy slid off, undid the surcingle and girth, and removed his saddle. "Sorry I didn't follow instructions, boss," he said. "She jumped out so quick and I found myself in front. I didn't want to disappoint her, so let her run her race. She was still on the bit at the finish and I think she'll get the mile."

"Well, that may be," said Edward, "but we'll enter her in the guineas next April. She won't have another run this year, and hope she'll mature over the winter and calm herself down."

My filly, thought Billy, *running in a classic here in Newmarket. Might they let me ride her? Shouldn't think so.* Then, remembering David's advice, he just put those ambitious thoughts out of mind.

Getting weighed in, he went back into the jockeys' room to change, and was surprised and thrilled when several well-known jockeys came over to congratulate him. His phone was buzzing with messages from David, Grace and Mum, but best of all was the one from Yve.

"So proud of you," it said. "Took me five months before I had my first win and now you win a listed race and your second win in a week. Our talent lives on. Yve."

Billy felt a flash of pride: pleasing his dad meant more to him than all the others put together. Wondering how Gordon got on, he looked up at the results of today's other meetings. Gordon had been third at Newbury and Jason Scott had won a class 3 race at Chelmsford City. Not a bad day, then, for Millgate Stables.

Wearing his working gear, he now felt slightly embarrassed, and slipped out, making sure the press weren't hanging around catching him unawares looking like this. He soon found Angela and Duncan drying off the filly after her wash-down, and they talked over the race together and were full of it, particularly Angela, who had been jumping up and down, urging the filly on, throwing her arms into the air and running up to the rails like a soul possessed. She said she thought her antics had been caught on camera. Not that she minded; she said it was good for the public to see and understand what a thrilling and exciting spectacle racing could be.

Horse dried off and cool, they tacked her up, led her out the yard through the exit gates, and onto the open heath, where Duncan legged Angela up, and with a laugh and a wave she rode off towards home. Duncan took hold of Billy's kitbag and they walked to the car park and drove back to Millgate.

–

On Monday morning the *Racing Post* ran a half page on the fact that Billy, at the age of sixteen, had two wins in his first two rides within the week and that the second was a top-class listed race. They followed this up with an edited version of their previous story of his background and his association with Yve.

Local ITV also showed the finish of the race on their morning show, which also featured Angela's excited antics urging the filly on, and in the canteen this morning there was more interest in her antics than the race itself. Everyone including Angela had a good laugh and a rousing cheer, creating a feel-good factor that lasted most the day.

After first lot, Billy was called into the office, and the secretary explained that Weatherbys had sent in a form to complete for the new bank account to be opened in his name. She'd had already entered his address, date of birth, nationality and gender. "They need it to transfer your riding fees, and the percentage of any win or place money due to you. Just sign as you would on future cheques at the bottom here, and, by the way, very well done yesterday."

FORTY-EIGHT

Things very soon got back to normal, although he wasn't expected to muck out or look after the normal three or sometimes four horses; he was now riding out four or five times a day, plus coming back in at four to help in checking for any injuries that might have been missed, skipping out, feeding, and bedding down for the night.

He didn't know when or where his next ride was coming from; after all the great publicity he'd enjoyed, he had hoped to have picked up at least one or two outside rides from other trainers but no such news had emanated from the office, David or the boss. Billy held his tongue and just got on with the routine.

Being used as a work rider when horses needed a strong piece of work, whether it be the youngsters or older horses, testing them upsides one another was valuable experience for him. It was important for a jockey to give an assessment of how a horse had performed when asked. Billy's was already being taken note of.

The following Wednesday, after his win, he was legged up onto a six-year-old due to run in four days' time to be tested by a three-year-old that had just won its fourth race three weeks ago.

Walking to the heath, they cantered the whole six furlongs of the all-weather track that took them behind the racecourse to the start of the gallop.

Presented by a two-furlong straight, it then has a steep incline to a left-hand turn, entering a final six-furlong straight running alongside the main Newmarket approach road.

David and Edward and another man, possibly in his middle thirties, had driven down, and parked the car in one of the laybys and walked over to stand twenty-five yards from the edge at the six-furlong marker. In the distance, they caught sight of Billy and Jason Scott walking their horses onto the gallop, and setting off upsides.

If any gallop can test a horse's fitness, this one can, and now they'd already reached the incline, and at full gallop both swung around the bend inches between them, so close their irons* touched on alternate strides. Entering the final straight, just two furlongs' distance from the three men, both horses were still neck and neck, but as they flashed by the three-year-old pulled away from Billy's, heading him by half a length. Under orders, neither of them rode a finish and just sat tight.

Pulling up, they walked to the end of Newmarket Drive* and walked around the collecting ring to wait for their boss to check all was well; a minute later, the car arrived.

"That was a nice bit of work, lads," said Edward. "No problems?"

"No, boss, sound* as a pound," Jason called, all smiles.

"OK, off you go, then, walk them home and as soon as you're back come into the office we'd like a word."

When out of earshot Billy asked Jason if he knew what it could be about.

"Haven't a clue," he answered, "and who was that other geezer? Never clapped eyes on him before; he's not one of our owners."

Riding into the yard, they jumped off, handed the horses over to the yard men and walked over to the office. Edward, David and the stranger were already there, each with a cut glass of whisky in their hand.

Edward opened their discussion. "Please take a seat... Now, as you might or might not know," he said, "Gordon Stokes is leaving us; he may well retire after a successful career, or perhaps go freelance. I'm not inclined to take on anyone to replace him. Jason, I am well pleased with the progress you've made. You've proved to be a loyal and proficient member of our staff since you were a young lad, and I am pleased to promote you from November the first as our retained senior jockey."

Billy caught sight of the shock and emotion reflected in Jason's eyes in this huge achievement. Henley continued, "And, as for you, Billy, we're having so many requests for your services we can't handle it. Janice has enough to do sorting out our own entries. So, I'd like to introduce you to Tim Stratford, who is one of the best and most trustworthy jockeys' agents, and, if you agree to use his services, he'll handle all future engagements for you, and pick out the best of them. It will cost you, of course, but I would advise you to take him on."

Billy shook hands with the agent and looked up at David for his approval.

"It's what you should do, Billy. I know Tim very well, and he'll look after your interests. He'll send us a letter of engagement for us to sign and we've already agreed it to be a six-month term, after which either of you can end it or, if happy, renew it. Once signed, we will register the agreement with Weatherbys. By the way, you already have five rides booked from Saturday to next Wednesday."

Beaming, Billy shook Tim's hand again and both he and Jason thanked them and, once outside, threw their arms around each other in a mighty hug and gave two shouts of total glee.

—

A couple of days later, on getting home from work, Grace handed Billy two letters, both addressed to him. One was handwritten and the other looked rather official.

Opening the handwritten envelope, before reading it he checked who it was from. His heart jumped: it was from Kate.

"Dear Billy," it read. "I've wanted to contact you for so long now, and held off as I didn't want you to think it was because of your success and of you being in the news. I enjoyed our talks on the bus to school so much and became very fond of you, but didn't think you had any real interest in me. I know I was pretty horrible to you as I was upset, and took up with a stupid lad Greg Matthews, and it didn't last more than a few weeks. As you probably know, I'm working for Henry Brothington. I don't like it here that much but I'm learning, and will soon be able to find another post as a trainer's secretary on my own. Forgive me for being so forward, but could we meet up after work sometime and have a good chat about things as we used to? My phone number is 07747 826 751. Hoping you'll ring me. Love Kate x"

Billy looked at the kiss at the end of the letter and surprised himself by the depth of the feelings that shot through him, and re-read the letter several times over.

Putting these thoughts away till later, he opened the other envelope. It was a bank statement in his name with four payments into the account from Weatherbys, these for his two riding fees and winner's percentage bonus, giving him a credit balance of £2,740. The envelope also included a credit card and a chequebook.

It being the first of October, and feeling flush, he wrote out a cheque covering his first payment for rent and keep, and when David returned from work proudly handed it over. David seemed rather touched and gave it to Grace to bank next time in town.

Billy had been worrying about something since the filly's race. "Why," he asked, "had he put on weight in the week between his two rides? What did you eat for lunch before your ride on Top Notch?"

"No, I had nothing, Angela and Duncan had a hot meal but not me."

"And what did you have before the 1.05 at Newmarket?"

"We all had a burger and chips at the canteen before we left."

"Well, there's your answer, then. You have to start thinking about your weight and what you eat; unfortunately, that's part of a jockey's life, and you should always be aware of your weight and how to control it."

FORTY-NINE

October again, and David, after studying the catalogues for hours, was off to the sales, checking over the eighteen yearlings he'd highlighted, hoping at least eight of them might measure up to his judgement and be bought within his budget.

Out of his twelve purchases last year, three had won, six had not run, two were to be sold off, thought not good enough, and one had broken down and would be rested until next season.

The winnings from the three youngsters plus those from the three-year-olds under his care won thirteen and placed in eight, winning a total of £580,000.

The agreed half of the 8.5 per cent due to the trainer brought his quarter-share to £24,650 and this, together with his salary, was far more than he could have hoped for.

Edward, with the older horses often entered into prestigious high-value handicaps, had won a total of £700,010 for his owners so, between them, with a total approaching £1,280,000, the yard had improved from the previous year and all were well satisfied with the new arrangement.

David sold all his remaining privately owned livestock and, being highly satisfied with the financial gains at Millgate, bought nothing for himself at the sales for the first time in many years.

Billy had twenty-nine rides up to the end of the year, winning nine times and placing in ten. These included two rides and a win for

Brothington due in no small part to Kate's influence.

The two of them were now meeting two or three times a week and every now and then they would go into Cambridge and walk beside the river and could often be seen holding hands.

Billy now had someone he could talk to. Talk out his thoughts and worries, and of how his determination to succeed still hung heavily on his mind. He was well aware he was now set for the very long journey that lay ahead, a journey without any guarantee it would get him to where he expected to be.

After much thought, and remembering David's advice, Billy set himself what he thought was an achievable target. He would ride out his apprenticeship by achieving ninety wins within three years, rather than it happening automatically at age twenty-six. So, once achieved at the age of twenty and losing his claiming allowance, he'd be a fully fledged jockey.

He would then set himself new targets of proving he was brilliant enough to be riding in top UK classics, vowing never to accept struggling on as a journeyman jockey, eking out a living in the winter months on the all-weather.

As for Yve, he didn't place in the Breeders Cup and only managed sixth place in the Prix de l'Arc de Triomphe. Fed up with so much travelling around the world, he retired and bought himself a 200-acre stud with a large country house, and bought, sold and bred horses of the highest calibre and best pedigrees money could buy. He moved the family there and now, feeling settled and content, he was happier than ever. He kept in touch with Billy, but, as each were set on different paths, they rarely met up, and never really formed a strong father–son relationship.

Just before Christmas, Billy asked Kate to come to Cambridge with him. He wouldn't tell her why. Rather than going in as normal on his moped, they went by bus and, once there, they looked for a posh-looking ladies' dress shop.

Feeling rather sheepish, they went inside, and a very smart woman was so nice and asked if she could help them to find what they were after. Kate didn't have a clue but obviously thought Billy wanted to buy something for her, but this place was way over the top. "It's for my mum," he said to the lady. "I want two lovely dresses for her."

"How nice," the lady said. "How old is she?"

"I think she's about thirty-five."

"And do you know her size?"

"She's the same height as my girlfriend but a little bit bigger on her front."

Kate tried to hide a blush: he'd called her his girlfriend and mentioned her top! The lady continued. "Can I ask, does your mum like formal wear, or does she prefer something more modern and a little risky?"

"She used to be a dancer, so I think it should be something pretty and casual."

"I think I know what she'd like and have just the right thing for her, and in a size eight." Leaving them for a few moments, she came back with two dresses over her arm.

Kate tried them on and Billy thought she looked beautiful. Kate loved them too, so they bought both dresses and the lady packed them neatly into a box and laid red tissue over them; she closed the lid and tied a blue ribbon over the lid. Billy took out a wad of cash he'd drawn from his account and paid. A fortune to him of £450, but to him worth every penny.

Leaving the shop, Kate said what a lovely thought buying his mum such lovely clothes, and asked him why.

"Because," he said, "when I was twelve and had to look after Mum, we had nothing, and could hardly afford even a loaf of bread. I told Mum not to worry because one day when I became rich I'd buy her lots of lovely dresses, and have never forgotten it."

"I love you for that," Kate said. She put her arm around him and kissed him on the lips.

GLOSSARY

3lb saddle	A jockey will have saddles from 1lb to 5lb in weight and will select one depending on the given weight he has to carry in the race.
800 guineas minimum bid	This is the minimum price a horse is allowed to be sold at a Tatersalls auction. This is to prevent them being bought for slaughter.
Action	Horses either have a high knee action or the opposite, showing the horse would prefer soft or firm going.
The all-weather	A track of fibre sand with a drainage base that horses can race over in all weathers and used all year through. Apart from rare occasions the all-weather is mostly used for lower-grade events.
Back end	The end of the flat season around the second week in November.
Black type	In a sales catalogue if any horse's performance is listed in heavy black type it refers to horses who have won the top classic group races and increases their value enormously.
Book 1	Book 1 is the first of four catalogues in Tattersalls yearling October sales. Book 1 is for the top-flight animals where only the best-bred are taken. Yearlings in this catalogue can go for hundreds of thousands of pounds, sometimes in the millions.
Boxes	Racing term for stables.
Breaking in	The term given for training a horse to accept a rider on its back and to respond to his aids.

Breeches	Worn with full riding boots.
Breeze-ups	Two-year-olds are galloped in front of buyers, before being auctioned a few days later.
Broken down	Leg injury preventing the horse from work.
Chifney	A severe bit used to lead around a horse that may be difficult.
Chip	Registering a yearling's name when it goes into training is injected with a chip. This will have the horse's name and breeding details. Whenever it is taken to a racecourse it is scanned to prove it is the same horse as the one entered.
Colic	A dreaded yet not unusual affliction when a horse has a blocked gut. Sometimes it passes; other times it can result in death.
Conditional jockey	This is the term for the jump jockey, equivalent to that of the apprentice on the flat.
Covered	A mare's visit to a stallion. She will then eleven months later hopefully have a foal.
Cut	Neutered.
Dark bay	A dark brown colour with a black mane and tail.
Dipper	The measure of hard feed a horse is given.
Dishing	A fault when its forelegs dish out or inwards at the trot.
Even break	Start of a race, the break out of the stalls.
Fetlocks	To explain in human terms, they are the horse's ankles.
The flat	Races not over jumps.
Full horse	Uncut.
Furlong	One-eighth of a mile.
Gait	Stride.
Gelding	A neutered horse.
Give it a run	Enter it for a race.
Guineas	A guinea is £1.05. The selling company take the 5pc as commission.
Hack canter	Slow, controlled canter.
Handheld canter	Holding a horse at a canter when the horse wants to increase to a gallop.
Handicap races	A handicap race will often range between the highest-rated horse at 10st down to the lowest at 8st 2lbs. The lowest-rated horse carrying 26lbs less in weight.
Handing in licence	When a jockey retires

Heat in legs	Shows stress or injury.
Hinds	Rear legs.
Hocks	The hocks are the rear joints of the horse's rear legs equating to the front knees separating its thighs to its shins.
Hop-up	A stone or wood platform for a rider to mount his horse. Otherwise he is given a leg up by another.
Irons	Stirrups.
Jods	Worn with legs to the ankle.
Ladies' hack	A quality horse suitable for gentle riding.
Lead horse	An older and quiet horse used to be ridden with a frisky young horse to calm it down and give it confidence.
Leathers	These are the leather straps hooked onto the saddle that carry the stirrups. They are pierced with holes so the length of stirrup can be adjusted to the rider's required comfort.
Licence	All apprentices and jockeys have to have a licence to ride and abide to the rules of racing.
Long reining	The reins are very long, and held by the person walking at a safe distance behind the still-unbroken horse with no rider on its back.
Long tom	A whip with a long loose tail that can make a loud crack when whipped into the air and brought down with a flick. Used to urge a horse on, mostly whilst being lunged without anyone on its back. Not used to actually hit the horse.
Lunge rein	Long rein used to exercise a horse in circles unridden.
Maiden	A maiden is a horse that has not yet won a race. A maiden race is specifically for those that have not won before.
Mare	A filly becomes a mare at four.
Newmarket Drive	The main entrance to the grandstands and racecourse. The trees lining the drive have details of many famous classic winners over many years.
Newmarket rise	The last furlong of the track rises, and is an added test to the runners.
Offside	The right-hand side of the horse. Riders mount on the opposite side, known as near side.
On the bridle or bit	When the horse takes a pull on the bit.

Parade ring	Where horses are walked around prior to being taken into the sales ring where they are auctioned. It also refers to prior to their race they are walked around the pre-parade ring before being taken into the parade ring, where jockeys mount up before a race.
Pinhooking	The business of those buying foals to sell on as yearlings.
Produce	The foals born to a sire and a mare.
Progeny	The issue of a mare's offspring.
Quarters	From hip to point of buttock, denoting power.
Racing boots	Lightweight boots, tight and difficult to pull on.
Ratings	An unraced horse has to run three times in maiden or novice races all at equal weights on which the handicapper will issue each a rating in pound weights. Therefore a horse rated seventy would carry 3lbs more than a horse rated sixty-seven.
Retained jockey	A jockey who is paid a sum for being on first call to race for the trainer's yard. Often, when the yard's apprentice loses his claim, if he is well thought of he may be retained as the yard's first or second jockey.
Ridden away	When a horse has been broken in and is able to be trained on.
Ride out one's claim	If an apprentice rides his ninety winners before the age of twenty-six, he loses his weight advantage and becomes a full jockey.
Seven-pound claimer	An apprentice not yet having twenty wins to his own name receives 7lb less than the horse's handicap allotted weight.
Shoes	Horseshoes fitted by a blacksmith.
Silks	Every owner has his colours registered with Weatherbys. Generally they are of silk.
Sire	A racehorse retired to stud for breeding.
Snaffle	Snaffle is a mild bit placed into the horse's mouth to which the reins are attached.
Sound	The opposite to lame.
Splints	A problem with young horses when slithers of bone break away from the cannon bone of the leg. Not considered an injury but the horse has to be rested until proved sound.
Stick	Whip.

Stick twirl	When riding a finish, the jockey has to change the position of the whip in his hand to reach the rear quarters of the horse. To see a top jockey doing it is a joy.
Surcingle	The girth attached to the saddle, the surcingle goes over the top of the saddle as a safety net should the girth break.
Tack room	Area where saddles, bridles, and grooming kits and horse appliance are kept, often used as the groomers' or owners' area for tea and biscuits.
Takes hold of the bit	When the horse pulls against the rider's hold.
Toe in the iron	It is now the fashion for a jockey to support his weight with only his toe through the stirrup (iron).
Trotted up	A person interested in buying the horse wants the groom to trot the horse away from him and then back to view the horse's action.
Underbidder	This is the person who made the last increase in his or her bid before making your own increased bid which was successful, as no one else increased it.
Upsides	Two riders riding up close to each other.
Valets	Jockeys in regular work will have engaged a valet who looks after him in the changing rooms, laundering his breeches and polishing his boots, and preparing his weight cloth and pre-weighing him to his designated weight before the official weigh out by the clerk of the scales.
Weatherbys	The institution that executes all racing administration and payments to jockeys and trainers for fees and percentages through Weatherbys Bank.
Weigh in/weigh out	Before they race, a jockey is weighed out with tack to the given weight of his race. On return he is weighed in to confirm the weight matches that of before.
Weight cloth	A cloth with components into which lead weight can be slipped to adjust a jockey's weight to coincide with the allotted weight he has been given for his race. The weighted cloth folds over the horses back under the saddle.
Will make a two-year-old	A smaller yearling not grown as quickly as others might be more suitable to race as a two-year-old, especially if its mare and sire also ran as two-year-olds. Large yearlings need their strength to grow and mature and be more suited to start racing as a three-year-old.

Wither	The protruding bone at the start of the neck in front of the saddle.
Work	The word work refers to a high-speed gallop when a horse or horses are being tested for fitness. Most often in pairs.
Work rider	An employee who is not a jockey but knowledgeable and experienced who will ride on the gallops when horses need to show their ability at a fast pace.
Yearlings	A foal becomes a yearling on January 1.

AUTHOR'S NOTE

Billy's meteoric short rise to fame and further opportunity is not unheard of in the world of horse racing, but extremely rare. Such success achieved at a young age is often paid for in adversity soon after, testing character and dedication to the limit. It is only the true champion who can steer themselves through the testing times to such recognition by his peers. Even then a jockey lives with insecurity. In racing whether it be trainer or jockey, one is only as good as one's last winner, and that winner is soon forgotten.

An apprentice is used by trainers as they claim a weight advantage, but after having ridden 90 winners they lose this allowance and become fully fledged jockeys, and very often they struggle to get booked to race. It costs an owner exactly the same fee whether a jockey is unknown or the most famous in the country. The best scenario for a young jockey is to be retained as the second jockey of a successful trainer he rode out his apprenticeship with.